CAMPY

A BALLSY BOYS PRODUCTION BOOK 4

K.M. NEUHOLD
NORA PHOENIX

Campy (Ballsy Boys Book Four) by K.M. Neuhold and Nora Phoenix

Copyright ©2019 K.M. Neuhold and Nora Phoenix

Cover design: K.M. Neuhold

Editing: Jamie Anderson

All rights reserved. No part of this story may be used, reproduced, or transmitted in any form by any means without the written permission of the copyright holder, except in case of brief quotations and embodied within critical reviews and articles.

This is a work of fiction. Names, characters, places, and incidents either are the products of the author's imagination or are used fictitiously. Any resemblance to actual persons, living or dead, businesses, companies, events, or locales is entirely coincidental. The use of any real company and/or product names is for literary effect only. All other trademarks and copyrights are the property of their respective owners.

This book contains sexually explicit material which is suitable only for mature readers.

1

CAMPY

I step out of the car and take a deep breath, letting the sweet scent of hay and the pungent aroma of animals and manure fill my lungs. It might not be what some people consider the best smell, but the sense of peace and happiness that washes over me is undeniably linked to the odor.

Gravel crunches under my work boots as I reach back into the car to make sure I have my neon-orange work gloves and a few bottles of water to tide me over for the next several hours. Five hours to be exact, the only five-hour chunk several times a week when I feel happy and peaceful. The only five hours where I get to be *me*.

The rest of the time, I'm Campy—porn star at the hottest gay porn studio in LA. But two to three times a week, I drive forty minutes to an hour outside of the city, depending on traffic, to Sylmar, California, where I volunteer at a wildlife, large, and exotic animal rehabilitation center and sanctuary. Those are the days I get to just be Cameron.

I make my way toward the main barn to sign in and find

out about any new animals we might've gotten since I was in last.

"Hey Cam," Julie, the shift lead, calls in greeting.

"Hey Jules. How's it going?"

"A bit busy with some new arrivals, but otherwise good," she says with a smile. "Hey, actually, you might be able to help with a little problem we're having with one of the new guys."

My chest warms a bit at her statement. I love being known around here as the guy who solves problems others can't. It helps me hang onto the hope that someday, I'll finally reach my dream of becoming a veterinarian.

"Yeah, what's the problem?"

"Well, we got this sheep in, her name is Ethel, and she won't eat."

"Hmm." I stroke my chin. "I assume she was checked for oral abscesses, parasites, the usual?"

"Yeah, she checked out as healthy. We figured it might just be stress from being in a new environment, but it's been a few days and everyone's getting a little worried."

"Can I see her?"

"Sure, come on." Julie waves me after her and we head down the main aisle of the barn, past towering cages filled with wild birds and a few barn stalls containing foxes, baby raccoons, and other cute furries. She pushes through the door leading to the first arena where a number of animals are housed with access to surrounding pastures.

Ethel is in the farthest pen with access to a small field to graze. She's huddled in the corner with her butt against the trough and the rest of her body as close to the wall as possible. Everything about her body language screams *insecure*, and it only takes me about thirty seconds to realize what the problem is.

I glance around the rest of the arena, assessing my options for a solution, and my eyes land on a pair of donkeys—Fonzie and Chachi.

"You know why it's so easy for one sheep dog to handle a huge herd of sheep all by itself?"

"Um…because it's instinct?" Julie guesses with a shrug.

"Because sheep have a very strong flocking instinct, it's how they survive predators. To a sheep, there's nothing worse than being alone, because being alone means they're vulnerable," I explain, and understanding dawns on her face. "Try her in with the donkeys, I bet they'll become fast friends."

"All right, let's try it."

A sense of satisfaction fills me as she grabs a herding board to move Ethel. The donkeys take to her quickly, and as I predicted, the change in Ethel's demeanor is almost instant. She starts bleating happily and within a few minutes she's happily chewing on alfalfa hay.

"You're amazing," Julie muses as she watches the animals together.

I wonder what Julie or the other people who work and volunteer here would think if they ever found out I was a porn star. Okay, *star* might be a bit of a stretch. In all honesty, I feel like at least half the comments on any video I'm in are about Pixie— *I need more Pixie! When will it be Pixie's turn to cum ;)? Pixie! Pixie! Pixie!*

Don't get me wrong, Pixie is a great kid and I can understand why guys are nuts for him. But damn if it doesn't hurt my ego just a bit. And if you'd told me three years ago I'd be salty about the fact there aren't enough guys jerking off to videos of me having gay sex, I would've probably died laughing. I mean, gay porn isn't exactly how most straight guys envision their future, right?

What? You didn't think the whole *gay for pay* thing was just a rumor, did you?

I'm sure people wonder how a straight man can do gay porn, and honestly, it's not as difficult as it seems. When I top, I imagine it's a woman I'm fucking...okay, except for this *one* time when I accidentally imagined John Stamos, but in my defense, I'd been binge-watching old episodes of *Full House* right before work and he just sort of popped into my head. But come on, it's *John Stamos*. At first when I bottomed, I would pop a couple Viagra before a scene, but over time I guess I've developed a bit of a Pavlovian response. My body knows I'm going to get to come and it doesn't seem to care how that happens.

So yeah, I'm a straight guy working in gay porn. But let's keep that little secret between the two of us.

With the high of solving the sheep problem, I get started on typical chores like mucking out stalls before moving on to feeding the raptors. Any birds of prey always seem to land on my shoulders because most of the volunteers are terrified of them. Not that I can blame them, but the eagles and owls are by far my favorites. Especially feeding the peregrine falcon, who prefers if you toss the meat into the air for him to catch.

"A little birdy told me they're going to offer you a full-time staff position soon," Julie tells me while I'm using a pair of scissors to cut up a frozen rat to feed one of the foxes.

My stomach swoops and I force a smile. I'd love more than anything to take on more hours here. But, unfortunately, they just don't pay anywhere near enough, and the hours would get in the way of me doing the one job that does actually make a dent in the mountain of bills that seem to get higher every day.

Maybe if I found a roommate to lighten my load even a

fraction I could afford to take more hours here and cut back at Ballsy Boys? I couldn't cut porn out entirely, it pays way too much, but if I could get that down to one day of filming per week? That's a lot of *maybes,* but it never hurts to dream, right?

Jackson

MY, MY, WE SURE AS SHOOTIN' aren't in Kansas anymore, or in my case, a small town in the Texas Hill Country no one has ever heard of. I'm barely able to hold back a gasp as LA pops up in the distance. Sure, I've seen big cities before, like San Antonio, Austin, and Dallas, and I went to Toronto when we shot the pilot, but this is different. LA is different. It will be, I promise myself all over again.

The view in the distance is hazy, but I can make out hills, high rises, and lots and lots of traffic on the most intricate pattern of highways I've ever seen in my life. It doesn't appear glamorous at all, but to me, it's what freedom looks like.

It may not be as pretty as the Hill Country where I hail from, but it sure as rain is a lot more inviting to me. I'll take polluted air, endless traffic, and exorbitant housing prices any day over blue skies, breathtaking vistas, and empty roads, because the latter come at a price I can no longer afford. I was dying, and to me, LA is life.

I have a shot at making a new life here, a life that's authentic and true, rather than spending the rest of my life choking in the straightjacket—pun intended—my parents have unwittingly forced me into. They love me, of that I'm sure, but they can't live with the reality of a gay son. The longer I stay there, the harder it will be for me to breathe, until I'm sure I'll wake up one day and discover I'm dead, even though my heart is still beating.

It's scary as all get out, this change I'm making, this dive off a high cliff, but I owe it to myself to see if I am strong enough to fly on my own. I've got the acting job, which pays enough to afford housing, and I've found a roommate with an apartment I can move into as soon as I arrive, so I'm all set. He actually offered to pick me up from the bus stop, but I already found out how to get to his place. That was mighty kind of him to offer, though, so I'm feeling good about rooming with him.

"There it is," says Anna, one of the girls I've been chatting with on the Greyhound bus, as enthralled by the view as I am. "The city of dreams."

"It's the city of *angels*," Tina, her supposed friend, corrects her, as she's been doing the whole trip now ever since they got on in Phoenix. She's pure vinegar pretending to be sweet as honey, that one. "Los *Angeles*, you know, meaning angels?"

"I didn't mean it literally," Anna explains, her patience unwavering.

Let me tell you, the way her friend has been dissing every single word out of her mouth, I would've been madder than a wet hen by now. Heck, I *am* mighty annoyed, and it's not even directed at me.

"It's a new start for us," Anna says. "It's the city of possibilities, of dreams. Anything can happen there."

She's right about that, as far as I'm concerned. LA is a new start for me as well, a place to try and be myself—whoever the heck that is. I have no clue, not after repressing myself for so long, but I intend to find out. And my new job is an awfully good place to start.

"What brings you to LA?" I ask Anna. We've chatted a bit on the endless bus ride—my jeans-clad behind has long since passed the *numb* stage—but not about what brings us here.

"I want to become a background dancer," she says, her face lighting up as she turns toward me. She's cute, with soft, brown curls tied back into a messy ponytail, and a pair of gorgeous brown eyes. "I've tried to audition from Tucson, where we live, but it's hard to get in when you can't show up for every audition in person. So I've given myself two years in LA to make it. I was hired as a server at an upscale restaurant some distant cousin I've never met owns. He says it's good tips, and hopefully, that'll tide me over until I get my break."

"She's a really good dancer," Tina says, the first nice words to come out of her mouth, and I'm pleasantly shocked until she continues. "But then again, so are many others. I hope she's cutthroat enough to survive."

Of course, she had to ruin it by running her mouth again.

"I'm sure if you're that good, you'll get your break eventually," I encourage Anna. "Now, don't get me wrong, I'm no expert, but a little kindness never hurt nobody."

She sends me a grateful smile. "What's your plan in LA?" she asks. "What temptation lured you away from Texas?"

I hesitate only for a moment. My publicist—and how weird is it that I even have one of those, can I just point that out?—said I can talk as much about the project as I want to. In fact, she flat-out ordered me to tell anyone and their mother about the show. They've announced it already, so there's no need to stay quiet about it anymore.

"I have a role in a new series that'll be broadcast in a few weeks, called *Hill Country*. We shot the pilot a few weeks ago in Toronto, and it's been picked up by a major network, so now we're starting on shooting the rest."

Anna's eyes widen. "That's amazing! How very cool for you. Is it a big part?"

I nod. "Yeah, I'm one of the four main characters. It's about a family in Texas who has to cope after the dad dies unexpectedly, and I play the oldest son."

Anna and Tina share a look. "You're perfect for that role, what with your accent," Anna says with a big smile.

I grin. "That's what the casting agent said as well. They preferred people with a natural Texan accent rather than teachin' someone, so that turned out well for me. I reckon I have a bit of a drawl." I lay it on thick and the girls both giggle.

"I could listen to you read the phone book," Tina says. "Though the rest of you isn't too shabby either. Maybe you could take me out sometime in LA? Check out the nightlife together?"

Here we go. This is the moment when I have to decide how much of a fresh start I really want to make. All my life, I've responded to scenarios like this the same way, but I'm so tired of it, so tired of pretending to be something and someone I'm not.

I take a deep breath and allow myself to feel the freedom. "As nice as that sounds, I'm gonna have to kindly decline, as I'm gay."

The rush that rolls through me after those words are said makes me light-headed. *I did it.* For the first time in my life, I've casually come out in a conversation. It may be stupid and insignificant to others, but as Anna and Tina both look surprised, I'm sitting on a rambling, bouncing bus, feeling doggone proud of myself.

My parents never allowed me to be myself. It wasn't that

they flat-out forbade me, more like they gave off a consistent air of disapproval. But, they're not here. Heck, they don't even know about my acting job, about me moving here. As far as they know, I'm still at the Southern Baptist college they pressured me into attending, God bless 'em.

Sure, I feel guilty about deceiving them, though I'm a tad more worried about my brother Brax's reaction when he finds out. We've always been close, and I hate lying to him. I wanted to tell him about quitting college and moving so badly, but I didn't want to put him in a position where he'd have to lie to Mama and Dad. He could never lie for crap anyway.

"Wow, I did not see that coming," Tina says, flipping her hair back. "My gaydar isn't usually that far off. Well, too bad. I'm sure we could've had fun together."

"I have no doubt," I say, even as I wink at Anna, who's clearly suppressing a laugh.

My name is Jackson Bedford Criswell and why, yes, I am gay.

2

CAMPY

"You coming out with us for a drink tonight?" Brewer asks as he towels himself off after his shower. I glance over my shoulder at him as I pull on my pants, wincing a little at the slight sting in my ass as I move. We filmed a very *enthusiastic* scene and I'm sure I'll be feeling it for a few days.

"I can't tonight, I'm meeting my new roommate."

"Bummer." Brewer sighs. "I feel like this is my last meal or something before I have to face the executioner tomorrow."

"You're filming a scene with Tank, not facing the firing squad."

Brewer and Tank have had a long-standing animosity, stemming from god knows where. Bear never had the balls, or maybe it's that he had too much brains, to pair them for a scene. But now that Rebel has stepped back from performing to do behind-the-scenes work for Ballsy Boys, he's decided he wants to fan the flames and see what happens.

"Same difference," Brewer mutters.

"What's he going to do? Fuck you to death?"

"Have you seen the way that man fucks? It's not that much of a stretch to think he could do it if he set his mind to it."

"Yes, I've seen the way he fucks, and I've also been fucked by him. You may walk funny for a few days, but I'm confident you'll survive," I assure him.

"Easy for you to say, he wasn't *trying* to hurt you."

"I think you're being dramatic, but if it'll make you feel better, I'll try to meet you guys after I finish up with my roommate."

"Cool, see you in a few hours then."

I wave over my shoulder as Brewer leaves, then I finish getting dressed and head out as well.

I'm not sure why I'm nervous about meeting this guy, but my nerves flutter in my stomach as I head home. Maybe it's because I've never lived with anyone before? God knows what kind of weirdo might show up. He seemed nice enough online when he responded to my listing, but this is LA. It's always safer to assume people are going to be weirdos, because you'll almost always be correct.

I quickly clean up the apartment once I get home, making sure I don't look like some kind of slob. Not that I'm even around enough to let the place get all that messy. If I'm not at the studio or the barn, I'm usually at my mom's checking on her, making sure she has meals and things are tidy for her. If I could afford it, I'd get her caretakers to help with the daily things, but it's not cheap. Although, soon it will probably be necessary, and fuck knows what I'll do then. Not to mention the MRIs she needs every six months to monitor her progression. At least the prednisone is cheap, but at her last doctor's visit, there was talk about trying some new treatment options that I'm sure will cost an arm and a leg...or in my case, my ass.

The sound of my door buzzer yanks me from my spiraling thoughts, and I'm glad for the distraction.

I cross the room and hold down the intercom button. "Jackson?" I check.

"That'd be me," a voice replies, thick with a Southern accent.

"Come on up." I hit the button that unlocks the outside door and unlatch my own door, leaving it slightly ajar while I head to the kitchen to grab a can of soda.

A minute later, the front door creaks open.

"Hello?" that Southern drawl calls out tentatively.

"Yeah, I'm in the kitchen. You want anything to drink?"

"Water's fine, thanks."

I grab a water bottle out of the fridge as well and head into the living room. The man standing awkwardly in the doorway with a suitcase set on the floor beside him fits the exact image my mind conjured up when I heard his accent. He's tall, a good head taller than me easily, and built like a brick house. He looks like he just hopped off a tractor, and I mean that in the best possible way. He's a good-looking guy, there's no denying that, even if I'm not into guys personally.

"You must be Cameron." He steps forward, offering me his hand with a polite, crooked smile.

It's odd, but I've gotten so used to being called Campy, unless I'm at the barn, that it takes me a second to offer him my hand in return.

"That's me," I agree. "So, uh, I've never had a roommate before. You'll have to bear with me."

Jackson lets out a little chuckle, filled with relief. "I'm glad I'm not the only one out of my depth. I swear, since getting off the bus I'm feelin' more and more like the dumb farm boy I always knew I was."

"I imagine it can be kind of overwhelming here at first. I grew up in LA so to me it's all pretty mundane at this point," I explain. "So, um, as we talked about when you emailed me, rent is three thousand a month, utilities included. So, you'll owe fifteen hundred on the first of every month. I got the first month's rent that you sent, so you're good until the first. You have a job yet?"

"Yeah, that shouldn't be a problem. I have a part in a new TV show. I mean, we're still filming the first season, so who knows if it'll even get a second season, but I have a paycheck for the next eight months guaranteed. And they gave me an advance, so I'm good for the money."

"Okay, cool. I'm not home much and I work odd hours, so you'll have the place to yourself most of the time. Do you have a girlfriend or anyone you'd be bringing around?" I check.

Something curious flits over Jackson's face, his jaw flexing before he bites down on his bottom lip and drops his gaze to his shoes. "Nothin' like that," he answers.

"Okay, if that changes, it's cool to have someone spend the night, just let me know ahead of time if possible. I don't want to run into a stranger in the kitchen in the morning or anything," I say, and he gives a quick nod. "Do you have any questions for me?"

He glances around the living room for a few seconds. "Can I look at the bedroom and everything?"

"Oh yeah, duh, of course." I usher him down the hall to show him the empty bedroom, stopping to let him look at the bathroom as well on the way.

He stands in the middle of the small bedroom looking

around for a few seconds before giving me another lopsided smile. "It looks great."

"Cool, welcome aboard, roomie."

"All I have right now is this suitcase of clothes, so moving in'll be easy."

"Oh, right. You probably don't even have a bed or anything, do you?"

"Nah, but I got my first paycheck yesterday, so that won't be a problem."

"Good. Let me grab you the extra key real quick because I won't be here when you get back. I told some work friends I'd go out with them for a drink."

"Okay." Jackson follows me to the kitchen where I grab the extra key out of the little basket on top of the fridge. "What do you do for a livin'?"

I freeze, the key in my outstretched hand. "Oh, um, this and that," I answer vaguely.

Jackson cocks his head but doesn't push for more.

"Before you go, any sightseeing tips?"

"Check out the beach."

"Thanks, I will. I'll catch you later," he says, taking the key from my hand and giving me a little wave before heading out to likely hit a furniture store.

"Later," I call after him.

Jackson

LA IS a whole different ball game from Texas and one I'm not sure I like. I figured it would be an adjustment, going from a small town in rural Texas to a city like this, but to say it's been a culture shock is an understatement. Don't get me wrong, I'm still all ready and rarin' to go, but I may have underestimated the cultural differences a little. Just a tad.

When I asked Cameron for some sightseeing tips earlier, just to get myself familiarized with the city, he sent me to the beach. Granted, that was on my list already, seeing as how it's one of the things I've been looking forward to. I've been to the Gulf Coast, but something told me it's not the same. And now that I'm sitting on a fluffy, soft towel on Santa Monica beach, I can confirm it's not.

It's busy here, even on a Wednesday afternoon, both the beach and the bicycle path crowded. There's a fair number of mothers with young children, presumably too young to be in school, but I also spot a lot of twenty-and thirty-somethings. A few are content to lounge and observe like me, but most of them are active in some way. They're walking along the beach, riding a bicycle, or doing a workout.

What surprises me most is how the people around me look. They're all toned and tanned and sexy, and even though I know I'm in pretty good shape, it's a little intimidating. They're so darn perfect. These people, they're almost like a different species.

Over yonder, a guy performs a complex series of yoga positions, each one bending his body in ways that shouldn't be anatomically possible, and something heavy sits in my stomach as I watch him. It's weird, because I'm about to live my dream, but now that I'm here, I don't know if it will ever live up to my expectations. Or maybe I should say that I don't know if I'll ever be good enough to fit in here.

I read an autobiography of the breakout star of a recent TV series, a young, gay guy who moved from Wisconsin to LA when he got the main part on that show. It became an instant success, catapulting him into celebrity status. Sadly, he struggled with that change and got addicted to all kinds of nasty stuff.

I wanted to read his book because I figured it would be a good cautionary tale for me, and now that I'm sitting here, some of what he expressed makes more sense to me. He called LA a *rat race*, complained about the intense pressure to fit in, to look as good as everyone else. I didn't fully understand it at the time, wondering how people in the same country could look so different, but as I'm sitting here on the part of the beach that's known as Muscle Beach, I get it.

I have never seen so many beautiful people at the same time, and it's disconcerting to say the least. Intimidating. Eerie, even, and I get where he was coming from now. How the heck can you compete with this and not go crazy?

I turn my head in surprise when someone plops on the sand beside me. It's a guy my age with a pair of piercing blue eyes.

"Enjoying the view?" he asks, gesturing at the yoga guy.

"It's quite the vista," I say, trying to keep it light.

He sends me a blinding smile, dragging a hand through his wind-tossed hair. He's the epitome of a surfer boy, right down to the colorful surf shorts he's wearing.

"His ass is a work of art," he comments, and it takes me a second to realize he's still talking about yoga guy.

I drag my view back to our yoga friend, who is now doing the most perfect downward-facing dog ever, the aforementioned rump sticking high in the air. Then it hits me. He must be gay. Surfer boy, not yoga dude, although he could be too. No one would comment on another guy's *ass* like that unless he were gay, right?

Something sizzles in my stomach. This is the kind of

casual meet up with gay men I've been dreaming about. And it's only my first day here. Maybe LA isn't so bad after all.

"It's certainly a nice ass," I say, forcing myself to use the word that my mama woulda smacked me on my head for and pushing down the almost automatic fear that I'm inadvertently outing myself. There's no need to be afraid here. I can be myself. This is going to take some getting used to, I realize.

"Well, yours isn't bad either," surfer boy says, and my head shoots to the side.

He's grinning at me cheekily, winking. Hot dang, he's certainly forward, isn't he? How does he even know I'm gay? Come to think of it, how can he even see my *ass* when I'm sitting down?

"And how you would know, curious minds and all that?" I ask.

"I may have been watching you for a little bit," he happily admits. "Before you sat down, even. Plenty of opportunity to check out the goods, I assure you."

What do you even say to a compliment like that? I don't think anyone has ever mentioned my ass before, at least not someone whose name I didn't even know. "Thank you?"

"I take it you're a new arrival," he says.

I smile back at him. His easy happiness is kind of hard to resist. "The greenhorn was that easy to spot, huh?"

"Aside from your wide-eyed observation of your surroundings, your accent was a dead giveaway, and let's not forget your cowboy hat. Don't get me wrong, I love it. In fact, I'd love to hear you talk some more, want to grab lunch together?"

My eyes widen. He's asking me out? He moves fast, doesn't he? I swallow and pray that I'll be able to keep my cool. "You want to maybe tell me your name first? I'm Jackson, by the way."

I extend my hand to him and he takes it with a widening smile. "Good god, you're adorable. Nice to meet you, Jackson. I'm CJ."

Adorable, that's good, right? Personally, when I hear adorable, I think more along the lines of golden retriever puppies or baby owls, but at least it's positive. I think I would've preferred *sexy* or *hot,* but I'll take adorable for now. Not that I even care what CJ thinks of me, obviously, but wouldn't it be nice to get some experience in flirting with men? He could be my practice, I decide.

I squeeze his hand a tad longer before I let him go. "The pleasure is all mine, darlin'."

CJ chuckles. "Oh, you're good. The way you just said *darling*, that was so fucking sexy. I could listen to you all day."

"All day is mighty presumptuous of you, but we could start with that lunch you mentioned?"

He winks at me again. "Sounds good, let me grab a shirt and some shoes. I'll be right back, so don't go anywhere."

I laugh as he jumps up and runs off toward what I assume is his car while I unashamedly stare at his ass. I can't really make it out in those baggy surfer shorts, but the rest of his body looks good.

"I see CJ already got to you?" a voice speaks up, and when I turn my head, yoga guy is standing in front of me, his body covered in a thin layer of perspiration.

Gosh darn it, the dude is perfect. Every muscle on his body is sculpted like a Michelangelo statue. How many hours of yoga a week does he need to do to be in that shape? I would kill for a body like that.

Then his words hit me, and I manage to drag my eyes away from his body back to his face. "Excuse me?"

The guy smiles. "CJ, he asked you out, right?"

What is with these people? How is it possible I managed to keep my sexuality a secret for so long and these guys can see I'm gay within seconds? Did coming to LA somehow boost my gay vibes or something?

"We're just gonna grab lunch."

He nods. "I figured as much. Come find me next time, okay?"

I frown, completely confused by what he means. "I'm sorry, I don't understand. You want to work out with me or something?"

The laugh he lets out is genuine, a booming, rich laugh that draws a couple of people's heads in our direction. "Fuck, you're adorable," he says, and there's that word again. *Adorable.* I'm still banking on it being a good thing, though I *am* starting to get worried a little. "Usually, I don't mind when CJ gets the new arrivals first, but I have to admit that in this case, I'm a little disappointed. Yes, honey, I would like to work out with you."

"Hey Dustin, you trying to steal my date?" CJ calls out as he makes his way back to us.

Yoga guy, whose name is Dustin I just learned, holds up both of his hands. "I wouldn't dare, and you know it, babe. I know the rules. Just let me know when you're done with him, okay? I wouldn't mind the leftovers, if you know what I'm saying."

There's a whole subtext here I'm only getting partially, I realize. I'm the new arrival, that much is clear, and these two both know I'm gay. How, I'm still not sure, but it means they're gay as well. And CJ is known for taking out newcomers? I don't know what that is about, but the comment about leftovers, that one I got. It leaves a nasty taste in my mouth, even though both men are laughing and joking about it.

"You know what they say, Dustin, save a horse, ride a cowboy. And we have found ourselves a mighty fine cowboy right here."

Okay, as naïve as I might be, that reference is hard to miss. Ride a cowboy? Really? I get that my accent and hat might make me appear like some dumb country boy, but I can't help but be a bit offended. The direct flirting, that's all fine with me, but I'm not a piece of livestock they get to haggle over. I'm better than that, I decide, no matter how much I would love to experiment a little.

"I'm terribly sorry to disappoint both of y'all, then, but this cowboy is gonna go hunt for greener pastures. Y'all can fight some more, but I'm callin' it a day. Have a nice day, gentlemen."

I tip my hat and saunter off, strangely satisfied when I leave them standing there all by themselves. I may be looking for some experience, but I still have standards.

3
CAMPY

I stumble out of my room, half-asleep and still a little drunk after going out last night with the guys and not getting in until almost three in the morning. I tried to leave earlier, but Brewer kept handing me drinks, telling me it might be his last night on earth before Tank kills him today. If I didn't have the barn today, I'd be half tempted to head down to the studio to watch their shoot out of morbid curiosity.

I shuffle to the kitchen naked as a jaybird, rubbing my sleepy eyes. When I see a large man standing at the refrigerator, I startle, letting out a surprised yelp before remembering that I got a roommate yesterday.

Jackson looks at me over his shoulder with concern.

"You all right?" he asks before his eyes go wide, flicking quickly over my naked body. I'm surprised to see a light-pink tinge creep over his cheeks. I wouldn't have pegged him as the blushing type.

"Shit, sorry," I mumble sleepily. "I forgot I don't live alone anymore, I'll go put some clothes on."

I hurry back to my bedroom to pull on a pair of pants

and a T-shirt before heading back to the kitchen. This time I find him messing with the coffee maker while bread cooks in the toaster.

"Sorry about that," I say again.

"No trouble." He waves me off, not looking at me this time. Great, I made him uncomfortable. Some roommate I am.

"So, did you get all your stuff moved in okay?" I ask, making polite conversation.

"Oh, yeah. Like I said, I didn't have much. I came here with a suitcase of clothes and blind hope."

"I think that's how most people come to LA," I chuckle, reaching for a coffee mug and filling it once he finishes with his.

"Was it how you came here?"

"Me? No, I was born here. Well, not *here* but about an hour outside the city. I moved here after high school for college initially and then stayed for work."

"Oh, right. You told me you grew up here, sorry. What do you do for work?" he asks for the second time in two days.

Fuck. I walked into that one, honestly.

"This and that," I answer, the same way I did yesterday. I really should come up with a standard lie I tell for times like these.

"Oh."

Now I feel like a jackass, so I decide to elaborate *slightly* more than I normally would.

"I didn't get a chance to finish my undergrad degree because some personal stuff came up. So now I do what I have to do."

"I'm sorry." The way he says it sounds like he truly is sorry, and not just like it's what he thinks he should say.

"Well, you know what they say, life's a bitch and then you die," I joke with a shrug to lighten the mood.

"My mama always said *every slip ain't a fall*. I guess she means you can always get back on your feet."

I force a smile, taking a sip of my hot coffee. "I hope she's right."

"She usually is," he assures me, and for some reason, it makes me feel a hell of a lot better than I've felt in ages.

"Sorry I didn't have a chance to clear off a shelf for you in the fridge before you moved in. I'll do that after breakfast so you have somewhere to put your own stuff after you go shopping."

"That's mighty kind of you. I don't mind sharin' either. We're roommates and I'd like to be friends."

"I'd like that too, Jackson," I agree, even though the idea of a friend sounds a little dangerous. I have too much I don't want to share with anyone else. What kind of a friend can I be carrying around secrets like I do? A familiar guilt tightens around my gut as every one of my lies feels like it weighs a ton, settling on my shoulders—lies to the guys I work with, to Bear, to my own mother. I met Jackson yesterday and he's already getting my standard heap of lies. I don't deserve friends.

After making some toast for myself, I move things around in the fridge so the top shelf is cleared off for him, as well as two of the four shelves in the door. I don't have much in there, so it only takes about a minute to do.

"It looks like I need to go shopping today," I mutter, mostly to myself.

"Oh? You mind if I tag along? I wasn't sure where the nearest grocery store was in this neighborhood."

"Sure. I need a shower first, then we can go, if that's cool?"

"Sounds good," he agrees.

I clean up my breakfast dishes and head to the bathroom to take a shower. Once I'm all clean, I grab a towel and wrap it around my waist so I can head to my bedroom. I've always hated dressing in the bathroom after a shower, it's too humid so it's impossible to get fully dry, then you feel mildly damp all day long. I much prefer to lie on my bed and air dry for a few minutes before putting fresh clothes on.

I step out of the bathroom and nearly walk right into Jackson on his way to his bedroom. His eyes go wide, doing that quick flick over my nearly naked body again.

"God, I'm sorry. You're going to move out before the end of the week if I keep walking around undressed."

"It's fine," he assures me in a husky voice. I could almost swear he likes the view. Maybe he does, not like I care one way or the other. I just don't want to make him so uncomfortable he decides to move out.

"Okay, well, I'll try to be clothed more often."

He gives a small nod but it doesn't seem like he's even listening to what I'm saying, before giving himself a shake and tearing his gaze away to hurry the last few steps to his bedroom.

∼

"Holy cow," Jackson mutters as we step into the massive grocery store, somehow buzzing with people even at ten o'clock on a Tuesday morning. "This is nothin' like back home."

"Yeah, I imagine LA is quite the culture shock for you."

"That's an understatement. I think there are more

people inside this grocery store right now than in the entire town I grew up in," he confides.

"Wow, that has to be overwhelming. I can't imagine living in such a small town like that, isn't it weird always feeling like everyone knows you and is watching everything you do?" I ask, grabbing a cart and starting in the direction of the produce section.

"I don't really know any different. It was difficult when —" he cuts himself off, going a little pale before giving me a forced smile.

"A little difficult when...?"

"Nothin', just datin' is tough when you know everybody's mama and daddy, have 'em breathing down your neck and all."

"Oh, I bet," I agree, studying the way his cheeks go from pale to pink as an array of emotions flit across his face. Something tells me Jackson doesn't have a ton of dating experience, and something about that makes me feel kind of dirty. Not that I've ever thought there was anything wrong with doing porn, but I have to wonder what he would think if he knew. He's probably one of those country boys who would freak out about all the gay if he *did* find out. He's not going to find out, though, because I sure as hell have no intention of telling him.

We chat more as we make our way around the store, each adding items to our own carts.

"Not to pry, but why are you gettin' two of everything?" Jackson asks as I add two loaves of bread to my cart. It's my turn to pale and force a smile. "Sorry, it's none of my business," he backpedals.

"It's fine. I do the shopping for my mom," I answer as succinctly as possible.

"Aw, and here my mama was tellin' me no city boys

respect their parents."

I breathe a small sigh of relief when the subject moves on to our favorite cereals. My gaze lingers on the sugary cereal aisle calling to me like a siren as I glance back and forth between the mostly healthy contents of my cart and the temptation.

"God, I miss not worrying about what I eat," Jackson complains as if he can read the thoughts directly from my brain.

"So much same," I agree. "You have to stay in good shape for the show, right?" I guess.

"Yup. I knew I'd have to look my best to make it in this town, but after we shot the pilot, I honestly felt a little dirty being told they were going to be rubbing dirt on my abs to film certain scenes."

I nod knowingly, certainly able to relate to his feeling like a piece of meat.

"You get used to that gross feeling, don't worry."

Jackson cocks his head.

"Do you act too?"

"Oh, um…" *Shit*. "Not exactly, it's hard to explain."

He frowns at my stuttering but doesn't press for more information. *Good going, Cam*, I scold myself. If I don't want him to find out I do porn, I need to be a lot more smooth than this.

"Well, I'm glad to know you're on a strict diet like I am. I was worried I'd be tempted if you had donuts around the apartment."

"Mmmm, don't say donuts, you're going to make me start drooling," I joke, and just like that, we're back to that less awkward place. I'm not sure what it is about Jackson, but I can see us being good friends…well, however good of friends we can be without telling him my numerous secrets.

4

JACKSON

It's the first day on set to start filming the rest of the episodes, and I'm so nervous I feel like throwing up. How I wish I could text Brax about this, ask for his moral support. Maybe I should tell him, I think, but then I remember how hard it was for him to keep my secret of being gay after I told him, and I reconsider. I can't do that to him. He's horrible at keeping stuff inside. It's like it eats at him or something. No, I'll have to get through this on my own.

We started the day with a breakfast with the whole core cast of the show, and I have to admit it was nice to get to know everyone a bit better. We shot the pilot episode months ago, but that was so tight on time we didn't get to hang out. Even now we didn't have the opportunity to exchange more than a few pleasantries, but it's still a good start.

As luck has it, I have a gay costar, *star* being a weird word for me here as the first episode hasn't even aired yet. I've literally had to introduce myself to pretty much everyone, so *star* is still a ways off for me. Humble beginnings and all that.

But Ethan's a legit star, someone who has been in this business for a long time, with an epic list of credits to his name. Ethan plays the uncle in the series, my dead father's brother, and he's a fifty-something guy who's been married for almost ten years, he told me. He was super friendly when we chatted for a bit during breakfast.

I can't even express how grateful I am to have at least one out and proud gay actor on the set. I'm not planning on advertising my sexuality, but I don't want to make a secret of it either. Call me crazy, but I have a sneaky suspicion that in a town like LA, sex and sexuality are topics that come up frequently in conversations, even on set.

Heck, this morning during breakfast there was an amount of gossip equal to that of lunch with the cheerleader squad at high school. Knowing that Ethan is there at least gives me hope I won't be vilified by everyone when I come out.

Before I officially came out to my parents—not a moment I think back on fondly—I read some articles and one thing stuck with me. It was an interview with a gay activist who had come out only a few years before. In the interview, he kept repeating that coming out wasn't something you did once, that it was a constant in his life. Every time he met new people, he had to come out all over again. Even at the time, I realized the truth of that statement, and so far, it's been spot on.

"Good morning everyone," Lucy speaks up. She introduced herself as the production assistant earlier, and she's one of those classic California girls, all blonde and tanned and bubbly. "Now that we've gotten to know each other a bit, let's start with our tour of the set and get you familiar with the set-up."

We all follow her like obedient little sheep as she leads the way toward the studio where they built the inside of the ranch, where many scenes will be shot. Even walking around on the studio complex gives me jitters in my stomach. I mean, I'm not that easily intimidated, but the *Dr. Phil* show is being shot in the studio right across from ours. To be even on the same complex as a legendary show like that blows my mind.

The inside of the studio is jaw-dropping in sheer size. There's a living room, a kitchen, and even two bedrooms to shoot the most important scenes.

"This is your bedroom, Jackson," Lucy says.

She gestures at a room that's set up in a rustic style, with decorations that could have been ripped from my parents' ranch. A Cowboys cap, a few rodeo buckles, the red-white-and-blue deco—it all looks awfully familiar. Still, something feels off, and as I look around the room I realize what it is.

"It's missing the Lone Star," I tell Lucy, then almost slap my hand over my mouth at my lack of filter. Surely there are smarter things to do on your first day than speaking up with criticism.

Lucy cocks her head. "What do you mean?"

I swallow. Might as well finish it now. "In Texas, most patriotic decorations don't focus on the Star-Spangled Banner but on the Lone Star. It's a Texas thing. Ma'am," I tack on for good measure. A little charm never hurt nobody.

"Interesting," Lucy says, but she doesn't sound upset or angry. Instead, she scribbles something down on a notepad she's holding. "I'll check with our designers. Thank you."

She takes us through the entire set, explaining which are actual doors and which are fakes, where the cameras and the lights will be, what we need to pay attention to. By the time she's done, my head is spinning. I mean, we shot the pilot, but that was a much smaller set where the cameras dictated your position. This is a little overwhelming.

"Don't worry," Ethan says, putting a gentle hand on my shoulder. "For the first few days, they'll mark your spots with tape on the floor so you'll know where to stand for perfect camera angles. After a week or two, you'll be completely used to it."

I shoot him a look of gratitude. "Thank you. I've never done a production this size. Most of my experience is with community theater and some commercials."

He chuckles. "I figured as much. You got lucky with Lucy, because she's the type of person who appreciates feedback like that, but in the future I'd recommend saying things like that in private. Generally speaking, people in the TV business don't appreciate being corrected in public."

I let out a long sigh. "Yeah, that makes sense. I said it before I could even keep myself from speaking up. Thank goodness she didn't throw a hissy fit, but I shoulda kept my mouth shut."

He shakes his head, letting go of my shoulder. "No, it was the right thing to speak up. Details like that can draw harsh criticism from reviewers, so it's good that you pointed it out. You just may want to do it in private the next time, is all I'm saying."

I look around to see if anyone else is paying attention to us, but the others are engaged in conversations with each other as well. Still, I drop my voice to a whisper. "So if I had noticed, hypothetically speaking, that an important detail is missing in the hallway or on the porch, who would I tell that to in private?"

He lifts one eyebrow in curiosity. "What did you spot?"

"It's supposed to be a working ranch, yeah? That means there should be something to put our boots on when we step foot inside. You don't walk inside the house with your boots on. There's a spot for boots on the porch or just inside the hallway. My mama would whack me with a wooden spoon if she saw me dragging mud and dirt inside."

Ethan's face breaks open in a big smile. "You've got a good eye for detail, son," he says. "I'll be sure to mention it to the right people so you're off the hook, okay?"

"Thank you. I appreciate it. I didn't want to speak up again and be *that* guy, you know?"

Our conversation is interrupted when the girl who is playing my younger sister joins us. Shelby, her name is, and she's from Louisiana. We talked for a few minutes this morning, and from what I can tell, she's a hoot. "I don't know about y'all, but I am fucking terrified. Just seeing this studio makes me feel what a fucking amateur I am."

Right, I forgot to mention. Shelby is quite fond of the F bomb. I've never heard someone be so inventive in the use of that particular word. It was impressive, actually, even more considering I still have trouble saying it.

Go ahead, laugh at me, but my parents were darn strict on language. You get your mouth washed out with homemade soap, see if you would ever curse again. As a result, I sound like a senior citizen when I try to use forceful language. Think I'm kidding? This kid in my class pranked me once by attaching something to my chair, so when I moved it, it sounded like a loud fart. You wanna know how I reacted? By loudly exclaiming, "Well, Heavens to Betsy!" That's how cool I was in sixth grade, just saying, and it's not like I've improved much since then.

"Same here," I admit to her. "Just seeing all the TV shows

that have been shot in this same studio almost made me shit my pants."

There, I said *shit*. Points for Jackson and his potty mouth. Let's not mention that I'm half expecting lightning from Heaven to strike me down any moment now.

Ethan shakes his head and laughs. "I'm going to thoroughly enjoy working with the two of you. I love working with new actors. Not to sound too jaded, but I much prefer people like you over those that have become even a bit famous and have developed this air of entitlement, you know? There are a few things I despise more than diva behavior."

He needn't worry with me. Diva behavior is still a long ways off, I can guarantee him that. I'm far too terrified of messing this up to get cocky.

Campy

"Hey, Cam!" Julie greets me as I enter the barn.

"Hey, Jules. How's it going?"

"Great! You were totally right about Ethel, she's happy as a clam now and the donkeys seem to adore her."

"Awesome." My smile widens and pride surges in my chest.

"Dr. Marx stopped by the day after you were here last, and I told him about Ethel and he said he would've made the same suggestion. He said to tell you *good call*."

I nearly let out a giddy laugh at that news. Not only does it show my instincts are spot on, but praise from Brett Marx is extremely hard to come by. I was bummed when my filming schedule ramped up a bit after Rebel stepped back and I ended up having to switch my barn days. When I'd first started working part time here, I used to come on the same day that Brett stopped by every week, and he would let me shadow some of his medical procedures and entertain my questions when he wasn't too busy.

I'd started to look forward to spending time with Brett almost as much as I looked forward to seeing the animals, which is really saying something.

But when I had to change my days and realized I wouldn't get to see him again, it had been almost physically painful, I guess because I'd developed a bit of hero worship toward him. And learning some hands-on things from him was the closest I was going to get to vet school for the foreseeable future.

The only downside of working with Brett had been that he was gay. Obviously, I don't care that he likes guys, but I was terrified he was going to stumble on my videos and stop taking me seriously once he found out about Campy.

Bile rises in my throat at the very thought. Compartmentalizing my life the way I have is an absolute necessity, but that doesn't make it any easier. Some days it feels like every other word out of my mouth is a lie to people I care about and I'm not sure that will ever sit right with me, even if I don't have a choice about it.

It had been even worse the time his boyfriend came by once to help out when we were shorthanded. Not only had I been doubly nervous about being found out, but something about the guy just rubbed me the wrong way. Brett could do *so* much better than that guy.

I bristle at the memory before shaking it off. It doesn't matter anyway. I'm not going to be working with him again anytime soon.

"Hi, Cameron," Alex, the owner of the rehab center,

greets me as he steps out of his office. "Can we talk for a minute?"

I glance at Julie and she gives me a smile and a thumbs up, and my stomach churns. *He's going to offer me a full-time position, and I'm not sure I can accept it.* With a nervous smile, I follow Alex back into his office.

"I'm sure Julie already told you, but good work with Ethel last time you were in."

"Thank you." I nod and lick my dry lips.

"You have good instincts and you're a hard worker. Am I correct in assuming you're applying to vet school?"

"I will be. Not yet or anything, I still need to complete my undergrad, but once I'm able to get the money together..." I trail off, knowing even as I say it that it's so far off. Even if I magically had the money for school, I wouldn't be able to afford to cut back working. If anything, my mom's needs are getting *more* expensive, not less. At this rate, I'll need to win the lottery if I want to go to vet school in this lifetime.

"I see. Well, I'm not sure what your school schedule will look like in the spring, but I'd love to offer you a full-time position here."

"In the spring?" I repeat, feeling a small flurry of hope. That might give me time to figure out if it's possible at least.

"Yeah. You know how it is in April, all the abandoned babies being brought in. Things will be busy, and I'll need to make sure we have more staff."

"But what about when fall and winter roll back around, will I be let go?"

"No, this wouldn't be a seasonal offer. What do you think, are you interested?"

My stomach flutters again and the word *yes* is on the tip

of my tongue. *Of course* I'm interested. But can I make it work? That's the bigger question.

"Can I get back to you on that? I'll need to figure some things out."

"Of course, take some time and think it over."

Walking out of Alex's office, I can't decide if I'm elated or about to collapse under the weight of my responsibilities. I want so fucking badly to take this job, to get back in school and start working toward my passion. But life doesn't work that way.

"Did you get the job?" Julie asks as soon as she spots me again.

"He offered it, I told him I'd think it over." She opens her mouth, but I don't want to answer any more questions so I whip open the freezer to grab a bag of dead rats. "I'm going to check on the raptors and get them fed."

"Oh, okay," she agrees. "By the way, if you pass the ducks, can you peek in and make sure Albert isn't picking on Kinsey again? Ever since Kinsey broke his wing, Albert has been a real dickwad."

I give her a salute to let her know I'm on it and head off to get some work done.

A few hours later, I'm leaving the barn smelling like dead rats and various kinds of animal shit, but the smile on my face is huge. There's just something about being here that makes my soul happy.

Walking to my car, I tilt my head back and look up at the stars. The city lights reach out here to an extent, but there are still visible stars, unlike within the city limits.

I hop up onto the hood of my shitty little car and lie back to look at the sky for a little while, basking in the feeling of peace and rightness being here gives me.

For some strange reason, I suddenly want to bring

Jackson out here sometime and share this with him. He grew up on a ranch, I bet he'd appreciate it. Then it occurs to me that bringing him here would open up a lot of questions I don't want to answer. Hell, it would mean giving him a fuck ton more insight into who I am than I've ever given any of the guys I work with. Maybe it's not such a good idea. It's a nice thought, though, sitting on the hood of my car all sweaty and smelly together, looking at the stars. Yeah, I think he'd enjoy that.

Eventually, it's too late to keep sitting here, so I climb off my car and get inside to head home, driving with the windows down and my music loud until I reach the city limits and the sense of peace and freedom leaves me.

One day I'll be a veterinarian and I'll live outside the city. I'll spend my days helping animals and everything about my life will make me happy. One day.

5

JACKSON

After shooting for six days straight, it's my day off today, and I'm too tuckered out to even contemplate going anywhere. It's hot as Hades outside, the oppressive heat covering the city like a gray, smelly blanket, and I have zero desire to leave this well air-conditioned room. I stepped outside for a few minutes to take out the trash, and I was sweating like a sinner in church.

And to think that when I was house hunting, I debated moving into an apartment without AC, thinking the LA heat couldn't be as bad as Texas. In hindsight, that was stupidly naïve. I'm happy right where I am, with Cameron as my roommate.

We've been roommates for a month now, and I still don't have a clue what Cameron does for a living. It's weird, because some days, he comes home with the distinct odor of animals on him. Hello, I grew up on a ranch. I know what animals smell like, and he's got that scent of hay, of dirty stalls, of animal slobber and fur all over him sometimes. He wears sturdy cargo pants those days, with boots that reek of manure, and he's tired but happy when he gets back

Other days, he comes home with his hair still wet from a shower, smelling fresh and soapy. Those are the days when he wears those ridiculously tight jeans that are so perfectly sculpted around his ass I have to force myself to look away. He has one pair that's faded to the point where I'm holding my breath every time he bends over...but I'm getting distracted here. Those days, he's plumb tuckered out, the kind of bone tired that has little to do with your body and everything with your head space.

I don't get it. It's like he's two different people, with two separate jobs. I'll admit, it's made me very curious, but I don't want to ask again. It's clear he doesn't wanna talk about it, considering he's blown me off twice now. If he wanted me to know, he would've told me, right? I have questions, though, lots of them. Like, the guy doesn't seem to have much of a social life either. There have been no girls sleeping over, not even visiting, as far as I can tell.

Again, not something I'm gonna comment on, especially since he could say the same from me. No, I haven't told him I'm gay. Truth be told, I didn't want to tell him at first. My money is on him being straight, and I don't want to ruffle his feathers. I fear he might not be too happy being roomies with a gay dude, especially with that habit of his of walking around almost naked. Not that I'm complaining, mind you, but he'd feel mighty uncomfortable if he knew I was gay. I think. Plus, I haven't found a natural segue yet from *hey, how was your day* to *by the way, I'm gay*.

But he's nice. Strike that, he's really nice. And super cute. Which obviously, I'm keeping to myself because of the aforementioned gay thing. But there's nothing wrong with my eyes, and he's a mighty fine sight. Especially naked or half-dressed. That boy needs to learn to put on some clothes when he saunters around the apartment.

But even dressed, I like hanging out with him. We've chatted a bunch of times about random stuff, and he's been patiently answering all my questions about getting around in LA, places to visit in my spare free time, and more.

Cameron told me he's working all day today, which is mixed news. I sure wouldn't have minded spending a little more time with him on my day off, I'll tell you that. Aside from him being easy on the eyes, there's this sense of mystery that has me captivated. But I'm also tired, so with him being gone, I'm fixin' to spend a lazy day inside. And after I did the dishes, cleaned up my room, and ran a load of laundry, I have something else on the agenda.

Porn.

Here's the thing. I never had much chance to watch any, since my dad put one of them filters on our internet back home. Heck, you couldn't even search for *breast cancer* what with how strict the settings were. College wasn't an improvement, since our college Wi-Fi network—strict conservative Christian college, remember?—had a similar filter. And since my phone was a prepaid one with a data limit, I never had much opportunity to watch any.

Sure, I watched some with friends whose parents weren't as strict as mine, but that was back when I was still pretending to be straight. Boobs just don't do much for me. My apologies, ladies. I know y'all work hard at making that porn, but it's leaving me plumb unsatisfied.

Since moving to LA, let me tell you, I've watched a lot. I found some stuff I never even knew existed. Hello, daddy kink. I gotta admit, watching one of them gray-haired bears —aren't I catching up on learning all the gay lingo?—pound an itty-bitty twink into oblivion is a mighty fine sight to see. I also tried some stuff that didn't ring my bell, which is fine. But this newbie gay Facebook group I joined had some recommendations for gay porn, which I bookmarked, duh, so I'm fixin' to try those out.

I install myself on my bed, buck naked of course, and place my laptop so I can see it. I haven't bought a TV for my room yet, but with Netflix and Hulu subscriptions Cameron and I share, this works just fine. I try out two sites that came recommended, and after watching some videos, my dick is already leaking like crazy. But I don't want to finish just yet. Years of playing with myself have taught me that edging is a hell of a lot of fun and totally worth it.

I pull up another rec, a paid site called Ballsy Boys that offers some free previews for nonmembers. There's a preview of a new shoot, and the picture they show is promising, with the cutest little twink ever taking a big dick. *Campy wrecks Pixie's ass*, the one-liner reads, and I chuckle at that nickname as I click. The video starts playing, and one second later, I freeze.

That's impossible, right? That sexy as all get-out naked guy on screen who is kissing the little twink like there's no tomorrow can't be my roomie. It can't be, and yet as the camera zooms in, there's no doubt in my mind. That tanned face with the blinding white teeth, that messy brown hair that always makes me want to drag my hand through it, and that toned body, I'd recognize him anywhere by now. It's Cameron, all right, though he apparently goes by Campy here.

Cameron is doing gay porn? I try to let it sink in as the video continues, Cameron and that cute twink—Pixie—kissing in a way that makes my stomach act all funny. Then they move on from kissing, and the camera travels lower, showing off Cameron's body. Oh my, he's perfect, all these tanned lines and hard planes. He's not bulky, but he's got the body of an athlete, all tight muscles and not an ounce of fat.

The camera zooms in on his cock, Pixie's hand wrapping around it, and I have to remind myself that oxygen is essential. *Breathe, Jackson, breathe.* Oh darn it, he's perfect. Every inch of his body is utter perfection, and that includes his dick, which is...perfect. I need a thesaurus, because *perfect* just doesn't cover it, but my mind is having a hard time functioning at all.

Pixie scrambles down and those full lips wrap around Cameron's cock. I can almost taste him myself, the slightly salty tang of his precum, the hint of sweat that never fails to turn me on, mixed in with the essence that's all him. I swallow thickly, my cock so hard it hurts. It's hard not to be jealous of Pixie, though I don't even know him, because he gets to taste him, gets to pleasure him. How I wished that were me.

Admittedly, I don't have a lot of experience in the sex department. I've had two partners, which I'm sure is an old-fashioned term, and I remind myself to look up how to better word that—one of the many things I need to learn about gay culture and sex.

One was when I was still in high school and messed around with a guy on my football team. No one knew, obviously. Texas, teens, and football players, it's like the holy trinity of *hell no*. But we had some fun exploring, kissing and frotting and giving each other sloppy blow jobs that got better over time. We never went all the way, too scared of the ramifications if anyone found out.

Then in college—a conservative Christian college, of all places, the irony of that wasn't lost on me—I met another guy who, like me, was shoved deep into the closet. After a month or two of dating in secret, we rented a motel room one night and went all the way. It was clumsy and yet sweet, both of us taking a turn at topping and bottoming.

I liked him and though I was nowhere near in love with him, it was still a blow when he announced his engagement a few weeks after that. Not to me, goodness no, but to a sweet girl he'd been dating for years but had "forgotten" to inform me about. Even worse was that he still wanted to see me. You'd better believe I turned down that proposal faster than I can throw a football. I wasn't quite that desperate.

So no, I don't have much experience. It's one of the things I set myself to rectify here in LA. But Cameron could teach me, right? Or Campy. Either one, though it's hard for me to think of him as Campy. I don't care what he calls himself, because the best news ever is that he's gay. I clearly have to work on my gaydar, but then again, so does he, as he hasn't pegged me as gay either.

Pixie lets out a soft little moan as Cameron fills him, sinking that perfect dick into his pink hole, stretching it wide open. I can't stop watching, greedily soaking in every grunt Cameron makes as he slides into him, first slow and then with a force that causes his balls to slap against Pixie's ass. The sound alone is intoxicating, and I can't resist the urge anymore to wrap my hand around my cock and start stroking myself in the same rhythm.

"Oh, you feel so good," Pixie moans.

Why yes, he does, I think, increasing the pressure on my dick. Cameron sneaks a hand around to wrap it around Pixie's cock, and I have no trouble imagining my own hand is his, firmly gripping my dick and stroking hard. He'd know to relax just a little on the downward move, then grip tightly on the upward one, fisting the crown. It's sopping with my juices, all slick and slippery, and I love the sound it makes as it mingles with the increased noises from the video.

Then Cameron lets out a low, deep moan, and I let go. My balls empty themselves as I come hard all over my chest, while Cameron and Pixie have their own cum-fest on screen. I have to wipe my hand on a tissue before I can turn off the video, and I sag back down on my bed, still shaking.

Cameron is *gay*. It's that thought that fills me more than anything else. He's gay. And as my heart rate finally settles a bit, my decision is made.

I'm gonna ask him out.

6

CAMPY

"Mom," I call out as I step into her small house about an hour outside LA. The house is quiet and dark, but her car is in the driveway so I know she must be home. "Mom," I call again, making my way down the hall to her bedroom.

I give a light rap at her door and hear rustling on the other side.

"Cameron?" Her voice sounds tired.

I push the door open and I'm not surprised to find her in bed, clearly just waking up.

"What time is it?" She rubs her eyes and tries to sit up, but winces in pain and sinks back down.

I hurry over to her and sit down on the edge of the bed. "Don't try to get up. Is the pain bad today?"

She nods weakly and tries to give me a reassuring smile. It breaks my heart to see my mom this way. Growing up, she was like Wonder Woman to me. My dad peaced out when I was a baby and she raised me on her own, working as a maternity ward nurse. Then, five years ago, she started experiencing fatigue and severe back pain. That's how it started, but it soon progressed to losing coordination in her hands at times, dizziness, and muscle spasms.

After her diagnosis, she was determined to keep working, but that only lasted about six months before she had to admit she wasn't able to do her job anymore. Even with the symptoms coming and going, there was no way to know when she would have a bad day, and she couldn't stand to have to call in so often on such short notice. She was devastated when she had to quit, and she's never quite bounced back emotionally.

"Have you been in bed all day? Do you want me to fix you something to eat?" She looks a little guilty and I know instantly she's been having more than just one bad day. "How long?"

"Oh, just a couple of days." She tries to wave me off and her hand tremors.

"Why didn't you tell me when I called? I would've been over here right away. Have you eaten or showered?"

"I didn't want to bother you. You're so busy working, making sure you can pay all of my bills." There's even more guilt and bitterness in her voice. "I don't want to burden you more than I already am."

"It's not a burden," I assure her. "If you can't get out of bed to take care of yourself, then I need to be here to help."

This is exactly why I need to find a way to afford a home health care aide to *at least* stop by daily. My original plan with Jackson moving in was to use the extra money I was saving on rent to cut back my hours at Ballsy, but this is more important.

"I'm going to hire you an aide. Once I get you fed and taken care of, I'm going to go online and start looking. I'll call off my barn shift and stay here the rest of the day, and for the next few days until you're feeling better."

"Cameron," she tries to argue but I fix her with a look that tells her to save it.

"I'll have to duck out tomorrow afternoon for work, but I'll come right back after."

She pats my hand and gives me a more genuine smile this time. "I'm so proud of my boy, working at a vet clinic and saving animals, and all the volunteering you do at that wildlife rehab."

I bite the inside of my cheek against the guilt rising in my throat. It's not like I could tell her how I'm really covering her medical expenses. I wish I could work at a vet clinic, but the paycheck would barely cover my own bills, let alone hers. I honestly can't think of another job I could do with my thin resume that would make her care possible. Better porn than drug dealing, right? I just wish I didn't have to lie to her about it. After everything she's done for me, *this* is how I repay her? By doing porn and lying straight to her face? Son of the year, ladies and gentlemen.

I help my mom to the shower and then go to the kitchen to fix her something to eat, keeping an ear out in case she calls for help. Once I have lunch assembled for her, I pull out my phone and call Jackson to let him know I won't be home for a few days.

"Hello?"

"Hey, Jackson," I say into the phone, hurrying over to help my mom to the table when she shuffles into the kitchen. "I wanted to let you know I won't be home for the next few days. I didn't want you to worry or anything."

"Oh?" He sounds curious, but clearly doesn't want to pry. It's that politeness in most people that makes it easy to avoid giving more information than I want to. People may be dying to know what's going on in your personal life, but they'll rarely come right out and ask.

"It's my mom," I explain, to my own surprise. "She has an illness and needs some extra help for a couple of days."

"I'm sorry to hear that, Cam. Is there anything I can do to help? I can make a mean casserole," he offers, and I find myself smiling. "Or I can bring some clothes by for you if you need?"

"Actually, clothes would be extremely helpful. Maybe my toothbrush too?"

"No problem. Text me a list of what you want and the address and I'll get it to you."

"Thanks, you're a lifesaver."

"Happy to help," he assures me before we hang up.

I shoot him a quick text with the info he needs and then join my mom at the table.

"Who was that?" she asks.

"My new roommate. I didn't want him to worry about me disappearing for a few days."

"Oh, I thought it might've been a lady friend. You had a smile I haven't seen before."

"No lady friends at the moment," I tell her with a laugh. I don't have time to date, and I can only imagine how a conversation about my career would go with prospective dates. I have a feeling most women wouldn't be thrilled to date a man in gay porn, or porn in general.

"Why not?"

"Because I don't have time to date."

She frowns. "You don't need to stay here and worry about me so much."

"You're my mother, of course I do. And I *want* to, so save yourself the guilt."

She stops arguing and finishes eating, then I help her to the living room so we can watch some TV together and relax.

A while later, there's a knock at the door signaling Jackson's arrival.

My stomach twists with nerves as I go to the door to let him in. I've never told anyone about my mom before, let alone introduced anyone to her. But he took an Uber all the way out here, so I have to introduce them, right?

I pull open the door and find Jackson standing there with a friendly smile holding a couple of grocery bags along with my duffel bag.

"You didn't need to bring groceries," I tell him as I step aside to let him in.

He shrugs. "I figured it couldn't hurt."

"Well, thank you." I take all the bags from him and lead him into the house.

"Mom, this is my new roommate, Jackson." I introduce them. "Jackson, my mom."

He crosses the room to shake her hand. "Pleasure to meet you, ma'am."

She swoons a little at his Southern charm, and I fight not to roll my eyes.

"Sorry I'm such a mess," she says, waving at her sweatpants and loose T-shirt.

"You look beautiful, ma'am. Cameron told me you weren't feeling well, and I assure you I look a lot more of a mess when I'm under the weather."

While they chat, I take my duffel bag to my old bedroom and the groceries to the kitchen. With the ingredients he brought, I can make a couple of meals to stick in the freezer that will be easy for her to reheat another day when she's not up to cooking. Jackson appears in the kitchen doorway while I'm putting things away.

"Your mom is a hoot."

"Yeah, she's funny," I agree. "She has MS, so it's not a

contagious illness or anything," I add, rushing to assure him.

"I can't say I know much about MS, but I hear it's no picnic."

"No, it's not. I'm going to have to hire someone to come by daily and help take care of her. And if I can swing it, there's a new medication the doctor wants her to try. It's...a lot to deal with," I confide and some sort of understanding dawns in Jackson's eyes.

"I'm sure she appreciates everything you're doing to take care of her." He reaches out and puts his hand on mine. The warm contact is comforting and I can't help but crave more, which is...confusing.

"I'm just doing what I have to." I shrug, not wanting to take more credit than I deserve. Anyone would do the same for their mother. And it's not like Jackson knows the extent I've gone to to make sure her medical expenses are covered, so why is he looking at me with so much awe?

"Is there anything else I can do to help? Maybe cook a couple of meals to put in the freezer for her?" he offers, pulling his hand away, leaving me missing the feeling instantly.

"I was just thinking about doing that, actually," I tell him, giving him a smile.

"You go spend time with your mama, I'll cook," he insists.

"You don't have to do that."

"I know I don't. Now, go." He makes a shooing motion to chase me from the kitchen and I relent, heading back to the living room to spend more time with my mom.

Jackson

. . .

THINGS ARE STARTING to make a heck of a lot more sense now. *I'm just doing what I have to,* Cameron told me, and after what I've discovered about him, that statement is loaded. He's doing porn to pay for his mother's medical expenses. That has to be the reason why.

It explains why he's not happy doing it, which I can only surmise from how he looks when he gets home after a shoot. And whatever else he's doing on the other days, that's what makes him happy. That's what he wants to do, if he could. Man, my respect for him just grew exponentially. He's one of the good ones, that one.

Seeing Cameron with his mom showed me a whole different side of him. Then again, I don't think I've even begun to scratch the surface when it comes to him. There's Cameron the porn star, aka Campy. I'll admit I never saw that one coming, but as I said, it makes a lot more sense now that I know about his mom. There's Cameron from the other job, the one I haven't quite figured out, though I do know it's something with animals. I'm sure that when I discover what he's doing on those days, it will reveal more about him.

I've seen Cameron the roommate—the busy yet attentive guy who so often forgets to put on some clothes before walking into the kitchen. And now I've met Cameron the son, and my heart mellows as I watch the tender care he has for his mama. He's reading to her now, snippets from a magazine she apparently loves but has trouble holding and reading. He patiently shows her the pictures, then reads the accompanying text.

She's so sweet and sassy at the same time, but it's easy to see how frail she is. I don't know much about MS, other than it stands for multiple sclerosis, but she looks mighty weak and fragile for a woman her age. She can't be much older than my mama, which makes sense 'cause Cameron is only a few years older than me, and yet she looks ten, fifteen years older.

As I chop vegetables and sauté some onions, garlic, and ground beef for a casserole, I wonder what I would do if my mama fell ill. Would I move back home? Even as I consider it, I know it would never happen. I couldn't. It would be like going back to prison, harsh as that may sound.

My parents love me, I have no doubt. But I also know they will never fully understand me, and they will never completely accept the fact I'm gay. That's something I've come to realize over the last few years, and as much as it hurts, I've decided holding on to false hope that they will change hurts even more. It's better to accept reality and adjust my expectations.

I do miss them, though, my folks and my siblings. I've been texting them, pretending to still be in college, and every time I lied about that, my heart hurt. It's not how I was raised, but what choice do I have? No, I made the right call. They'll find out, but when they do, it'll be a done deal and nothing they can do about it. It's my life, and my choices are my own. This was a dream I couldn't allow to escape.

Then again, I've always been a practical guy. Oh, don't get me wrong, I'm a dreamer all right. I've never backed down from something I really wanted, but I do know the difference between what's attainable and tilting at windmills. Says the man who moved to LA to try and see if he could make it as an actor, and I grin at myself.

"That smells good," Cameron says.

He's leaning against the door to the kitchen, his arms

crossed. His face shows weariness, deep lines that shouldn't be there. He must be so worried about his mama.

"How is she?" I ask.

I mix in the red sauce with the meat and vegetables, then add a dollop of cream and some dried herbs.

He shrugs, not quite pulling off the gesture. "She's resting a bit now." He hesitates, then adds, "She's not well, but then again, she hasn't been for a long time. I need to get her more help, but it's not going to be easy."

I transfer the meat and the vegetables to the oven dish, then generously sprinkle grated cheese on top. "Because it's going to be hard to find good, qualified help or because she's gonna resist it?"

He lets out a deep sigh. "Both, but especially the latter. It's hard on her, losing her independence more and more. She's only been ill for a few years, but this disease is progressing fast with her."

I close the oven and set the timer, then turn toward him. He looks lost, forlorn, and my heart aches for him. "I'm so sorry. And there's nothing doctors can do for her?"

"They've tried a bunch of different meds, but she is not reacting well to any of them. Some make the pain less but seem to make her mobility worse. Others make her nauseous or have no effect at all on her symptoms."

I hesitate, but I have to ask. "What's her prognosis? Is there any chance of her getting better?"

The look on Cameron's face breaks my heart. "No. Her disease is too progressive for that. All we can hope for is to find a treatment that stops it from progressing further, but she'll never be healthy again. I just want her to be pain free as much as possible, you know? I don't care if I need to have someone take care of her full time. I just want her to be comfortable, to live as much as possible."

I don't know what to say. It must be so heartbreaking for him to watch his mom deteriorate like this. "I wish I coulda met her when she was still healthy. I bet she was an amazing mom."

For the first time, Cameron's eyes light up. "She was wonderful. She still is. We've always been close, and she's worked her ass off her whole life to make sure I was taken care of. With my dad out of the picture, it was just her and me, and she did such a great job. I've always felt loved and safe, and I never even missed having a dad. She was... She is everything to me."

I don't know why I do it, but on impulse, I step in and hug him. It only takes a few seconds for him to hug me back, and when he puts his head against my shoulder, it almost feels like a triumph. He's not a man who easily leans on others, that much I do know about him. He's proud, but in that moment, as he leans on me just a little bit, I'm grateful that I can be there for him, and even more determined to ask him out. I just need to figure out how and when.

When I let go, he sends me a grateful smile. "Thank you so much for being here, for helping me. Us. I really appreciate it."

I smile right back, even as I turn toward the counter again to start preparing another meal his mom can heat up in a few days. "You're welcome. Now, I was thinking of making a nice pasta Alfredo as well, since it freezes well. Do you think that's something your mama would like?"

7

JACKSON

It's two weeks after my big discovery about Campy—and coincidentally, also two weeks after I started my subscription to the Ballsy Boys—and Cameron and I have been spending quite some time together since he got back from his mom's.

I cooked two more meals for his mom and after that, I left. Cameron wanted to stay with her a day or two, just to make sure she was okay. He's been home since, and we've hung out.

It's only reinforced my decision to ask him out, but I need a little time to prepare myself. Not to mention I need to figure out how to ask someone out in the first place, because I have no experience yet. Both my relationships—if you can even call them that when they're all hush-hush—kinda developed organically, so there was no asking out involved. It's a whole new territory, but I'm determined not to mess it up. Cameron undoubtedly does have a lot of experience with dating and stuff, so I need my A-game here.

Again, I wish I could text Brax. He's got more dating experience than me by a long shot, though with women.

Can it be that different, though, asking girls or guys out? But I'm afraid if I text him, it'll lead to questions I don't want to answer. How am I gonna explain finding a gay guy at a conservative Christian college, for example? No, I can't. I do text him a meme of Bert and Ernie he'll love, just to make him laugh.

Luckily, I know just who I can ask for advice. During lunch break, I seek Ethan out. "Hey Ethan, can I sit with you?"

He shoots me a friendly smile and pulls a chair back. "Anytime, kid. Seems like you're getting the hang of it, eh?"

I smile at his Canadian accent slipping back in, though on set he has a mean Texan drawl. He's one of the few non-native Texan speakers on set, but his husband is from Texas, so that explains a lot. "I sure hope so. It's been a steep learning curve."

He nods as he chews on his tuna sandwich. "It takes a while to find your footing, but you're doing a great job."

"Can I ask you something personal?" I ask, not sure how to make a natural segue.

"Sure."

I swallow. Now that the moment is here, I'm wondering if this was such a good idea after all. We don't know each other that well, so maybe it's inappropriate for me to bring up such a personal subject? Ethan patiently waits, something telling me he has an inkling of where this is leading. That gives me the courage to speak up.

"As I told you, I'm gay," I start, and then the words come by themselves. "I only recently came out, and I don't have much experience dating yet. There's this guy that I wanna ask out, and I was wondering if you could give me any pointers on how to do that?"

Ethan smiles. "That's good. Is he out? I mean, do you

know for a fact he's into men? 'Cause that makes a big difference."

That's one question I can answer with certainty. I'm not gonna divulge how I know this for sure, because it's clear Cameron doesn't want others to know about what he does, which I can understand. "He is."

"Well, that makes it a whole lot easier. And he doesn't have a boyfriend as far as you know?"

I chuckle. "He's my roommate, so I'm pretty darn sure he doesn't."

Ethan laughs. "Your roommate, eh? Going for the roommate-with-benefits thing?"

I hadn't even thought of all the possibilities that dating Cameron would bring, considering we live together, but now that Ethan mentions it... My head fills with visions of me and Cameron showering together, of lazy nights on the couch watching TV, of me cooking for him.

"That'd be great," I say with enthusiasm, and Ethan's smile broadens.

"There's no hard rule here, but a good approach is always to come up with something you know he would appreciate. Like, is he into movies? Does he like clubbing or dancing? Is he more an active date type of guy, like going for a hike? If you can figure that out, it helps to ask him for a specific date, not just a generic invite."

Hmm, he's got a good point. Cameron is so busy, though with what I'm not exactly sure, so I think a relaxing date would work well. But what does he like? Then I think of the documentaries I've seen him watch on efforts to save white rhinos from extinction and on an all-female wildlife protection unit somewhere in Namibia, I think, who are trying to save elephants from being killed for their ivory. That, combined with the way he smells certain days, gives me an idea.

"I think I wanna ask him to the zoo," I say. "He loves animals."

Ethan chuckles as he gently shakes his head. "You, my dear Jackson, are the cutest thing ever. You look like a badass cowboy, but you've got a big ole' soft heart. You'll do just fine, my boy. Just be yourself. I can't see how anyone could resist you."

I feel my cheeks heat up at that unexpected praise. "Thank you."

Ethan sends me a blinding smile, the one that made him famous, but then he sobers. "I'm excited for you to discover more of yourself as you venture out into the gay community, but promise me you'll be careful, Jackson. No offense, but you grew up sheltered, and not everyone is as nice and decent as you. As within any community, there are bad apples, and I don't want to see you get hurt."

I nod solemnly. "I promise. Any advice on how to pick out those bad apples?"

Not that I have any doubt that Cameron is the real thing, of course. He would never intentionally hurt me, of that I'm sure.

"Trust your instincts, that's the best I got. If your gut tells you someone or something's fake, listen to it. You'll save yourself a heap of trouble if you do."

That seems like good advice, and I promise myself to take it to heart.

"Thanks, Ethan. I appreciate it."

"You know what? Once you've asked him out, we'll have you and him over for dinner at our place. My husband, Rick, does a mean Texas barbecue, which you should appreciate, and between you, me, and Rick, we'll charm the socks right off your guy."

Now that sounds like a perfect plan, and I shoot a big smile at Ethan. "Awesome. I've been dying for a good barbecue anyway, and I'd love to meet Rick."

"That's settled then," Ethan says as he wraps up his trash and gets up from the table. "Let's get back to work so you can ask your man out afterward."

Campy

Heart shoves his tongue into my mouth with aggressive sloppiness that looks way better on camera than it actually feels. I give an over-the-top moan, hoping it sounds muffled in a sexy way by his tongue rather than giving the impression of being gagged by it. I hope for his sake he's a better kisser in real life than he is when filming.

"Cut," Rebel calls and I cease thrusting, both of us ending the kiss abruptly to look over at Rebel, standing off set just behind the cameras. "Campy, you're looking a bit stiff."

I cock an eyebrow at him and Heart snorts, his hole clenching around my dick as he laughs.

"I thought that was the point," I deadpan.

"You know what I mean." Rebel rolls his eyes at our childish snickers. "You don't look like you're having fun. Is there a problem? Do you need anything?"

I give a sharp shake of my head. I'm usually much better at acting than this. In the year I've been at Ballsy, no one has ever been able to spot the fact that I'm *not* into dudes. But the past few weeks, the stress has been getting to me. Everything feels like it's being piled on until I'm about to collapse under the weight of it.

"Sorry, just a little distracted. I'll get my head in the game."

Rebel gives me a look and for a second I'm worried he's going to press me on what has me so distracted. But to my relief, he just gestures to the cameramen and shouts, "Action!"

Heart instantly starts moaning loudly, and I have to bite the inside of my cheek to keep from laughing at his theatrics. *Head in the game*, I scold myself.

I pull my hips back and then snap them forward, pegging Heart's prostate and eliciting a genuine moan this time, his fingers digging into my back and his eyes rolling back in a way our viewers love.

I let my eyes fall closed for a second, searching for mental inspiration to get through this scene with more enthusiasm. Typically, I'd bring up the image of a beautiful woman—sweet, girl-next-door types always do it for me. But for some reason, the first image that pops into my head is Jackson. Why my brain decides to conjure up my burly, manly cowboy of a roommate with a crooked smile and kind eyes when I'm balls deep in Heart is beyond me. It surprises me enough I lose my rhythm for a few seconds.

To make the whole thing even more shocking? The images of Jackson do the trick in the inspiration department, making my cock harder and my balls churn. The fact that I need to get through this scene keeps me from analyzing it too closely, I just thank fuck for my renewed enthusiasm and fuck Heart like I mean it.

His moans reverberate against all the acoustically ideal

set walls and mine join in. I force my eyes open, hoping to dispel images of Jackson before I come. Heart is blushing and panting, my own harsh breaths matching his. I reach between us and wrap my hand around his cock, jerking him in a fast rhythm that's bound to make him blow in no time. I never thought I'd become an expert on how to get men off, but obviously life can take us in unexpected directions.

His channel clamps down around me and his eyebrows scrunch together, a look of almost pained pleasure on his face—also known as Heart's famous O face. His cock swells in my hand and he cries out as his cum spills over my fingers and shoots onto his chest.

When he finishes, I pull out and quickly do away with the condom, tossing it onto the floor before fisting my own erection and jerking off onto Heart's chest, so when my orgasm washes over me, my release adds to the streaks already there, mixing together and looking entirely filthy in the best way.

Always one to go the extra mile, once the last drop of cum is milked from my cock, I lean forward and gather our combined releases on my tongue and then pull Heart into another sloppy kiss, sure to let some of our seed drip down over our lips and chin to create a nice fantasy scene for viewers to finish to.

He smirks when I pull back, a strand of sticky spit connecting our lips for a few seconds before falling away.

"Cut," Rebel calls, and I let out a little sigh of relief.

"Way to rally," Heart says, clapping me on the shoulder before climbing off the bed and catching a towel tossed to him by the main cameraman, Joey.

"Thanks, Joey," I call when he chucks one at me as well.

"We good?" Heart checks and Rebel gives him a thumbs-up.

Together, we make our way upstairs to the showers and changing room, both eager to wash the scene off.

"Is everything okay with you, man?" Heart asks as we enter the locker rooms.

My stomach twists. I fucking hate how thoughtful and caring all the guys are. I know that's a dickish thing to think, but every time they ask me if everything is okay or offer to listen if I ever need to talk, I feel like a piece of shit. They genuinely want to be friends and form a connection so we can work better together, and I have to hold them at arm's length to protect my secrets. What would they think if they knew I wasn't even gay? What would Bear think? And worse yet, how much would they pity me if they knew the reason for my lie?

"Oh yeah, great," I lie, forcing a smile and it's obvious he doesn't buy it, but I take advantage of the fact we've reached the showers to end the conversation by jumping into the nearest one and turning on the water. I wince at the icy spray, bouncing around for a minute while it warms up.

"Did you seriously get into a cold shower to avoid talking about whatever's bugging you?"

"What? I can't hear you."

He mumbles something before starting his own shower. I close my eyes and tilt my head back into the now-warm cascade of water. Whatever the deal was with thinking about Jackson today, I'm sure it had to do with spending some time together. It's not like I've *never* thought about a man while fucking before, it's just not a regular thing and it's never been someone I know. Usually it's a celebrity or something. And, sure, on occasion a scene I've filmed will pop into my head when I'm jerking off, so *technically* I've thought about some of the guys I work with while getting off, but it's not like it means anything. Thinking about Jackson didn't mean anything either. I'm not homophobic, *obviously*, I'm just not gay.

When you think about it, it's not that surprising Jackson popped into my head. After all, we have been spending a *lot* of time together recently. For the most part, our schedules match up nicely, both of us getting home near the same time most nights, both tired after filming and content to sit together and watch TV or movies while we eat dinner. He's even been taking time to call and check in on my mom when I have busy days and can't manage it.

I've never had a roommate, but I've heard enough horror stories from other people to know I got lucky with Jackson. He's not only a great roommate, he's becoming a good friend. Given all that, it makes sense I'd think of him randomly like that. It doesn't mean anything more.

I mean, yeah, he's good looking too, but that's not why he came to mind. There are plenty of good-looking guys in the world and I've never fantasized about any of them. I'm not about to start with my roommate who somehow manages to be both adorable and drop-dead sexy at the same time.

I rinse the soap off, ignoring the fact that my cock is hard again as I shut off the water and reach past the curtain for a towel.

I push the curtain back and startle at finding Heart standing on the other side, freshly showered and clearly not finished bugging the shit out of me.

"Can I help you?" I ask dryly.

"I just wanted to make sure you knew I was serious, if there's anything you want to talk about, I'm here."

The sincerity dripping from him throws me off for a second.

"I appreciate it. I really am okay, but thank you."

"The offer stands."

I nod, wrapping my towel around my waist and stepping out of the shower as Heart turns and walks toward the lockers, bare assed. The sight of his pert ass wiggling as he walks does nothing for me, even though I've fucked him so many times I've lost count. *See? Definitely not gay.*

8

JACKSON

I've done my research, and it turns out, LA has a zoo. I don't think it's the most impressive one ever, but it'll do the job, I hope. On my phone, I also compiled a list of gay-friendly restaurants—thank you, internet—and with that, I think I'm all set to ask Cameron out. All I need now is courage.

Actually, I need some wisdom as well. Do I tell him I know about his job? It could get mighty awkward, but if it comes up later, I'd feel horrible for pretending I didn't know. Also, he'll want to know how I spotted he was gay, for sure. I'm not gonna lie to him. That doesn't seem like the way to start a relationship. No, honesty is the best approach here.

I saw Cameron leave the house this morning, and if I interpreted his clothes correctly, he had a shoot today. That means he'll come home tired and hungry, and since I'm off today on account of it being Sunday, I can prepare dinner. He seemed to like the casserole I made for him and his mom, so I'm gonna do something similar. Also, casseroles are hard to mess up. Even I know that, as they're basically the backbone of Southern cooking. That, and anything fried and barbecued, but the latter is hard to do in our apartment.

Grabbing some bags to put the groceries in, I head out. It's not the best part of LA we live in, I've discovered. When I saw on the map that Cameron lived close to Hollywood Boulevard, I was all excited. That's where the Hollywood Walk of Fame is, after all, and I thought it would be a nice neighborhood. Boy, was I wrong.

The part near the Chinese Theatre is nice, but other than that, it's a bit seedy. Lots of people loitering, in various stages of being drunk and/or high, or dressing in a way that makes me suspect they're earning their money a certain way. I did see *Pretty Woman* quite a few times, which in hindsight should've clued me in to me being gay, since I was way more interested in Richard Gere than in Julia Roberts.

Even our street, a few blocks from Hollywood Boulevard, can get a bit rowdy at night, and we regularly have homeless people sleeping near the entrance to our building. That's something I'm not used to—my country background showing up again. Cameron said not to give them any money on account of the landlord not wanting any homeless people hanging around permanently, so I haven't, but I do occasionally give out sandwiches to this one guy who's a regular.

It's a twenty-minute walk to the farmers market, but I don't mind. If there's one thing I miss since moving here and taking the acting job, it's being outside. I used to work outside on the ranch as much as I could back in Texas, before I went to college, that is. I've always loved being outside, and riding horses sure is no punishment either. I really need to figure out a way to get some outside exercise in here, I muse as I walk to the market.

This market is rapidly becoming a favorite of mine, since

it reminds me a little of the farmers markets back home. It's much bigger and more crowded, but I love seeing the same pride in homegrown produce. I grab some leeks, fresh herbs, and potatoes, then stock up on fresh fruit. Cameron loves pineapples, I've discovered, so I buy two of those as well as some other fruit to make a fruit salad for dessert.

On the walk back, one of those open-tour minivans drives past me, the driver calling out something about a seeing a genuine cowboy in LA. I tip my hat the best I can with my hands full of groceries, which earns me spontaneous applause from the passengers.

I guess I do stand out with my boots, hat, and jeans. I flat out refuse to wear shorts, no matter the temperature. I only wear shorts when I have to, like in sports, but even then I'll take them tight football pants over those crazy, unflattering baggy basketball shorts any day. My behind looks a sight better in tight-fitting jeans, and why yes, I checked it out in the mirror multiple times to verify.

And I rarely venture out without my hat, as it keeps the sun from my face. I suppose a baseball cap would do the trick, but I never felt they looked particularly good on me. Call me vain, but my cowboy hat suits me whereas a cap seems so...ordinary. But once the series airs, I may have to reconsider. Not that I expect to be instantly famous, but you never know, and with my hat I may become a bit too easy to spot.

By the time Cameron comes home, the casserole is bubbling in the oven, the cheese already browning nicely, and the fruit salad is chilling in the freezer. I take it out as soon as I hear his key in the door, because it tastes much better at room temperature. It's stupid, but I can barely refrain myself from meeting him in the hallway, kissing him senseless, and then asking how his day was.

Luckily, I don't have to wait long till he steps into the kitchen, his hair still damp and his body wash drifting toward me. He looks tired, as he often does on days he has a shoot.

"Hey, what's cooking?" he asks, sniffing the air.

"Potato-leek casserole," I say with pride. "It's almost done."

"It smells amazing," he says, sending me a smile. "Though I'm not so sure I've ever had leeks."

"They're good," I say. "You have to make sure they're well-done, though, so I always let them simmer softly for fifteen minutes before putting them in the casserole."

"You're a regular Martha Stewart," Cameron jokes. "That casserole you made at my mom's was amazing as well. One of these days, you'll have to teach me your secret."

I swallow, overcome by that urge again to hug him. He looks fragile, underneath that strong body, and it's the weirdest thing. "Bacon," I say instead. "You just add bacon. That makes everything taste better."

He grins. "True that."

A few minutes later, we sit down in front of the TV with our food. Cameron prefers watching something while he eats. I think it helps him relax.

"What do you want to watch?" he asks.

I gesture at the remote. "You pick something."

He lifts an eyebrow. "You know that means watching some boring nature documentary, right?"

"If it's boring, why would you watch it?" I fire back.

His eyes drop to the floor. "I like watching them," he admits. "But we can totally watch something else. I'm not expecting you to like those."

"I don't mind nothin'," I say with a smile, laying the accent on a bit thick. He always smiles a little when I do that, and I think he secretly likes it. "I like animals and nature."

His eyes light up. "Have you ever seen the BBC series Planet Earth? It's amazing. I haven't seen the second season yet."

I shake my head and minutes later we're watching jaw-dropping footage of tropical islands where all kinds of animals try to survive. I learn things about Komodo dragons and pygmy sloths, I kid you not, and it's pretty cool. Even cooler is that Cameron gobbles down his portion of casserole and then goes for seconds. He likes the fruit salad as well, and he looks a lot more relaxed by the time he's finished his food.

"Wanna watch another episode?" he asks.

I gather all my courage. "Actually, there was something I've been meaning to talk to you about. Something I wanted to ask you."

"Oh?"

He shifts on the couch to look at me, those gorgeous brown eyes studying me inquisitively. This is it, the moment of truth. *Just be yourself,* Ethan had said, and with that in mind, I opt to go for simple.

"I've loved gettin' to know you a sight better these last few weeks, and I gotta say, it's been a pleasure, so I was wonderin' if maybe you wanted to go out with me? I was thinking we could go to the zoo, since you like animals so much?"

His mouth drops a little open, and so I plod on, terrified to stop now. "And I looked up some gay-friendly restaurants, so afterward, I could take you to dinner?"

I have to breathe, and when I do, Cameron's face transforms in a way that makes my stomach drop.

"Jackson," he says. "I'm really flattered, but I think there's a misunderstanding. I'm not gay."

Campy

JACKSON COCKS HIS HEAD, confusion clear on his face. He studies me for a few seconds before his confusion turns to hurt and embarrassment. My heart constricts painfully at the expression. I want to scoot closer and wrap my arms around him, maybe even agree to go out with him if it will make him stop looking like a kicked puppy.

"If you're not interested it's fine, but you don't hafta lie, Cam."

It's my turn to be confused. "I'm not lying," I assure him. "I'm not gay."

Jackson's face gets a little red and he huffs out a breath, shaking his head and looking down at his hands. "I've seen the videos."

I can feel the blood draining from my face and turning to ice in my veins, and my lungs refuse to cooperate as I try desperately to drag in a full breath. So far, I haven't had any problem keeping Campy completely separate from Cameron. It helps that I don't have much of a social life, but I naïvely had the feeling of those two parts of myself being neatly compartmentalized, neither bleeding over into the other at any point. What if Jackson isn't the only one who's seen the videos? What if someone from the wildlife center stumbles upon them? What if my mom finds out some day? Even after I quit doing porn, they'll still be out there for anyone to find.

"Breathe, Cam," Jackson's steady voice breaks through

my fog of panic. "That's it, deep breath in and hold it for a few seconds." His hand rubs soothing circles on my back as he coaches me through breathing for a few minutes.

"I'm not gay," I say again once my breathing is under control.

"Then I'm confused," Jackson says.

I look up, meeting his eyes with a pathetic expression. "Can you think of another job I could do that would allow me to not only cover my own bills, but keep up with my mom's mortgage, living expenses, and medical bills? Because I can't."

Jackson's mouth falls open. "When you told me about your mom, I figured it was why you were in porn. But, you're not even gay and you're doin' that for her?"

I give a weak, one-shoulder shrug. "Gay porn pays a hell of a lot better than straight porn."

Jackson blinks a few times and then runs his hands over his face and through his hair. "I'll be honest, I couldn't do that with a woman for all the money in the world. Nothin' against women, but I literally don't think I could get it up."

I chuckle, relaxing a fraction. "I didn't think I'd be able to either when I first started. It was sort of a Hail Mary, praying I could pull it off. I took Viagra my first few shoots and after that I noticed I didn't really need it," I explain. "Coming is coming as far as my dick is concerned, I guess," I chuckle and Jackson winces at my crude words. "Sorry."

"Don't apologize." He waves me off, standing up and taking our empty plates to the kitchen.

"Jackson," I call after him, jumping up to follow him.

"Don't, Cam. It's okay, honestly. I'm sorry I assumed, and I'm sorry I watched that video, it clearly makes you uncomfortable."

"No, it's fine. It's not like I don't know guys watch them,

that's kinda the whole point." Jackson avoids my gaze as he washes our plates and stacks them in the drying rack. Then he starts wiping down the counter and I get the feeling he's just finding ways to keep from looking at me. "Jackson," I say his name again, putting my hand on his shoulder and feeling his muscles stiffen under my touch.

"I'm a little embarrassed is all," he admits. "Can we leave it alone so I can lick my wounds in peace?"

"Why would *you* be embarrassed? I'm the one with countless sex videos who admitted to using Viagra not two minutes ago."

He finally stops cleaning and meets my eyes. "I've never asked a guy out before, I feel stupid I got it wrong."

"You didn't get it wrong. If I were gay, I'd be thrilled to go on a date with you. The zoo sounds like fun, actually. I kinda wish I was gay so we could go."

Jackson rolls his eyes and tosses the rag down. "Cam, you don't have to pretend to be gay to get stuff you want. We can go to the zoo anyway if you really want."

"Yeah?" I ask with a flutter of hope. "I'd like that."

He nods resolutely. "Then we'll go." He pushes away from the counter and moves to skirt around me. "I'm going to head to bed, if you don't mind."

"Okay. We're good though?" I check.

"We're good," he assures me.

9
JACKSON

Out of every possible reaction I had imagined to me asking Cameron out, him telling me he wasn't gay wasn't anywhere on that list. Somewhere deep down, I'd considered the possibility of him rejecting me, for whatever reason. Maybe 'cause I'm not his type. Maybe 'cause he has an ex he's still pining over. Maybe 'cause he's too focused on his work and his mother, I don't rightly know. But him rejecting me because he's not gay, I didn't see that one coming. And it's thrown me for a loop.

I know he explained it to me, doing gay porn simply for the money. And don't get me wrong, I'm not judging him. On the contrary, I'm in awe of the things he does to make sure his mama is taken care off. Say what you want, but he's working two jobs and spending a lot of time as her primary caregiver, and that's something I admire.

At the same time, I have to admit I don't get it. I meant what I said to him, I don't think I could get it up, no matter how much money you offered me. I think women are absolutely wonderful, and I love hanging out with them. Heck, I can even admire their curves and bodies from a more artistic point of view, but the reality is that they don't do anything for me. The idea of being intimate with a woman, it's just not something I'm interested in, no matter the price tag.

And this isn't as theoretical as it sounds. When I considered going into acting, I realized that if I was ever cast for TV or for a movie, the chances of me having to do some kind of intimate scene with a woman would be astronomical compared to doing one with a guy. Believe it or not, but I did debate this with myself, if pretending to be intimate with a girl was something I could live with once I had come out.

But acting is different from porn. Isn't it? Cameron seems to think they're the same, that all he does is act, but I'm not sure if that's the case. Sure, even with my limited experience in watching porn, I can tell that acting is involved. Or it should be, lemme put it that way, seeing as how some of the videos I've seen can't rightly be called acting, not even when you're horny and just looking for some inspiration to jerk off to.

Acting is selling a dream, making believe. Porn is... Well, now that I think about it, maybe they're not that different after all. If I act like I am in love with a woman, my job is to sell it to the audience to the point where our romance is believable and connects with them. Maybe Campy is right that his job is to sell that he's enjoying the sex. I don't know. It feels different to me, but I can't explain why.

What I do know is that I'm simply flabbergasted that he's not gay. Hell, that scene I watched with him and Pixie, how could he not be into that, the way he looked, the way he acted, the sounds he made, the way his body responded?

Oh great, now I'm hard all over again. I let out a frustrated sigh. This has been pretty much my reality ever since I asked him out two days ago. Every time I think about him,

I get aroused all over again. Maybe I'm a weirdo who gets a kick out of being rejected, what the fuck do I know?

Aw, darn it, he's got me cursing now, that's how upset I am. I'm such a softie. Truly, I got no game at all. Zero.

I take my phone out, my fingers itching to text Brax. What if I...? No, I can't. It'll lead to too many questions. Instead, I reply to his earlier text about an exam he failed and mention I'm having a crappy day as well. Shared misery and all that. He sends me a Cookie Monster meme back to cheer me up and it does, for a little bit. Then my thoughts wander back to Cameron.

At least we have that trip to the zoo to look forward to. I'm kind of mixed about that now, since the whole idea was to figure out a date that would make him happy. Now that it's not actually a date but more of a friends thing, isn't it kind of weird? Then again, he suggested going, or maybe I did? That part is a little fuzzy to me, my brain still in shock from his unexpected bombshell.

If he and I can't date, at least we can be friends. Heaven knows I could use a friend here to help me navigate the LA scene, because even the few experiences I've had so far—my mind immediately travels back to that beach encounter with CJ and Dustin—have shown me I may lack the necessary suaveness to do this on my own. Campy may pretend to be gay, but at least his experiences with the Ballsy Boys should've given him some kind of edge on how to handle dating in this town. I hope.

Well, I guess it's time to put myself out there. If Cameron isn't going to be my date, I'm determined to find someone else. I asked about the best dating apps in that new gay group on Facebook, and the opinion was pretty unanimous that I had to be on Grindr. Since I don't do anything without researching first, I go and do a little googling, and from what

I discover, taking a good profile picture is crucial. That, I can start with.

I take off my shirt and look at myself in the large mirror I've hung on the back of my door. Before you think that I'm completely vain, I use that mirror a lot to practice my lines and check myself for posture. Trust me, I'm not one of those guys who stares at himself for hours just for fun. There are far more interesting things for me to look at than my own face and body.

Like Cameron's. Oh my, he looks good half-naked. Or naked. That video showed off his...assets in fine, HD quality. The little dimples in his ass cheeks, for example. The smooth planes of his chest. His strong, toned body, so perfectly proportioned. Not that I can ever watch his videos again. Can I? That would be weirdly perverted.

I can't deny I'm in good shape. I trained my ass off in the weeks before I came here, knowing that I have scenes coming up where I'll be half-naked. Sure, it's a drama series, but they're not afraid to draw in female viewers with a little male nudity. Not full frontal, duh, but apparently my upper body was deemed worthy enough to attract females, so they've written a few scenes for me where I walk around in the house with just jeans on. I think it's gonna look exceedingly stupid, but what do I know?

The result of me training and watching my diet is that I'm in good shape, even if I don't come close to some of the guys on Muscle Beach. But I don't look too shabby without my shirt on, and I try to take a few pictures that show my body. Should I include my face?

I take a selfie with and without my face, but I can't decide which I like better. What is the custom here, anyway?

Should I ask Cameron? Why the heck not? If he's willing to help me, this is something practical he could do for me.

And it's not like he has anything else to do right now, because I can hear him watching one of his documentaries in the living room.

I walk over to him, phone in my hand. "Hey dude, can I ask for your opinion?"

He pauses his show, then gives me thorough look. "Did you lose your shirt?"

"Har. No, I was taking pictures to put up on Grindr, but I can't decide if I should do a body shot or a body and head shot. What do you think?"

His eyebrows shoot up. "Grindr, huh? Good for you. Show me what you've got."

For a second, I think he's asking me to show poses, but then I realize he's asking for my phone. I pull up the headless shot I did. "This doesn't look bad, right?"

He studies it for a few seconds, then shakes his head. "You can do better. If you do a few push-ups or weight exercises just before, you'll look more pumped. The difference is enough to make you look just a bit more muscled than you are in reality."

"Interesting. I didn't know that."

"It's what Bear makes us do before he takes pictures of us for the website," Cameron says.

I frown in confusion. "Bear?"

"Oh, sorry, right. Bear is my boss, the owner of the Ballsy Boys studio. Every few months or so, he wants us to do new pictures for the website so it always stays fresh. So right before the photographer shows up, he has us do some push-ups and lift a few weights. What can I say, it works."

"Okay, point taken. Anything else?"

He swipes back and forth between the photos with and without my head. "I think it all depends on what you're looking for. Headless shot with just your upper body will definitely attract men who are interested in your type. You should have a good response to that, but chances are it will be mostly guys who are looking to hook up. If you include your face, that may signal you're interested in more than just a body yourself."

I let out a sigh. "I had no idea dating was this complicated. How in the name of all that's holy should I have known the type of picture you post sends a message about what you're looking for?"

Cameron smiles at me. "Dude, there's like a whole language on Grindr, from what I understand. You'd better get up to speed on the lingo, pronto. The guys have told me there are definite codewords you need to know."

I roll my eyes. "Codewords? You do realize I'm tryin' to find a date, not spy on a foreign government, right?"

"Hey, I'm just the messenger here, bro. You might want to read through a ton of Grindr profiles to see if you encounter any words or expressions you don't know. Either Google them or I can ask the boys, I don't care. I'm just trying to look out for you. I don't want to see you get hurt."

I blink a few times, since that last sentence is unexpected. "Thank you. I appreciate that. And I didn't mean to get snappy with you. I do appreciate all the advice you're givin' me."

"No problem. And if you want, I could take a good profile picture of you, once you decide what you want to do. I'm not a professional photographer, but I've picked up enough tips from shooting videos and doing the occasional promotional photo shoot for Ballsy Boys that I think I could do a decent enough job."

Getting Cameron to take my picture while I'm half-naked? The thought is equally arousing and terrifying, but I'm not gonna say no. No-brainer.

"Thank you. I'll do some research on whether or not I want my head in the shot and I'll come find you when I know what I want, okay?" He nods and I quickly add, "After I've done a round of push-ups and what not to get pumped, apparently."

He grins at me, and my stomach does this little trip it always does when he smiles at me like that. "Can't wait," he says, and how I wish that were true.

10

CAMPY

I lean over the railing beside the black rhino enclosure and watch the large animal lazily rub its head against what looks like a giant scratching post. I sigh wistfully, wishing like hell I could be doing something to reach my goal of becoming a wildlife veterinarian. For a second, I feel a wave of resentment toward my mother, followed by nearly suffocating guilt. It's not like she *wants* to be sick. Neither of us chose this, we're just doing the best we can to get by.

I glance over and catch Jackson watching me with a frown.

"Everything okay?" he asks when he notices me noticing him.

"Great," I assure him, and aside from my inner turmoil, it's true. The zoo has been a complete blast. I can't remember the last time I came here, probably not since my class field trip in seventh grade. My mom always worked too much for outings like this when I was younger. She put her happiness on hold so she could support me growing up, and it's my turn to do the same for her.

Jackson doesn't look convinced but nods anyway, and

then steps out of the way of a few children who come running up to the railing to see the rhino.

I follow him, skirting around kids on our way to the next exhibit. My smile becomes more genuine when I see giraffes are up next.

"Giraffes are my favorite," I confide as we stop in front of the large sign full of facts about giraffes. "Did you know they have the same number of vertebrae in their neck as people do? Each one is just massive."

"Really? That's crazy."

"I know, right?" I can feel my inner animal nerd bubbling to the surface but I can't seem to want to tramp it down. "And, did you know that they only need about two hours of sleep every day?"

Jackson's eyes seem to sparkle as he listens to me list off nearly every fact I can think of relating to giraffes, simply nodding and making interested noises as I run my mouth. When I finish, I notice a warmth in his eyes that does funny things to my chest.

"Can I ask you a question?"

"Yeah, sure."

"If money was no object, and you could be anything in the world, what would you want to do with your life?"

"Be a wildlife veterinarian," I answer without a thought.

His smile turns a little sad. "I kinda figured."

"I will be," I assure him, wanting to chase away whatever's getting him down. "Eventually I'll get the chance to go to vet school and then I'll get a job working at this zoo, helping all these animals. And I'll own a ranch outside the city and take care of injured wildlife there too."

"That sounds really nice, Cam."

"It will be," I say resolutely. "When I'm not at Ballsy, I

work part time at a wildlife and large animal rehab, and I absolutely love it."

"Ah." His eyes light up again like he's just solved a puzzle. "Now *that* makes sense."

Jackson's hand twitches and, for a second, I think he's going to reach out and take my hand. To my surprise, I sort of want him to. Then a kid barrels into me and knocks me off balance. Jackson reaches out to steady me and the moment is broken.

"Let's go look at those giraffes," he suggests, pointing toward the walk-up. "Then you can tell me everything you know about tigers, because those are *my* favorite," he says, winking at me.

"Oh, did you know that a tiger's stripes are unique to each cat, like human fingerprints?"

"Really?" he responds with interest, letting me go off on another tangent, seemingly happy to listen as long as I want to talk.

After seeing our favorite animals, we wander past an ice cream cart and I catch Jackson looking at it wistfully.

"Come on, let's be really bad and splurge, just this once." I grab his hand without thinking and drag him over to the cart.

"I really shouldn't," he says, but the protest is weak. It's obvious he wants me to talk him into breaking his strict diet this one time.

"You brought me out here on a date, which means you're subject to my whims if you want to make a good impression."

"Seein' as you're not gay, this isn't a date."

"Do you want the ice cream or not?"

He throws another longing look at the creamy treats and then nods eagerly.

"I'm going to hate you tomorrow when I have to do extra cardio to burn off the calories, but let's splurge."

"That's the spirit. Besides, we're walking around in this ridiculous heat all day, you're already burning the calories, so the ice cream is basically free."

"I like the way you think."

When we reach the ice cream cart, I drop his hand.

"What do you like? It's on me."

"I'm boring, vanilla's my favorite."

"That's not boring, vanilla is my favorite too. I don't know why vanilla gets so much hate. Vanilla is seen as plain or boring, but the thing about vanilla is it's versatile. You can add sprinkles or hot fudge, hell you can even get crazy and add marshmallows or fruit. Vanilla can be whatever it wants to be, it doesn't need to be boxed in like the other flavors do."

"You've spent a lot of time thinking about ice cream," Jackson says with a chuckle.

"Yeah, well, this stupid diet and all." I shrug. "Few people want to see jiggling love handles when they turn on a porn."

The ice cream vendor gives me an odd look and I realize what I just said out loud. I give him an apologetic smile and order two vanilla cones, tipping him a little extra before turning and handing Jackson his treat.

"I don't think that's true," he says as we find a bench under a shady tree to sit and enjoy our indulgence. He starts licking his ice cream and my brain seems to short circuit, my eyes stuck on the way his tongue laps at it, coming away with streaks of white cream with each lick and sending my mind to an entirely filthy place.

"What's that?" I ask in a bit of a daze, having completely lost the thread of our conversation.

"People not wanting to see love handles in porn. I don't think it's true."

"You don't?"

"No. Don't get me wrong, it's nice to see brain-meltingly hot people, but it's also nice to see people who are more relatable. It adds to the fantasy, don't you think?"

"I never really thought of that," I admit. "I'm surprised Rebel hasn't thought of that actually, he's the marketing genius."

Jackson just nods, not seeming to have anything else to add. I watch for a few more seconds as he continues to devour his ice cream in an entirely too sensual way. The worst part is, it's obvious he's not *trying* to be sexy. It's not like when someone holds eye contact while licking a popsicle in an exaggerated way. He looks sinful doing it without even trying and I'm not sure what to think about that.

"So," I clear my throat, needing to find something else to focus my mind on other than his tongue, "have you always wanted to be an actor?"

"Pretty much. I always loved movies, and as soon as I realized being an actor was a job people could have, I knew that's what I wanted. I loved the idea of getting to be so many different people, finding ways to think and understand different characters, and the challenge of bringing them to life. My dad was horrified when I came home from school in the seventh grade and I told him I got the lead in the school play and wouldn't be able to help with ranch chores on the weekends because I'd have rehearsal," he confides. "Guess it was just a dress rehearsal for coming out to them."

Once we finish our snack, we decide to head over to the aquarium and get in line to pet the stingrays. I know this isn't a *real* date, but I'd be lying if I said this wasn't the best day I've had in a long time, and leagues better than any real date I've gone on.

When it's our turn to reach into the shallow tank, I glance over to see a look of delight on Jackson's face as his fingers graze the smooth skin of the ray. He looks up and our eyes meet, causing a little flutter in my chest. There's something about the simple joy of this moment that settles over me and makes me wish I could freeze time and live here forever, where there's no worries over money, no sick mom, no dreams miles out of my reach. It's just me and Jackson, and his adorable, crooked smile.

Jackson

THE NON-DATE WITH Cameron is everything I thought it would be. I've never seen him this animated, and I am amazed at how much he knows about animals. Some of it is completely random facts that are amusing, but he's also shared knowledge that shows how much he understands about wildlife and the challenges they face in our modern society.

We're in front of the wolves' exhibit, and I suddenly remember the documentary he was watching about the wolves in Yellowstone. "Didn't they reintroduce these in Yellowstone a few years ago?" I ask, glad I can actually contribute something remotely intelligent to the conversation. "I remember you watching something about this."

He looks at me funny for a few seconds, as if he's amazed I remembered. "Yeah, that documentary showed the impact their reintroduction has had on the ecological system in

Yellowstone. They are native to the park, but they vanished from there, mostly because of humans."

"So they brought them back?"

"Yeah, there are now multiple packs in the park. They're tracking at least some of them, which is super cool. I saw this map that showed where each of the pack members have ventured, and most of them stayed within their own pack land, so to speak. But there was this one wolf who clearly didn't give a shit and who wandered all across the park."

"Little rebel wolf," I say, grinning.

"Right? I just hope he won't go outside the park itself, because he might get shot. Inside the park, they're protected, but outside they're not. If he crosses into Montana... Humans still are the biggest threats to wolves, as they tend to shoot them on sight."

"Well, if they're ranchers, you can hardly blame them. Wolves are a big threat to livestock."

We've found a spot on a wooden bench in the shade, and guzzle down some much-needed fluids.

"You grew up on a ranch in Texas, right?" Cameron asks.

"Yeah. A small one to Texas standards, but a decent one compared to the rest of the country, I think. We mostly have what's called black baldies, a cross between Angus and Hereford, plus some Texas Longhorns, 'cause my dad likes 'em. They don't make any money, but they're very Texan, which makes him happy."

"Didn't your dad want you to take over for him?"

I shake my head. "I got lucky, because I have a younger brother, Brax, who from a young age showed interest in the ranch. It's never been an issue for him, me, or my dad. It was quite clear he was the one who would take over. He's in college now, studying animal science and learning all he can about sustainable farming. So there never was any pressure on me, luckily."

I offer Cameron a healthy snack bar I brought, and he gladly accepts it.

"Your brother's name is Brax?" Cam asks with his mouth full. "That's a rather unusual name, isn't it?"

I can feel my cheeks heat up with embarrassment. "It's short for Braxton. He's named after General Braxton Bragg, a Confederate general in the Civil War."

Cameron almost chokes on a sip of water. "You're shitting me. Your parents are *that* Southern, huh?"

"Well, they're Texan, at least my dad is. My mom's family hails from South Carolina, originally, and that's where those names come from, family tradition. My dad gave in to her on that one, though I'm sure he woulda preferred naming us after Texan legends, you know?"

Cam raises an eyebrow. "Texan legends?"

I shrug. "Davy Crockett, James Bowie, Sam Houston, ..."

"Dude, I have no idea who those people are," Cameron says with a laugh.

I nod, all but biting my tongue to keep myself from going into a whole *Remember the Alamo* spiel. It's fascinating how that doesn't mean anything outside of Texas.

"Not that I've ever heard of Braxton...Bragg, you said? And why Jackson?" Cameron continues, looking a bit puzzled. Then it hits him and I can see understanding dawn in his eyes. "Jackson. You're named after..."

"Yup, Stonewall Jackson. Just like my mama's older brother and her dad and my great-grandpa, proud family name on my mama's side for the oldest son. My great-grandpa was born in 1923, a late-in-life surprise for his father, who named him after the hero of the south, Stonewall Jackson. And my middle name is Bedford, after

Nathan Bedford Forrest, another Civil War hero, according to the South, that is."

To his credit, Cameron doesn't laugh at me. Not much anyway, though I can see his eyes twinkle with mirth. "You got any more siblings?" he asks.

"Two more brothers, Stuart and Beau, both named after generals. I also have a baby sister, Scarlett, just to stick with the whole Deep South theme we have goin' there."

Cameron puts his hand in front of his mouth. "I'm not sure whether to laugh or say sorry or both."

I shrug, strangely comforted by his reaction. At least he's not upset about it, like I had any choice in it. "It is what it is," I say, as always trying to be pragmatic about it. "But it's not uncommon where I grew up to have that devotion to the South, though usually, it's more to Texas than to the South, but that's my mama's influence, I guess."

"I think I might like it, being a rancher," Cameron says after a short pause, a wistful edge to his voice.

I try to picture it, Cameron on a horse, dressed in jeans, boots, and a hat. I have to admit, it's not hard to visualize him like that. "You'd be a good fit, what with your love for animals. It's a hard life, though. And it's a lot of routine work. I didn't mind helping out my dad, but I knew even as a teen that I needed more excitement, more creative expression than being a rancher offered."

Cameron chews on his bar, looking pensive. "The conservative environment probably didn't help," he comments.

"There was one openly gay teen in my high school, and you don't want to know how they treated him. There was absolutely no way I was coming out while living there. It would've ruined me socially. It made me feel like a coward at times, but—"

"It's not cowardice to choose the right time to come out," Cameron interrupts me, his intonation definitive and strong. "I think that's a choice everyone has to make for themselves. For some people, it may make sense to come out early, and for others, it may take longer. Hell, being a teenager is hard enough in and of itself, trying to figure out who you are and how you fit in. I can't even imagine adding discovering your own sexuality to that mix."

"I told my parents right after graduation," I say. "That didn't go over well. Technically, considering how conservative they are, it could've gone a lot worse, I guess. They still love me, and they never would've kicked me out, but there's this cloud of disappointment, you know?"

"So how do they feel about you coming to LA?"

A rush of shame fills me. "They don't know."

Cameron's eyes widen. "You haven't told them?"

"Nope. I started acting in high school, and they weren't happy about it. Then in college, I managed to score some roles in commercials, and I starred in a few parts in the community theater in my college town. The guy who mentored me there, he told me about the opportunity for the part on Hill Country. They were holding auditions in Texas, since they were looking for actors with a native Texan accent. I auditioned, and I got the part, much to my surprise. But I never told my parents."

Cameron's eyes have grown big during my story. "Where do they think you live, then?"

"They're under the impression I'm still at college, finishing up my bachelor's degree in English Lit."

"Damn," Cameron says, and something flashes over his face that's hard to read. "That's a big secret to keep from them."

My shoulders drop a little. "I know. I don't expect it to

stay secret for much longer, but I didn't know how to tell them. They're already so disappointed in me for being gay, and to add to that by telling them I dropped out? I guess I'm not *that* convinced of their unconditional love for me."

Cameron sends me sympathetic look. "I don't blame you. It's something I never quite understood, religion. Or I should say, conservative religion. My mom, she grew up Catholic with very strict parents. When she got pregnant with me outside of marriage, they disowned her, even after my biological father left her to raise the baby on her own. They never contacted her again. I mean, who does that to their child? How can you call that love?"

"I'm with you. I grew up Southern Baptist, and the list of things we weren't supposed to do was long, let's leave it at that. Even before I fully realized I was gay, I was so discouraged by the sensation of always falling short. No matter what I did, I could never be good enough. There was always this talk about sinning and needing a Savior and not being worthy, and it kind of got to me. It left me wondering, if we are so worthless and useless, why would God even bother with us? Then I realized I was gay, and it got even more complex."

Cameron nods solemnly. "Politics and religion, man, two things people rarely change their minds on. Also the two things that rarely make sense."

We sit in a comfortable silence for a while, until I let out a sigh." Sorry for dragging us down. Tell me what you know about wolves, because I'm sure it's more entertaining than me talking about my frustrated youth."

11

CAMPY

My veins fill with ice as I head into the Ballsy studios and nearly walk right into someone I never expected to see again—or more accurately, *hoped* I wouldn't.

"King." I mutter his name like it's a dirty word.

"Well, if it isn't Rex... Oh wait, you go by Campy now, don't you?" he spits out and my stomach jolts with fear as I glance around to make sure none of the guys were around to hear that.

"What are you doing here?"

"Interviewing for a position. Maybe I'll get to wreck that lying ass of yours."

The room feels like it's spinning and for a second I'm sure I'm going to pass out.

"I don't know what you're talking about," I manage to reply through clenched teeth. I'm finally in a position to cover my mom's medical bills and a few words from King to the right people could blow everything I've built here over the past year.

"Sure you don't. See you around, Rex," King says before

sauntering out, making sure to give me a hard shoulder bump on his way past.

On unsteady legs, I head straight for Bear's office. I'm not sure what my plan is, but King *can't* work here, and not just because he could destroy my career. He had numerous complaints at Diablo Studios from the women who worked there. He was overly aggressive with them both on and off the set.

I knock at Bear's door and he calls out for me to come in. When I open the door, I find Rebel seated near Bear behind the desk, which makes sense since I'm sure Rebel is now being included in casting decisions.

"Hey, Campy, come on in." Bear waves me over.

"Everything okay?" Rebel asks, eyeing me with concern.

"Um, kind of." I force a smile and drop down into the chair on the opposite side of the desk from them. "That guy you were just interviewing, is he going to be offered a job here?"

"King?" Rebel clarifies and I try to keep my face blank, not wanting to give away how well I know him. "No way, dude has *trouble* written all over him, and not in a good way."

I let out a relieved breath. "Okay, cool." I make a move to stand so I can go get ready for filming today.

"Why, did he say something to you?" Bear asks before I can make it to the door.

"Just sort of hassling me. Didn't strike me as the type who would fit in here," I answer vaguely.

"He gave us the impression he knew you," Rebel adds casually and my heart thunders again.

I shrug and reach for the door handle, my stomach churning. Bear took a chance on me when he hired me, and if he found out I've been lying to him this whole time, I can only imagine how badly that would go. Hell, I lied my ass off in the interview itself, claiming I'd never done any porn before and claiming to be gay. When he asked why I wanted to work at Ballsy, I put on a roguish smirk and said, "Who wouldn't want to get paid to have sex with all these hot guys?" Practically every word I've ever said to Bear and the rest of the Ballsy Boys has been a lie, and that fact weighs heavier on me every day. These lies are like quicksand, pulling me deeper and deeper until I have no doubt I'll be suffocated by them eventually.

"Nope. Gotta go get ready, don't want to keep Pixie waiting for me," I say quickly before rushing out of the room without giving them a chance to respond.

My head isn't in the game the entire time we're filming, and it's obvious to everyone.

"Cut," Rebel calls and I bite the inside of my cheek, embarrassment swamping me as I pull out.

"Want me to suck you a little?" Pixie offers quietly, not commenting directly on the fact that I've lost my erection for a second time while fucking him.

"Yeah, sure." I tug off the condom and toss it into the garbage bin behind the bed, placed there for that very purpose.

Pixie shimmies into a position that will work and wraps his pretty pink lips around my floppy, only half-hard dick. The suction of his mouth does wonders to pull my mind off my worries about King and back to my dick where it belongs while I'm working.

Pixie runs his tongue up and down my length while simultaneously bobbing his head and sucking. The kid is a master of multitasking. I let my eyes fall closed, focusing solely on the feeling of his mouth on me.

Once I'm hard and aching again, he pulls off and smiles up at me.

"Think you'll be good to go now?"

"Yeah, thanks, sweetie." I tug him up to press a gentle kiss to his puffy lips.

"It's not exactly a hardship," he assures me, giving my cock one more firm stroke before turning around so he's back on his hands and knees.

One of the crew appears by my side with a fresh condom, which I take and roll on quickly.

"Rolling," Rebel calls out and the set goes quiet again as I slide back into Pixie's ass, determined this time to stay focused.

We manage to wrap the scene a short time later with spectacular cum shots from both Pixie and myself and no further mishaps.

Standing in the locker room shower, I close my eyes and let the hot water pelt my face, thinking about how easily King could destroy me. Maybe if I'd been honest from the start that I'd done straight porn before, this wouldn't be a big deal, but it feels huge. I've created an entire persona in Campy, and he doesn't fuck women, he's gay. He also doesn't have dreams of becoming a veterinarian, or a sick mother to take care of. Maybe in some ways, Campy has been a chance to escape from my real life.

Jackson

As soon as I see who's calling, I know that I'm in trouble. I shoulda told them, but then again, how could I? They would've tried to talk me out of this. And they might've even succeeded. My mama has making me feel guilty down to an art, and I have a mighty hard time saying no when she gets all emotional. I couldn't let them stop me, not with this opportunity.

My heart beats furiously as I pick up the phone. "Hi, Mama."

"Jackson Bedford Criswell," she starts, and my stomach drops. She's middle-naming me, a clear sign I'm in a heap of trouble. "Where in tarnation are you?"

I lower myself on the couch, my legs suddenly not strong enough to support me. "I'm in LA, Mama."

The quality of the audio changes, and I realize she's put me on speaker phone. Things are about to get even worse. "We just got a letter from your college saying you have dropped out," my dad says. "And when we called the office, they said you moved out weeks ago."

I could point out that he shouldn't open my mail, since I know that letter was addressed to me and not to them, but that's beside the point now. The bottom line is they know, so now I need to at least try and explain.

"That's right. I've moved to LA to pursue my acting career."

"Oh Jackson," my mom says, the disappointment in her voice cutting through me like a knife. "Why didn't you tell us? Do you realize what a shock it was to find out you had already left the campus, that we didn't even know where our own son was?"

I cringe at her words. When she puts it like that, it's easy to understand why they would be upset, even aside from me quitting college in the first place. She's right, I should've told them sooner. If something had happened to me here, they wouldn't even have known where I was.

"I was scared you would try to talk me out of it," I say, and before I can add an apology, my dad cuts in.

"Of course we would've tried to talk you out of this. It's a fool's dream you're chasing, son. I know you think you're good at acting and maybe you are, but the chances of you making it in that business are —"

"I have a lead role in a new drama series," I interrupt him, frustrated by his lack of faith in my abilities. "I shot the pilot a few months ago, and it got picked up by a major network. They offered me a role for at least the first season, but if the ratings are good, it could be extended for years to come. I didn't drop out of college on a whim, Dad. I did it because it's not a fool's dream I'm chasing. It's a dream I'm realizing."

There is a long silence at the end of the line, and I close my eyes in anticipation of their reaction.

"What kind of series?" my mom asks, and I hear careful interest, which is ten times better than I had expected.

"It's a drama series called *Hill Country*, set in Texas, actually. It's about a family on the ranch and the dad dies unexpectedly, so the mom and the kids have to deal with that. I play the oldest son. They were looking for native speakers, and I guess I fit the bill."

"Well, I'll be," my mom says with a hint of pride. "How about that? And you said you had a lead role?"

"Yes, Mama. There's the mom, me, my sister, and an uncle. So four lead parts, and I'm one of them."

"What about the *values* in that series?" my dad asks, and I have no trouble understanding the code word *values*. My dad has always been stricter than my mom, and church ranks right up there with Texas, family, and football.

"It's not a Hallmark Channel movie, Dad. There's cursing and nudity and sex scenes," I say. I could sugarcoat it, but I don't want to. I'm proud of this series, and there is little sense in me trying to hide what it is.

"Son, that's not how we raised you," my dad says, following his predictable script.

And this discussion is the one I feared, the one I've been trying to avoid ever since I knew I was gay. Sure, they weren't happy when I came out, even though they still love me. But their biggest fear wasn't me being gay. It was me choosing a gay life, me rejecting the traditions of the religion I grew up with.

"Dad, I know this isn't easy for you to hear, but I need you to listen to me. I respect your religious beliefs, but you have to respect that I feel differently."

There's an audible gasp, which has to be my mom. My dad is too controlled to respond like that.

"Are you saying you don't believe in God anymore?" my mom asks.

I close my eyes for a second, fighting back the wave of frustration at this crazy simplification of something that is so much more complex. "No, Mama, I'm telling you that I don't believe in your particular brand of religion anymore. It's not about believing in God. It's about believing in a God the way you and your church paint him, as a God who would send me to Hell just for being gay."

Another gasp, then my father's stern voice. "That's not what our church teaches, and you know it. God loves the sinner, and your sin is nothing worse than anyone else's. Being gay doesn't get you sent to Hell. You just have to fight it and not give in to your gay impulses."

I shake my head, clenching my left hand into a fist as I'm fighting to stay calm. There are few things that infuriate me more than this utter bull, and the worst thing is that he genuinely believes it. He's not trying to be judgmental or mean. He legit believes this, which never fails to baffle me, because other than that, he's such a compassionate, smart man.

"We'll have to agree to disagree on that one, Dad. Being gay is not something I can turn on or off. It's who I *am*. And I refuse to believe in a God who could create me like this only to tell me that who I am is not good enough for him. I don't think that's how God works, not if God is supposed to be a God of love."

"Jackson," my mom says in that pleading tone that has so often made me keep my mouth shut in the past.

"No, Mama, I've kept quiet long enough. I know that you guys love me, but I also know you struggle with the fact I'm gay. I respect that, because I do understand where you're coming from. But you guys have got to accept that I feel differently. I don't think I should have to apologize for who I am, let alone agree that who I am is inherently wrong. I love you guys, but you need to accept that I'm never coming back to the religion you raised me in."

The silence this time is even longer, and I can picture them in my head. My dad, basically an older version of me, pulling my mom close as she tries to keep her composure. It's funny, my physical appearance is more like my dad's, but I definitely inherited my mom's emotional temperament.

"That's not the path we had hoped for you," my dad says finally. "But we love you no matter what, Jackson. I hope you know that."

"I do, Dad. And I'm sorry for disappointing you. I wish..." My throat closes, making it hard to talk.

"Give us some time to process, okay?" my dad says. "We'll call you in a few days to talk more. We love you, son."

I agree, and they hang up before I can say anything else. I let myself fall back on the couch, the phone dropping from my hand. My throat hurts so much that even swallowing is painful.

"Tough conversation with your parents?" Cameron asks.

I hadn't even heard him come in, focused as I was on my parents. Not that I mind that he's heard it.

"Yeah. They just found out I dropped out of college and moved to LA. *Not happy* is an understatement, as you can imagine. Plus, I basically told them I quit their church as well, which was the icing on the cake."

Cameron lowers himself next to me on the couch. "Parental disapproval," he says softly. "That's a tough one. I'm sorry, man."

"You're so lucky with your mom," I say, resisting the urge to curl up against him.

It's as if Cameron reads my mind, because he drapes his arm around me and pulls me close. I don't even hesitate before dropping my head to his shoulder.

"You can borrow her anytime," he says, and somehow that makes me feel better.

12

CAMPY

I step into the apartment after a long day of filming. My muscles are sore, as is my ass, and all I really want is to collapse on the couch and veg out in front of the TV the rest of the night. But, unfortunately, I have interviews with caretakers for my mom, so relaxing isn't on the horizon for me tonight.

Jackson is sitting on the couch with his feet up on the coffee table and his laptop out. That little crooked smile of his is just peeking through as his fingers fly over the keyboard. For some reason the sight fills me with a mixture of happiness and something else...something hot and unpleasant. I want to say it's jealousy, but that doesn't make sense, does it?

"Hey," I greet him as I kick off my shoes.

"Hey, Cam. How was your day?"

"Exhausting."

He looks up with curiosity burning in his eyes, and strangely enough I find myself wanting to tell him about it.

"I got pounded, *hard*. I feel like I ran a marathon with a dick in my ass."

When Jackson's eyes widen, I worry for a second that I crossed the line into overshare territory, but seconds later he's cracking up.

"Could you make that sound any less sexy?" he complains. "I was gettin' a little excited at first, but then you made it sound so...grueling."

"Dude, it *is* grueling." I plop down on the couch next to him and groan as my tired muscles protest and my ass twinges. "Porn is *not* glamorous."

"So I'm learning," he chuckles before returning his attention to his computer and typing again.

"What are you up to?" I ask.

"Just chattin' with this guy," he answers with a shrug, but I can see the blush on his cheeks and the little smile again. And now the hot, unpleasant feeling is back.

"Oh?"

"No big deal. I've been tryin' this dating app, but I'm not sure I'm really findin' the right kind of guys."

"What do you mean?"

He reaches for his phone, unlocking it and pressing on an icon before handing it to me.

"I know you don't date guys, but is this typical?"

I look down to see the message center of whatever dating app he's enrolled in. Off the bat, I can tell a majority of the messages are dick pics and almost all the rest are some version of "want to fuck?"

"Jeez, not even a *hello* from these guys? They just jump straight to asking if you top or bottom."

"Right?! Okay, I was startin' to think maybe I was crazy, but these guys are forward, right?"

"Yeah, this is kind of gross, honestly." I wrinkle my nose, handing his phone back to him with disgust.

"I had no idea how hard it would be to date. I always figured once I was out of my homophobic little town it would be easy as pie to find a man."

"Yeah, dating in LA isn't great, no matter your sexual orientation. Porn isn't the only reason I've been single most of my adult life," I confide.

Jackson frowns and closes his laptop, looking completely dejected. "Hey, maybe I can help you," I find myself offering before I can think better of it.

"Help me?"

"Yeah. You're new in town, but I have all kinds of connections. I'll ask the guys at work where they recommend scouting for decent ass."

Jackson snorts and shakes his head. "I told ya, I don't want *ass*, I want—" he cuts himself off with a sigh. "I'm bein' too picky, aren't I?"

"Not at all. Leave it to me, we'll find you the man of your dreams, I guarantee it."

He still looks skeptical, but he nods and his smile starts creeping back into place. "You're a good guy, Cam. I'm lucky I got you as a roommate."

"Back at you, Jackson. Now, I've got to get over to my mom's to interview some caretakers."

"Want some company?" he offers.

"You don't have to."

"I know I don't. Truth be told, I kinda miss my own ma, yours reminds me of home a bit. And I'd be happy to cook up some more casseroles or do a little cleanin' for her. I hate thinkin' of her unable to do for herself."

His words make my breath catch in my throat. I can't seem to form words, so instead I just nod in agreement.

Setting his laptop on the coffee table, Jackson stands up

and quickly slips his shoes on, and then grabs his cowboy hat off the hook by the door and places it on his head. I'm not sure what it is about that hat, but it's so damn endearing.

We lock up and head down to my car.

"You can put whatever you want on the radio," I offer. "This car is old as shit so it doesn't have anything fancy like a hook-up for your phone or something, but the radio works fine. Although, I'm not sure LA has any country stations that come in."

He snorts a laugh and uses the dial to search, stopping on a station playing eighties rock.

"I got stuck listening to country music my whole life, I'll take George Michael or Madonna any day."

"I knew you were cool," I joke, reaching over to crank the volume higher so we can both sing along to "Faith" at the top of our lungs.

When we get to my mom's house, I'm thrilled to see she seems to be having a good day.

"Jackson!" she greets him excitedly. "I'm so glad you came back to visit me."

"Gee, thanks, Mom. I guess I'm chopped liver?" I joke.

"Of course I'm happy to see you too, my wonderful, perfect son," she lays it on extra thick, her words making my insides squirm with guilt, and I roll my eyes but hug her tightly.

"How are you feeling today?"

"Not bad," she assures me. "All this business about having a health care aide is too much. I don't need it."

"Yes, you do, and you're not going to talk me into changing my mind."

"Jackson, can't you talk any sense into my son?" She turns puppy dog eyes on my poor roommate.

"Sorry, ma'am but I happen to agree with your son on this one. But, I'll tell you what, how about if I bake you some apple tarts from a recipe my mama sent me. I bet that would cheer you up."

"You would win that bet," she agrees and I send Jackson a grateful look.

The next few hours are spent interviewing a handful of nurses while Jackson keeps my mom too occupied to protest, for which I'm immensely appreciative.

At the end of the night, there's a kitchen full of meals and treats, and I've chosen a nurse to come over every day to take care of my mom's physical needs as well as cleaning the house and making sure she's eating.

It's difficult to pry my mom away from Jackson once it's time to go, but I eventually manage it.

"She is somethin' else," Jackson says as we climb into the car.

"I think she has a crush on you," I tease and he blushes.

"Maybe if I swung that way."

"Ew, no, you can't even jokingly say you'd consider banging my mom," I complain and Jackson just chuckles. "Seriously though, thanks for coming. You made it a lot easier. I have a feeling she would've spent the rest of our stay putting up a protest if you hadn't been there to distract her."

"It's no problem, I was happy to help."

I glance at Jackson out of the corner of my eye as I drive and my heart gives a little flutter. Whatever man is fortunate enough to catch Jackson's eye is going to be one lucky bastard.

∽

A FEW DAYS after promising Jackson I'd ask around for him, the perfect opportunity comes up. Bear orders in lunch for the whole cast and crew and we all gather around a couple of tables to share a meal and talk.

It's one of the things I both love and hate about working at Ballsy Boys. Bear makes it a priority for all of us to be friends, to get to know each other more than just sexually. It scares the shit out of me that I'll slip up and let some Cameron bleed into Campy. But at the same time, it's nice to hang out with the guys. I just wish I didn't have to keep such a high wall between these two parts of my life.

"Hey, Pix." I turn my chair so I'm facing Pixie a little better. "Do you date?"

Out of the corner of my eye, I see Bear's head whip in our direction.

Pixie gives a little one-shoulder shrug. "Yeah, sometimes."

"I mean, have you dated much since you moved to LA?"

"Do you mean like *dating* dating, or hooking up?"

Bear growls from his place a few seats down and I turn my head in his direction, trying to figure out what his malfunction is. I find him with his attention fixed on Pixie, his jaw clenched and his shoulders tense.

"Looking for a relationship type dating," I clarify.

"Oh, no." His gaze darts toward Bear and I frown, looking between the two of them. Clearly, I'm missing something. "The only man I've been interested in like *that* since I've moved is a stubborn asshole, so I've hooked up here and there, but that's it."

Bear growls again and I'm half convinced I should get out of the way before he lives up to his nickname and mauls somebody.

"Why are you asking?" Bear asks and suddenly, all the guys have their attention on me.

"Oh, well, my...*friend*... hasn't been having much luck on the LA dating scene so I told him I'd ask around for him to see where the best places are to meet guys who aren't douche bags."

Brewer cocks his head curiously. "Why would you have to ask around? Where do you normally go to find hookups?"

Fuck me sideways.

"Oh, well, um..."

"Can we drop the *friend* bit and just admit you're looking for a boyfriend?" Heart suggests.

"It's not—" I start to protest

"His friend's looking for boyfriend material, and you're more into hookups, right?" Rebel supplies, saving me from floundering.

"Yeah, um, exactly."

"Oh, in that case, I am *not* your man." Brewer holds his hands up and Tank scowls. "Hey, I'm a one-man kinda guy now," he points out, leaning over and pressing a kiss to the grumpy man's lips. Okay, that's fucking weird to see. I knew they started dating recently, after their video together blew up, but it's just too fucking odd to process.

"Yeah, you don't want to ask me because if I had the first clue where to find a boyfriend, I'd avoid it like the plague," Heart adds.

"Before I met Troy, I used to hang out at this quieter gay bar near my place sometimes. I'll write down the name of it for you," Rebel offers.

"Thanks. I can't believe you're the only one at the table who isn't a commitment-phobe. I guess it explains why we're all in porn," I joke.

"Yeah, thank god for that because if I was half as afraid

of commitment as Troy was, I never would've pinned him down," Rebel says with an indulgent smile that causes a strange, longing ache in my chest. It *would* be nice to have someone to care about the way Rebel cares about Troy. But fuck, who has time for all that mess? Not to mention the porn issue. It's just not in the cards.

13

JACKSON

I check myself in the mirror in my bedroom, turning around several times and craning my neck to make sure I can see myself from every angle. Then I shrug. I guess this outfit will have to do. The jeans fit me nicely enough, and I like the way they curve around my ass. The moss-green button-down is a level more formal than I usually wear, but it brings out the color of my eyes—or so the sales guy assured me when I tried it on.

I figured my cowboy hat would be too much for the city folks here, but I'm wearing my favorite pair of boots. My hair is styled, I'm clean-shaven and freshly-showered, and I dabbed on some expensive-as-all-get-out cologne. This is as good as it's going to get for a first date.

When I walk into the living room, Cameron is spread out on the couch, barely awake enough to follow the program he's watching. He's pale compared to his usual tan, and the bags under his eyes betray he's not getting enough sleep. The man is working his ass off—almost literally, I fear. I know he needs the money, but I can't help but wonder how long he'll be able to keep this up.

He looks up from the screen and gives me a thorough once-over. "You look all spruced up. Where are you heading?"

"I have a first date," I say. "It's the first guy who was actually willing to chat with me and go through the getting-to-know-you phase rather than wanting to know my sexual preferences and whether or not I was available to hook up tonight."

Cameron pushed himself into a sitting position, his eyes narrowing. "What do you know about him? Where are you meeting him?"

Aw, how sweet, he's kind of stepping into the role of an older brother. Not that the thoughts I'm having about him are brotherly, not even close. With how tired he's been, he keeps forgetting to throw on some clothes when he steps out of his bedroom. As a result, I keep running into him in various stages of undress. As if I needed any more reminders of how perfect that body of his is.

"His name is Neil, and we're fixin' to meet at a gay bar called Bottoms Up? I think that was the name. I have the address. He said it was a well-known gay bar and safe enough for both of us."

Campy nods, but his face still shows a hint of annoyance I'm not quite following. "Yeah, I know that one. We often hang out there with the Ballsy Boys. I guess you could say it's kind of our go-to spot, and a lot of our fans know to find us there as well."

I gently shake my head at the astonishing contradictions in his life. "You're comfortable hangin' out at a gay bar while you're straight?" I ask, and then I realize how stupid that question is. Of course he's comfortable there. He hangs out with gay men all day at that job. Heck, he's pretending to be one of them, acting like one.

A flash of guilt clouds his eyes. "It's doesn't bother me, but I never flirt or give off the wrong signals, you know? Whenever we hang out there, I just chat with the other guys."

"Who's your favorite?" I ask.

I may not watch Cameron's videos—though it's costing me a lot of willpower to stay away from them—but I have watched all of the others. I can honestly say I don't have a preference, because they all look sexy as fuck to me.

I mean, I haven't had enough sex to know if I'm a top or a bottom, but if I had to take a guess, I would say I'm versatile. And looking at those videos kind of confirmed that, as the idea of sinking into that cute little Pixie guy aroused me just as much as the idea of being taken by Tank—though I may have to practice a little more if I want to take a dick that size and not get wrecked.

Cameron's eyes twinkle. "To chat with or to fuck with?"

I grin. "Fair enough. Both."

"I like talking to Brewer. He looks like this total party boy, this shallow piece of ass, but if you get to know him a little, he surprises you. He and I share an affection for weird documentaries, so we always have enough to talk about."

Huh, interesting. From the few videos I've seen of Brewer, he did appear like a total shallow player. "And for sex?" I ask.

Cameron shrugs. "Pixie is always fun to work with, and I can't deny that fucking him is a pleasant experience. If I'm bottoming, I might have to say Brewer as well. Nothing against Tank, but the guy has a massive dick, and my ass prefers two sizes smaller."

I mentally shake my head at the absurdity of this conversation. It still doesn't compute for me. How can Cameron talk about enjoying gay sex and yet maintain he's not attracted to men?

When I suspected I was gay, I did a little research. Not at home, of course, since our internet filter wouldn't have even allowed me to see the results. No, I went to a friend's house and pretended to do research for a project for school. Anyway, I discovered that unlike what I had always been told, sexual attraction or however you want to label it is not a black-and-white thing.

I thought you were either gay, straight, or bi, but it turns out there are a lot of variations and shades. There's even a scale or something to determine how gay you are. I don't know if they hand out, like, pink unicorns to those scoring a hundred percent on that scale, but if they do, I must be pretty close.

But it seems to me that no matter what Cameron says, there is no chance in hell he would score zero. Maybe I'm overthinking things, but I can't imagine admitting you like fucking a cute guy like Pixie and then in the same breath maintain you're not attracted to men. And dang it, he's got me using curse words again.

Cameron looks at me expectantly and I realize he asked me something. "Sorry, what?"

His grin widens. "I was curious to see who your favorite is."

"I don't watch your videos," I hasten to say. "I admit I did subscribe, but I'm not watching your videos. That would be too weird. I only watched the one, the first one where I discovered who you were."

He shrugs. "That makes sense. But I'm sure you've watched the others."

We're certainly venturing into personal territory here again, and I can only hope I won't blush. "Well, as you said, I think being with Pixie would be a pleasant experience. And maybe Rebel? I know he's not active anymore, but I watched some of his older videos, and he's super hot."

Cameron nods, an adorably serious expression on his face. "He is. He knows how to work that dick too. He's always been a viewer favorite."

"Anyway," I say, checking the time on my watch. "I have to go if I want to make it there on time."

"Are you taking an Uber? You have my number in your phone, right? Call me if you need to. If this guy turns out to be a total dick, don't be afraid to ditch him. You can call me and pretend there's an emergency or something."

I think his care for me is super sweet, even if it's a little over the top, and so I dutifully nod. "I will."

"Wait," Cameron says when I'm already halfway out the door. "Show me a picture of that guy, just so I know what he looks like."

I dig my phone out of my pocket and swipe until I've found the profile pic the guy used. I turn the phone toward Cameron and let him see it.

"I hope that's his real picture. It looks kind of too good to be true, don't you think?"

Frustration dances down my spine. "You don't think a guy like that could be interested in me?" I ask, my tone a little sharper than I intended.

"No, of course not, that's not what I was trying to say. It's more that so many of these guys try to pretend they're better than they are in real life, at least that's what I've heard. So all I'm saying is that I hope you won't be disappointed."

I study him for a second or two before I take my phone back. "Well, there ain't a heck of a lot I can do about it now except wait and see. I'll tell you afterward how it went."

I hurry out the door now, having learned that getting

anywhere in LA takes an inordinate amount of time with the crazy traffic. Luckily, I have an Uber within two minutes, and the guy turns out to be content focusing on driving while listening to some nineties radio station. Works for me.

The entire trip to the bar, I wonder why Cameron is so overprotective of me. Is he just being nice or is this a projection of something else? Maybe he's so powerless with his mother's illness and watching her struggle that he's focusing on something he can influence?

It doesn't quite make sense to me, but I can't think of another reason why he would be so invested in finding me a suitable date. He's a nice guy, but we haven't known each other that long, you know? It's kind of...odd.

But as the Uber pulls up to the bar, I let it go. I want to focus on Neil, and as I get out of the car and hesitantly make my way inside, I hope with all my might he's exactly who he presented himself to be.

Campy

I can't keep a scowl of my face and the unpleasant feeling from my stomach as I watch Jackson leave the apartment for his date. I turn up the volume on the wolf documentary I'm watching, hoping that will drown out the worries and irritations buzzing in my mind about whoever this Neil dude is Jackson's meeting up with.

When that doesn't work, I grab my phone and mash the button to call Brewer.

"Hey, boo what's up?" he asks, picking up on the third ring.

"What are you up to tonight?"

"Nothing much, maybe hanging out with Tank, why?"

"I was thinking of going out to grab a drink, but it's no big deal if you're busy."

"I could probably make time for *one* drink," he concedes. "Don't rat me out to Tank though."

I grin, even though he can't see it. "I wouldn't dream of it."

"See you at Bottoms Up in forty-five minutes?"

"Sounds good," I agree before hanging up.

I'm not going to spy on Jackson's date, I'm hanging out with my friend. I'm not even the one who suggested Bottoms Up, I reassure myself before switching off the TV and going to my bedroom to get dressed.

As usual, we get to skip the line when we get there. Greg, the bouncer, greets us with a smile and a few flirty words before letting us right through. In the dim light of the club, I start scanning immediately for Jackson. I'm not sure why I thought it would be easy to spot him, this place is always packed and the flashing lights don't help matters.

My eyes scan the bar anyway, and surprisingly it doesn't take long before I spot him sitting at the end of the bar with his date.

"Who's that?" Brewer asks, following my gaze.

"My roommate, Jackson."

"Did you know he was going to be here? Why didn't you just come out for a drink with him?"

"He's on a date," I explain, and Brewer looks confused for a few seconds before understanding dawns.

"Ooo, is this like a stakeout? Do we not trust this guy? Is he not good enough for hottie roommate?" He grabs an empty stool across the bar where we'll be able to watch Jackson without him noticing us, and politely asks the man beside him to give up his seat to me.

"It's not a stakeout, I just wanted a drink."

"Riiiight."

I clench my teeth and sit down way harder than I need to. For the first time ever, I can see why Tank always said Brewer was obnoxious.

"Seriously, I'm not here to spy on his date." Maybe if I say it enough times I'll believe it too. "That guy totally sent a picture that was a good ten years old though," I grumble, studying *Neil*, if that's even his real name.

"He's not bad looking though," Brewer says, tilting his head as he studies Jackson's date as well. "I mean, it's kinda dark in here to tell for sure, but he's pretty attractive."

"Whatever," I grumble, flagging down the bartender, Ryan, for a drink.

"Hey guys, how are you doing tonight?" Ryan asks.

"Great," I mutter.

"Good, we're spying on his roommate on a date," Brewer shares and I elbow him in the ribs. "Ow, hey. Watch it."

"We're not spying on anyone. Look, this is Jackson's first date in LA, he doesn't even know this guy. For all we know, he's a serial killer. I just wanted to make sure he was safe."

Ryan's eyes soften with understanding and so do Brewer's.

"Point him out, I'll keep an eye on them to make sure his date doesn't do anything fishy."

"Really? Thank you." I breathe a sigh of relief and nudge my chin in Jackson's direction so Ryan can pick him out.

"Oh, he's pretty hot. Are you sure this isn't even a *little bit* about jealousy?"

I scoff and shake my head. *I'm not gay*, I scream inside my own head, biting my tongue to keep from shouting it out loud. "It's not like that."

"Whatever you say." He shrugs. "I'll keep a close eye on them, I promise."

"Thank you."

He brings Brewer and me our usual drinks, and as promised, Brewer takes off after finishing just one, asking over and over if I'm sure he shouldn't stay with me longer. I wave him off, telling him I'm going to take off soon too.

I don't take off soon. I sit and watch as Jackson chats and laughs with the man for hours, which could be days for the way time passes in the loud, dark club. Eventually, they get up together and head for the door.

A weight sits heavy in the pit of my stomach as I imagine Jackson going back to this guy's apartment and having hard, sweaty sex all night long. My cock perks up at the thought of Jackson's skin glistening with sweat, and I shake my head at myself. I'm so good of an actor I even have my own body fooled at this point.

I toss a handful of bills onto the bar as a tip and drag myself out of the club. No reason to sit here any longer thinking about Jackson and his date, I might as well go home and try not to think about it there instead.

The drive home feels like an eternity and when I get up to our apartment, I'm surprised to find Jackson sitting on the couch, watching TV.

"Hey, I wondered where you went," he says as soon as I step through the door.

"Oh, um, just out for a drink with Brewer. How was your date? I didn't think you'd be home so early."

"It was good." He shrugs. "He was handsome and polite enough. There wasn't much of a spark though. The goodnight kiss felt like I was kissin' my brother."

I wrinkle my nose, the knot that has been in my stomach all night finally loosening. "I'm sorry."

"It's fine. The right guy is out there, I just need to find him."

His eyes flick to mine for a fraction of a second and a little zap of heat goes through me.

"Yeah," I agree, turning quickly to head down the hall to my bedroom. "Plenty of fish in the sea, and all that. Night, Jackson," I call over my shoulder before closing my bedroom door and leaning back against it, letting my head thump back against the wood. *What the fuck is wrong with me?*

14

JACKSON

"Jackson, what the *fuck*?!" Brax explodes into my ear as soon as I pick up the phone.

That issue I have with cursing and using rough language? My younger brother *so* doesn't have a problem with that, somehow managing to turn it off magically when he's home.

"Hey Brax," I say weakly, mentally bracing myself.

"I don't even know what to say to you," Brax says, anger still dripping from his voice. I know from experience it's best to stay silent and wait till he gets it out of his system.

Brax and I have always been close. It's funny, because on the surface, we have little in common except a shared parentage. I played football in high school, but I was also part of the drama club and a straight-A student who loved to read.

He can't throw a ball if his life depended on it, but put him on a horse and he's amazing. He's won an endless collection of ribbons in rodeos, for barrel racing when he was a kid, then for roping. He even tried bareback bronc riding a few times, but after he broke his arm with a particu larly nasty fall, he decided that wasn't worth the risk. He's always been more of a hands-on person, preferring to learn by doing much more than by reading. I'm amazed he even went to college, but then again, he takes ranching as seriously as I take acting.

Despite our differences, we've always found enough to connect over. Video games, for one. TV shows we both loved to watch. Working on the ranch in companionable brotherhood. He was actually the first one who knew I was gay, even before my parents. He didn't bat an eye, just gave me a slap on my back and told me that he'd still kick my ass in gaming.

I was the first to know that he had a girlfriend, and then that he'd gone all the way with her, as he explained. I was also the one who listened to him pour his heart out when she got pregnant, two scared kids who were determined to do the right thing. She had a miscarriage before they could even tell our parents, and I don't think he ever told them.

It's why I feel so crappy about keeping this from him, and I'm pretty sure he's about to tear me a new one for it.

"Dammit, Jax," he says, using his old nickname for me. Jax and Brax, almost like twins, we used to joke. "Why the fuck didn't you tell me? Didn't you know I woulda supported ya?"

"I know you would've."

"Then why, man? I don't understand how you could lie to me like that."

The underlying *I thought we were close* hits me deep, and in that moment, I realize I was wrong. I shoulda told him, shoulda given him the chance to support me. "I'm sorry, Brax. I had my reasons, but I was wrong."

He lets out a long sigh. "Okay, then. Talk to me. What the fuck is going on? Mama said you got an acting role?"

I tell him about *Hill Country* and the part I'm playing.

"That's an amazing opportunity," he says, and it's only because I know him so well that I recognize the slight edge he still has to his voice.

"I wasn't scared you wouldn't support me," I say quietly. "I was scared you wouldn't be able to keep quiet about it. You know how Mama can put pressure on us when she's suspicious."

Brax groans. "Ugh, don't I know it. She's like a pit bull when she senses something. And I suck at lying to her," he says, and I hear the tone of his voice change. "You were always better at that."

That's kind of a mixed compliment, but I get what he means. "That's why I didn't tell you. I didn't want that pressure on you."

He's quiet for a bit, then says, "Okay, I hear ya. It's all good, Jax. Now, tell me about LA. How hot are the girls? Oh damn, like you would know."

I snicker. "I still got eyes, bro. They're really freaking perfect. Those stereotypes about pretty California girls? All true."

"Aw, nice. And the guys, are they equally hot?"

This is why I love my brother. He's been wonderfully supportive, even though it must've been hard for him as well, adjusting his mindset to having a gay brother. He's not as conservative as my parents, as evidenced by how liberally he sprinkles his conversation with R-rated expressions, but still.

"They're really cute," I say, and my mind immediately goes to Cameron.

The whole night with Neil, all I could think of was Cameron. It wasn't a fair comparison in any way, but I couldn't help it. Neil was super nice and friendly and the conversation flowed easily, but my heart was never in it. I think he knew, too, especially after that kiss. It was nice, but nothing more than that. Not the fireworks I was hoping for, that's for sure.

"Jax!" Brax yells in my ear, and I realize he's been trying to get my attention.

"Sorry, I got lost in thought for a sec."

"Anyone specific you were thinkin' about?"

As much as I want to, I can't tell him about Cameron. I'm not ready yet to share something so private. So I opt for a watered-down version of the truth. "I'm trying to date."

"Oh, awesome. Any luck?"

"Yesterday's guy was a bit of a bust, but I'll keep trying."

"I really need to come visit you sometime," Brax says, and I frown, wondering about the strange segue from me dating to him coming to visit. Then again, Brax has never been known for making the most logical jumps in his thought process.

"I gotta come check those California girls out," he adds and that makes more sense. Of course, his mind would still be stuck on something I said five minutes ago.

"Anytime, bro. I'd love to have you here."

We chat a bit more, and my heart is so much lighter now that I know things are okay between us.

"I'm proud of you, Jackson," Brax says when we're about to end our call because I want to start cooking for when Cameron comes home. "I've always known you were crazy talented, but I'm so damn proud of you for living your dream. You're an inspiration to me, you know that?"

I ponder that statement long after we've hung up. When I realized I was gay, I waited to tell Brax for a long time, because I didn't want to corrupt him. Bear with me here, because I didn't understand a whole lot about being gay back then, like the fact that it wasn't contagious. That took me a while to figure out, that it wasn't a choice, like I'd always been told, nor a lifestyle. Nor a sin.

I was scared that by telling him, I'd influence him in a wrong way, maybe upset my parents as well and get accused of leading him on a wrong, sinful path. Not once did I consider I might be an inspiration to him. The thought lifts a cloud off my soul that I wasn't even aware was still there, and I find myself hoping Brax can make it to LA sometime soon.

15

CAMPY

I tap on Jackson's bedroom door and hear the rustling of fabric on the other side. My throat feels tight, realizing he's naked on the other side of the door. *Of course he's naked, you idiot, he's getting dressed to go out and find some dick.*

"One sec," he calls and I lean against the wall to wait. When he finally pulls the door open, my mouth goes dry at the sight of him in a pair of tight, worn jeans that hug the muscles of his legs with the familiarity of a lover, his defined abs on full display, complete with a dark happy trail leading down to the edge of his pants.

"Is a button-up shirt too much?" he asks, plucking at the sides of the unbuttoned shirt. It's all too easy to imagine him slowly undoing each button...or better yet, the feel of the buttons popping as I tear the shirt open while our tongues tangle frantically. "Cam?"

"Huh?" I force my eyes away from his chest and abs, and look at his face. What the fuck is wrong with me? I mean, yeah, the dude is good-looking and he's a great person, but drooling over *anyone,* let alone another man, just isn't me. "Sorry, I was spacing out."

"I asked if a button-up shirt was too much? Should I keep it more casual?"

"No, I think it looks nice. Just make sure you roll up your sleeves so all the guys out there with forearm fetishes can get their kicks."

Jackson blinks at me until I snort a laugh, then he shakes his head. "I don't understand half the stuff that comes out of your mouth."

"Yes, but one day you'll be as corrupted as I am, and I won't get to amuse myself with your adorable innocence anymore, so let me have my fun while I can."

Jackson deftly buttons up his shirt, and then reaches for his pants, unbuttoning them with deft fingers.

"What are you doing?" I rasp, not sure if I should turn around or enjoy whatever show he's about to put on.

"I'm just tuckin' my shirt in," he explains, doing just that before re-buttoning his jeans. "Sure you don't wanna come with tonight?"

"You don't want me there," I argue. "I'd cramp your style."

"Nah, you'd be my wingman. Please?"

"You really want me to tag along to the bar so you can pick up men?"

"I keep tellin' you, I don't want to pick up *men*. I want to find someone...special," he explains, his voice getting kind of misty and wistful. "That sounds so corny, doesn't it?"

"No it sounds nice," I assure him, and I mean it. It really does sound nice to have someone special to share life's burdens with, someone to come home to every night and kiss every morning. It sounds *really* nice, actually.

"So you'll come?" he asks again.

"If you're sure you want me to."

"I'm sure."

"Okay, give me a few minutes to get changed and we can go."

It doesn't take me long to put on some decent jeans, a nice shirt, and add a little gel to my hair so I look presentable. I'm not sure why I even bother with that much, it's not like I'm the one trying to get laid tonight. But you never know who will see *Campy* out at the bar and I don't want to be caught looking like I just stumbled out of bed...at least that's the reasoning I give myself before one quick mirror check.

"You look good," Jackson says, his eyes flicking quickly over me when I return to the living room.

"Not as good as you look," I argue, realizing a few seconds too late how that sounds, but decide backpedaling would be worse than leaving it be.

"Thanks. Ready to go?"

"Ready."

~

REDD'S IS a lot quieter than Bottoms Up, which is where the guys and I usually go to unwind after a busy week of filming. It's easy to see why Rebel thought to suggest this place, it certainly has less of a *casual hookup* vibe than Bottoms Up does and it makes me suddenly immensely glad he found what he was searching for for so long in Troy.

"This is kinda nice," Jackson comments as we grab a table not far from a couple of pool tables and dart boards.

"It is," I agree. "I'll get the first round."

"Nope," Jackson argues, waving me back into my seat. "I dragged you out, drinks are on me. Beer okay?"

"Yeah, great. Thanks."

I watch as Jackson saunters up to the bar, leaning over it and catching the eye of half the men in the place, myself included, as we all memorize the way his jeans mold to the curve of his ass.

While Jackson waits for our drinks, a man approaches him. He's the definition of a twink— petite, pretty. A bitter taste rises in my throat as I watch him put his hand on Jackson's bicep and bat his eyelashes. I can't see Jackson's face to tell what he thinks about the man. Are twinks even his type?

Finally, the bartender slides two beers across the bar and Jackson takes them. He says something to the twink whose face falls a little before he recovers with a bright smile and watches Jackson walk back in my direction.

"Not your type?" I ask casually as he sets my drink in front of me and then takes his seat.

"Hm?" he makes a curious sound while taking a sip of his own drink.

"The cute guy who was throwing himself at you. You weren't interested?"

"Oh, him?" Jackson glances back toward the bar where the man is now standing with some friends. "Not really. I usually like bigger guys, closer to my own size. Except..." his cheeks flush and he takes another hurried gulp.

"Except me?" I guess.

"Except you," he agrees. "Sorry, it's weird, I know. In my defense, I really did think you were gay when I was droolin' over you."

"You don't drool over me anymore?" I tease with a grin over my glass as I bring it to my lips. Jackson's blush deepens and he shakes his head but doesn't confirm or deny whether he still checks me out. "Can I ask you a question?"

"Sure."

"If I'm not your normal type, what did you like about me? Physically, I mean."

"Cam," he groans my name and gives me a *can we not do this?* look.

"No, I'm not trying to make it weird. It would just be good for me to know what physical attributes of mine I should make sure I'm playing up for the cameras. Maybe one day I can be as popular as Pixie is with our viewers," I joke, my stomach an odd jumble of nerves as I wait to hear how he'll answer.

"I dunno. You just have somethin' about you that kinda drew me in. You're slim, but a bit muscular still. And…I don't know, you have a nice…um…you know," his eyes dart down and then back up and I bite my tongue against laughing.

"Okay, so my body is decent and you like my dick. Is that seriously it?" I'm not sure why, but I'm a little disappointed there isn't more to it.

"No. It's hard to explain, I guess." he shrugs and then finishes off his glass, already looking around for a server to ask for another. "Can I be honest with you about something?"

"Of course." I find myself leaning forward, across the table toward him.

"I was surprised when you told me you weren't into guys at all. In the video I saw, you seemed really into it, like *really* into it."

"I'm usually thinking about other things to kind of help me out," I confess, my heart pounding as my mind wanders back to the last scene I filmed with Heart when Jackson popped into my head.

"Oh." He seems kind of disappointed. "That makes sense. I'm going to get another drink."

"Okay. Hey, when you get back, let's see about reeling

someone in for you. There are a couple of beefcakes over by the pool tables, we can see if they want to play a round."

Jackson glances at the two men leaning against the pool table not too far away.

"You're on," he agrees.

Jackson

CAMERON CALLED them a couple of beefcakes, but that's not how I would describe them. The two men near the pool table are tall, muscled, and casually dressed in shirts and tight jeans. If I had run into them on the street, I probably wouldn't have guessed they were gay.

Cameron is right that they're more my type, though they might be a little older than I had in mind. They look like they're about my size, with plenty of strength to handle me. Yeah, if I had to make a list of a body type I'd be interested in, these two would fit the bill. And judging by the way they take in my body as I walk over to them, I think that feeling might be mutual. I walk a little taller as a result.

"Hey," I say, suddenly wondering what I'm supposed to say. Do I just invite them to play pool? Is there a requisite amount of small talk I have to make first? Someone really should write a dating guide for new gays, I decide. I could sure use a little guidance.

"Hello there," one of the guys says, giving me another slow, thorough look, ending it with a little wink. "You look positively edible."

I can't help but smile at that straightforward compliment, voiced in a low, sexy tone with a hint of a twang. "Why, thank you. You ain't so bad yourself."

His face lights up. "A Southern boy," he says, his accent betraying his own Southern roots a bit more now, though it's still too faint for me to determine where he's from. "Where do you hail from?"

"The Texas Hill Country, you?"

"Galveston. How nice to meet a fellow Texan."

I cock my head. "You sound like you've been gone for a while, though."

He sends me a full smile, his white teeth almost blinding. "You wouldn't break my heart right off the bat, would you? I've been gone twenty years, but I still consider myself a Texan."

I whistle between my teeth. "Twenty years? Wow, that's a long time to be away from home."

Wistfulness fills his face. "Don't I know it. Trust me, I hadn't planned on staying away so long, but this town is hard to leave. You'll find that out when you've been here for a while. What brings you here?"

All this time, his companion has been content to merely listen, and since it doesn't seem to bother him, I send him a friendly smile and answer the question. "I'm playing a part in a new TV series. My guess is that's quite a common story here, but that's why I moved to LA. Hoping to make my dreams come true, just like everybody else here."

"Good for you." He extends his hand to me. "It's a pleasure to meet you, Texas. I'm Reed."

I take his hand, returning his firm handshake, then do the same to his friend, who introduces himself as Corey. "The pleasure is all mine. I'm Jackson."

"You're perfect, is what you are," Reed says, sending me another one of his blinding smiles. His flirting is so on the nose, it doesn't even make me feel uncomfortable. At least with him, I don't have to worry about misinterpreting. He's a *what you see is what you get* kind of guy, and I can't help but admire his balls.

"You here by yourself or is that your boyfriend?" Corey asks, not sounding even remotely Southern. He gestures at Cameron, then narrows his eyes. "He looks kind of familiar. Is he an actor too?"

I'm not sure what to say, unsure if Cameron is usually open about his porn career or not. I think I better let him handle that himself, and I gesture at him to come over.

"Guys, this is my roommate. Cam, this is Reed and Corey."

"You're one of the Ballsy Boys," Corey says, shaking Cameron's hand. "I thought you looked familiar."

I almost hold my breath. Did I mess up by asking him over? But Cameron sends them an easy smile. "I am. I take it you're a fan?"

Corey and Reed share a look, then burst out in a laugh. "I don't think there is a gay man in LA who isn't a fan," Corey says. "It's a pleasure to meet you, man."

"You guys want to play a round of pool?" Reed asks.

We readily agree, and a few minutes later, we're having fun, trying to beat each other. Reed keeps flirting with me, and it amuses me to no end. I have no idea if his level of directness is normal, though if I look back on the two guys I met at the beach, maybe it is, but I think it's funny as all get out.

Truth be told, I don't see myself ending up with him in any way, and I think he knows it too, but it sure is fun to watch him flirt with me and to flirt back a little. He feels safe in a way that's hard to explain. Harmless.

He starts with words, and after a few minutes, he touches me for the first time. It's just a quick hand on my shoulder, then one on my lower arm. I allow it, curious to see how this will progress. He's so good at this that I might pick up a move or two.

It's my turn, and I have to bend over the table to take my shot. It doesn't escape my attention that three pairs of eyes are glued to my ass. Much to my surprise, Cameron's are as well, but maybe he's following the stares of Corey and Reed?

"Hot damn," Reed says. "It's been a long time since I saw someone wear jeans quite like you do. It should be illegal, the way they stretch over your ass when you bend over."

I look at him over my shoulder, sending him what I hope is a flirty smile." You like? Them's just my old jeans, you know?"

He clears his throat. "I never knew a simple piece of cotton could have that effect on me."

He brings his hand to his dick, which is clearly outlined in his jeans, and rearranges it not too subtly. That move is so bold I can't help but smile. It's a heady feeling, to know that you can impact another man in such a way.

But when my gaze travels from Reed to Cameron, I'm surprised to see anger on his face. Is it too much for him, this blatant flirting? He should be used to it, right? I wonder what's bothering him, but I can't spend too much time on it, what with not wanting to lose a game and keeping up with Reed's flirting at the same time.

Corey wins the first game for him and Reed, and we all immediately agree to play another round.

"I'll get us some more drinks," Cameron says and stalks off.

"Someone's got a bee in his bonnet," Reed says, and the idea of Cameron wearing a bonnet is funny enough to make me snicker.

Corey gives Reed a smack on his shoulder. "He's jealous,

you moron. Every time you dialed up the flirt, his face got darker."

It takes a second or two for that statement to sink in. *Jealous?* He thinks Cameron is jealous because Reed is flirting with me? That doesn't make sense at all, and yet at the same time, a sliver of hope fires up inside me. It would explain certain things, wouldn't it?

But no, it seems too far-fetched to even take seriously. Cameron isn't attracted to men, that's what he keeps telling me. Heck, he didn't even wanna come tonight. I practically had to drag him here.

If that's the case, then why does he keep bringing the conversation to such personal topics, like asking me what type of men I'm attracted to? Or what I like about his body? Those aren't the kind of questions a straight guy would ask, now would he? I'm horribly conflicted about all of this, and all I know is that I won't be able to figure this out right now. But Corey certainly has given me food for thought.

"We're just roommates," I tell them with as much conviction as I can muster, but Corey's face shows he'd not impressed.

When Cameron comes back with drinks for all of us. I decide to dial up my flirting with Reed a little as well, just to see how he'll react. I basically copy some of Reed's own moves, touching him, smiling at him, and letting my gaze linger on his body. Heck, who knew that flirting was so darn easy?

Corey manages to crush us in next game as well, scoring another victory for him and Reed, and they head over to the bar for the next round of drinks. Something tells me I need to be careful with my alcohol intake now. I need to keep a clear head for this.

"I don't think he's what you're looking for," Cameron says when they're out of earshot.

Something inside me jumps up in joy at his tone. "Really? He's hot as can be," I say, careful to keep my face straight.

"Sure, but he's way too practiced at flirting. He's looking for a hookup, not for a happily ever after."

I have to admit he's probably right about that, which makes me wonder if I'm misinterpreting things. Maybe he really *is* only looking out for me. I let out a sigh. "I guess you're right. It's a shame, 'cause I do like him."

Cameron bumps my shoulder. "We're just getting started, man. No worries. I've got you."

Confused doesn't even come close to describing how I feel. Cameron's mixed signals are driving me insane, going from *he likes me and he's jealous* to *he's just looking out for me*. Can you blame me, what with him going from hot to cold and from sexy and flirty to brotherly concern?

And my own feelings for him, those are even harder. I like him, I have from the moment we met, and I tried to switch to friend-mode when he told me he wasn't gay. But all the hanging out we do and him being my wingman isn't making it easy to think of him as just a friend. Not when both my body and my soul want more.

Just before we leave—Cameron is already heading to the door—Reed grabs my hand and pulls me close, whispering in my ear. "Come find me if your roommate decides he doesn't want you after all. I hang out here a few nights a week..."

He kisses me on my cheek and I nod. "Thank you."

"My pleasure, Texas. Now, go get your man."

My man. Now, there's a thought I like.

16

CAMPY

I watch with a scowl while that middle-aged, horn dog of a cowboy paws at Jackson, whispering something in his ear before kissing him on the cheek. I clench my teeth together and call on all my restraint to keep myself from marching over there and kicking the guy in the balls to get him off Jackson.

He's not interested, dude, take the hint already, I rant internally, glaring daggers at his hand resting on Jackson's lower back.

Although...Jackson isn't pulling away or telling him off. And he *has* been doing quite a bit of flirting himself tonight. Fuck, maybe he *is* interested in the guy. That thought makes my stomach churn and the unpleasant, hot feeling in my chest flare.

Am I jealous of this man with his hands *still* all over Jackson? But why? Why the hell do I care? We came here to find him someone to fall in love and live happily ever after with, so why does the thought of him actually doing it make me want to punch something?

Jackson finally peels himself away from Cowboy Grabby Hands and makes his way toward me.

"You know, you didn't have to ditch him on my account. If you want to go home with him, feel free," I snap, surprising both of us, judging by the look on Jackson's face.

"What are you talking about?"

"You and Red seemed pretty cozy, I just hate to break that up."

"Reed," Jackson corrects and I scoff.

"Whatever." He frowns and I immediately feel like a giant asshole. "I'm sorry, I'm being a dick. Seriously, if you want to hook up with Reed, you should."

Jackson studies me for several long seconds and I start to feel myself squirm under his inspection.

"No, it's okay. He was nice and all, but I'm not interested."

"He's your type though," I point out.

He shrugs. "When there ain't any sparks, type don't matter."

"That's true," I concede.

"Funny how that goes both ways," he muses. "When there *are* sparks, type don't matter then either." The deeper meaning of his words makes me squirm for a second time, his eyes feeling like they're boring into my soul and seeing all the irrational jealousy and confusing thoughts on full display.

"Yeah. Are you ready to go?" I ask quickly.

"I'm ready." He steps forward and pushes the door open, holding it for me.

On the sidewalk, we hail a cab and ride silently for a while.

Everything in my head is such a jumbled mess. I wish there

was someone I could talk to about everything, but there's no one. I can't talk to any of the guys at the studio because it would mean outing myself as straight. I can't talk to Jackson because, *hello, awkward*. I can't tell my mom because too many questions would be raised about things I'm not going to tell her. Jackson is the only person with a foot in both parts of my life.

I glance over at him and find him leaning his head back, watching the buildings as we drive past. The lights flickering across his face give him an oddly ethereal look and the serene smile on his lips warms my chest. He notices me looking and tilts his head in my direction.

"I haven't been able to decide if the city is beautiful or if it's just a giant concrete wasteland contributing to air and light pollution."

"I think it's both, honestly," I offer. "I've lived here so long, sometimes I forget stars even exist, because you can't see them here. When I stay late at the wildlife center, I sit on the hood of my car for a few minutes afterward just to look at the sky for a while."

"That's kind of sad."

"Yeah, it is."

"I don't want to forget stars exist. Maybe if I make enough money on the show I'll buy a ranch outside the city where I'll be able to go outside and see the stars whenever I want."

"Take me with you?" I ask wistfully, only half-joking.

"Of course," he agrees solemnly.

We fall back into silence, this time far more companionable, the rest of the way home.

"Sorry this night was a bust," I say as we climb the stairs to our apartment.

"It wasn't a bust. Just 'cause I didn't find no one to go

home with doesn't mean it wasn't fun. At least I got to practice my flirtin' a bit."

"Is that all it was with Reed? Practice?"

"Sure, I told ya I didn't feel a spark."

I nod, unexplainable relief flooding me.

"Maybe next time," I offer and Jackson smiles.

"Yeah, maybe next time."

We both head into our own rooms and I take my time changing out of my clothes and into pajamas, still wrestling with my thoughts and wishing like hell there was someone I could talk to about all this.

I wonder what would actually happen if I told anyone at the studio. I do my job like a professional, surely Bear wouldn't fire me for not being gay, right? But they might see me differently, feel differently around me. But more than that, if I told them this secret, what would keep the barrier between Cameron and Campy? As strange as it seems, being Campy is my escape from my life. Once they know Cameron, I won't have anywhere to hide anymore.

Jackson

EVER SINCE COREY'S REMARK, I keep thinking about it. Is Cameron jealous? I can't make up my mind about it, going back and forth between it's absolutely ridiculous to even consider it and all the evidence is pointing that way. How on earth can I find out the truth?

I have to push this issue down, because I have a tough scene to shoot today. It's an emotional scene between me and my TV mom about my father's death, and the mess we've discovered he has left us. It's the type of scene I fear and love in equal measure. They certainly challenge my capabilities as an actor, but they also give me a massive high after doing it well that's unlike anything else.

It takes us five takes until the director is happy with the result, and that last one went so well I knew we nailed it before he even yelled *cut*. Me and Brenda, who plays my mom, high-five each other. It's a weird sight, I'm sure, as both of us are still teared up from the emotions the scene required, but the joy of performing well races through me.

"Jackson!" the director, Patrick, calls out.

I turn around, hoping for praise but inwardly bracing myself for anything else. If there's one thing I've learned in the last few weeks, it's that this is a brutal business. You have to have thick skin to survive. It's a good thing I'm made from strong, Texas stock.

"Yes, sir?"

Patrick grins at me. "How many times have I told you not to call me *sir*? It makes me feel ancient, kid."

I could point out that at pushing the end of his sixties, he could easily be called ancient compared to me, but I don't think that will earn me any favors. "Sorry," I offer instead. "Force of habit."

He gestures me closer, as around us, assistants are setting up for the next shoot, which we'll do after lunch. "You did really well today, Jackson. It's been a pleasure watching you grow. I have a good feeling about this show."

My face splits open in a beaming smile. "Thank you. I love the material we're working with. The writers have done such a phenomenal job on giving us these great lines. Like the scene we just did, that was so easy for us to act out since it was written with emotional oomph. It makes it very easy to perform well."

Patrick nods at me, his face a little more serious now.

"You know, that's the most perfect response ever to a compliment like the one I gave you. I don't know if someone taught you that or if it's your ingrained humility and politeness, but an attitude like that will get you far. I don't kiss ass, as I'm sure you've figured out by now, but you're a pleasure to work with, kid. Even if this show doesn't do well, I'm confident you'll find another gig soon."

I'm stunned by this unexpected praise, and he's right, I do realize how much it means coming from him. Patrick has a bit of a reputation as a director. He does a great job, as the many awards he's received over the years show, but he's a perfectionist and he demands the best from the people he works with. For him to pay me a compliment like this, it means a lot.

"Thank you," I say, then I have to clear my throat to even make myself audible. "That means a lot coming from someone with your reputation. I really appreciate it."

He nods at me again. "A few more weeks and then we'll know if all our hard work has paid off. You are coming to the pilot party, right?"

He's referring to the party the network is throwing to celebrate airing the pilot episode. Of course, we're all on pins and needles as to how that one will be received. The network has guaranteed us a full first season either way, but if the pilot and the first few episodes do really well, we could be signed for a second season soon. Both Patrick and the producer, a rather grumpy and businesslike guy named Max, have assured us the network executives love what they've seen of the show so far.

"Yes," I say, barely able to swallow back the *sir* that I almost tacked on automatically again. "I wouldn't miss it for the world."

"Good. Make sure to bring a date. Those parties are a great way to impress a girl."

And here we go again, one of those subtle remarks that makes me wonder if I have to say something or not. Is it important? In the bigger scheme of things, maybe not, but I have promised myself I would be true to myself in this city. I don't ever, ever want anybody to be able to say that I lied to them or even pretended.

I take a deep breath. "That would be a boy, sir. Patrick, I mean. I would bring a boy, if I had a date. I'm gay."

He shrugs, his face showing complete indifference to that news. "Well, a guy then. Whatever. Just make sure to bring someone, because it's guaranteed to get you laid."

I'm not sure what to say to that, but I appreciate the thought, I guess.

When lunch is called, I grab a tray and head over to Ethan's table, as I've been doing a lot. I really like his company, and we always find something to talk about. And it's not like it always has to do with us being gay either. The man has a lot of experience in Hollywood, and he has told me some amazing stories about the movies and TV series he's worked on. He's a veritable fountain of knowledge, and I drink it all in. On his part, he seems to appreciate a captive audience, as he always seems glad to have my company.

"So," I say, studying the egg salad sandwich in front of me that looks like a sad rip-off of the one my mama used to make. "Patrick just mentioned the pilot party. He said it's custom to bring a date. Do I have to?"

Ethan shrugs. "It wouldn't hurt, but it's not like a requirement. Most people will, though. Are you comfortable with everyone knowing you're gay?"

My answer is fast and certain. "Yes. That's not the problem."

Ethan sends me a smile. "What is the problem then? Dare I guess it has something to do with your illustrious roommate?"

I let out a deep sigh. "Remember when I told you I was absolutely, one hundred percent certain he was gay?"

Ethan raises an eyebrow. "Uh oh."

"Yes, *uh oh* is right. It turns out he was not what he seemed and now says he's straight."

Ethan gently shakes his head. "Careful there, boy. In my experience, guys who say they are straight are a recipe for a lot of heartbreak. You may want to move on to someone else who has figured out what he wants."

I drop the remnants of my miserable sandwich on my plate. I'm sure my frustration is clearly visible as I raise my eyes to meet Ethan's, who is looking at me with sympathy. "I wish it were that easy. The thing is, I…"

"You've kind of fallen for him already," Ethan guesses correctly.

I wipe my hands off on a napkin and lean back in my chair. "Pretty sad, right? The first guy I meet here and I'm stupid enough to develop a crush on him."

"Maybe it's just a proximity thing," Ethan suggests. "After all, you're seeing him every day if he's your roommate."

I let out a bit of a bitter laugh. "Yeah, don't remind me. He forgets he has a roommate half the time and walks around half-naked. That's not making it easy either."

Ethan chuckles. "I can see why that's a mixed blessing. Maybe you should try to date more."

I throw my hands up in frustration. "I'm trying, but so far that's not going well. The thing is that I really don't want to hook up with guys, you know? I know that may sound outdated or whatever, but it's just not me. I may be an actor and living here, but I guess I'm just an old-fashioned cowboy at heart."

"You can take the cowboy out of Texas, but you can't take Texas out of the cowboy," Ethan says, but there is no scorn or judgment in his tone. Instead, he leans forward, sending me an almost fatherly look. It's how I had hoped my father would look at me and talk to me, but that's a whole different story.

"Look, kid, navigating this whole relationship thing, it's hard. I got lucky when I met Rick, I know that. But like you, I was sick and tired of the whole casual scene. Not to brag, but it's not hard for guys like you and me to score a hookup, you know? We're actors, we're not ugly, and we're charming enough to make a good impression. If you wanted to, you could get laid every night. The problem is that you want more, and so did I."

"I do. I want the white picket fence, you know? I don't care if that makes me horribly old-fashioned, but it's the truth. I don't see myself hopping from bed to bed. I see myself settling down with someone, buying a home, raising a family. And when I look at Cameron..."

My voice trails off as my heart unexpectedly clenches. Oh my, I hadn't realized he'd managed to settle that deep in my heart. This is more than a crush. It feels bigger than that, deeper. Could it be...?

"You see him in that picture," Ethan finishes, his voice soft and understanding.

"I do. It doesn't make sense at all, because he has given no indication he's interested in something permanent, even if by a miracle he would suddenly admit he was attracted to me. So what do I do now?"

Ethan grabs my hand and squeezes it, a gesture so comforting that it almost brings tears to my eyes. "Here's the thing, Jackson. The heart wants what it wants. You can try to convince yourself you want something else, but you know better. That means there's two things you can do. Either you decide you're going to give it your all and you're going to try and convince this Cameron of yours that you're his man. Or, you'll accept that you'll be pining for him for a while until your heart is finally able to let go. I can't tell you which choice to make, that's up to you. But I'll be rooting for you."

17
CAMPY

I stumble into the kitchen half-asleep, following my nose to the smell of coffee brewing.

"Mor—" Jackson starts, cutting himself off with a choking cough.

My eyes pop all the way open as concern wakes me the rest of the way up.

"Are you okay?" I hurry around the counter to check on him.

"Fine, I just...uh..." his eyes dart down and then back up again. I look down and realize I walked into the kitchen completely naked.

"Oh, shit, sorry." I spin and hurry to my bedroom to tug on a pair of sweatpants. I don't know why it's so hard for me to remember to put on pants when I wake up. In my defense, I didn't get much sleep and I'm fucking exhausted, but still, pants shouldn't be that difficult to remember.

"Sorry," I mutter again as I make my way back into the kitchen, this time with my junk covered.

"It's okay. It's certainly one way to make sure I'm awake in the morning," he assures me with a wink.

"Speaking of dicks out and swinging," I transition skillfully as I pull out a mug and fill it with coffee, "Rebel asked for help moving his boyfriend into his place today, you up for some manual labor?"

"That sounds great, actually. As weird as it sounds, I kind of miss working up a good sweat doing something other than lifting weights."

I am *not* going to think about Jackson sweaty. I'm not. I'm *not*.

"Awesome. All the guys will be there, so it'll be a good chance for you to meet them."

Jackson's eyes go wide. "Oh gosh, if my mama could see me now," he jokes, shaking his head. "She would tan my hide. Helping a bunch of porn stars move furniture, who'd have thought."

"Well, it's not like we're going to be naked or fucking while we're doing it, if that makes you more comfortable," I tease. "But listen, the stuff about my mom..."

"I won't say anything," he promises.

"Thank you." I breathe a sigh of relief. "None of the guys know, it's just easier that way."

"I understand, you can trust me," he assures me, and I really do. Trust him, that is. If I didn't, I never would've let him know about my mom to begin with.

"Thank you. And, um, the whole *not gay* thing..."

"My lips are sealed, Cam, I promise."

"Great. Ready to go in an hour?"

"No problem."

After I finish my coffee, I get dressed in some clothes I won't mind getting sweaty and then meet Jackson in the living room. He looks hot in a pair of well-fitting jeans, a T-shirt, and that cowboy hat of his he loves so much. The guys are going to take one look at him and cream their pants, and something about that makes me bristle a little.

"Do I not look okay?" he asks, insecurity creeping into his voice as he looks down at himself.

"No, you look fine."

"Then why are you frowning at me?"

"I was just thinking that you're going to have some of the guys wanting to climb you like a tree, looking like a sexy cowboy like that," I explain, and Jackson smiles and preens a little. "Let's go before your head gets so big it can't fit through the door." I slip on my shoes and wave him toward the door.

When we arrive, Rebel, Troy, Brewer, and Tank are already there. I introduce them to Jackson, who tips his hat and drawls an appropriate Southern greeting.

I can practically see the hearts forming in Brewer's eyes as his mouth falls open. I swear I even see a little bit of drool forming.

Tank glowers at him, leaning in to whisper something in Brewer's ear that has him scowling right back and shoving Tank away. I'm not sure I understand those two together, but if it's working for them, then more power to them.

"So, where are you from?" Rebel asks Jackson.

"Texas," he answers and then launches into an explanation of what he's doing in LA. A bit of pride swells in my chest, listening to him talk about his show. Maybe it won't be picked up for a second season, but there's something so admirable in the fact that he's out here, so far from home, pursuing his dreams.

Pixie and Bear show up as we're starting to haul stuff down the stairs and out to the moving truck. In all honesty, I'm not sure why Pixie came to help because he's not exactly a "hauling heavy boxes" kind of guy, and it seems Bear agrees because every item Pixie picks up that's heavier than a pillow is promptly taken from him by Bear.

"You know, I'm not an invalid, right?" Pixie gripes the fourth time Bear repeats this pattern, taking a box right out of his arms before he can get anywhere near the stairs with it.

"I don't think you're an invalid, but I'm not about to let you fall down the stairs because you've decided to pick up a box that weighs almost as much as you do," Bear argues and Pixie rolls his eyes. Bear looks at him like he's contemplating bending him over the arm of the couch and spanking him for his attitude.

"Wow, you could cut the sexual tension in here with a knife," Jackson rumbles in my ear, watching the exchange just like I am.

"Sexual tension? No way, Bear is old enough to be Pixie's dad," I argue and Jackson shrugs before moving past me with a box in his arms.

I notice for a few seconds the way his biceps bulge from the weight of the box and heat settles in the pit of my stomach.

"You planning to stare at your roommate all afternoon or are you going to grab another box?" Rebel teases and I snap my eyes away from Jackson and pick up the nearest box while Rebel grabs one end of a dresser and Brewer takes the other.

On our way down the stairs, Brewer faints and chaos ensues.

Jackson

. . .

I'M CARRYING a box out of the kitchen when I hear Rebel frantically calling out for help. "Somebody, help me!"

I drop the box on the floor and rush down the stairs to help Rebel hold up the heavy dresser he and Brewer were carrying. Brewer is barely conscious and looks white as a sheet, except for the dark circles under his eyes, that is. He looks like he might be ill or something.

Tank inches past me and grabs him, lifting him up without breaking a sweat. Rebel and I quickly get the dresser out of the way so Tank can carry Brewer into the living room.

When we get back upstairs, Tank is tenderly holding him, feeding him some juice. He's got a little more color in his face, but he still doesn't look well.

"I think he's dehydrated a little and definitely exhausted. I think we need to call it a day. He needs some sleep," Tank says when Bear suggests calling a doctor.

A little discussion ensues with people insisting Brewer shouldn't be by himself and Tank assuring them that he won't be, that he'll take care of him. We watch them leave, Brewer asleep in Tank's arms as he gently lowers him into his car.

"Is Brewer ill?" I softly ask Cameron, not wanting everybody else to overhear. Maybe he is and this is a known issue I'm not aware of.

Cameron shakes his head. "No, not that I know." He shoots a worried glance at Tank's car as they drive off. "He didn't look good, did he?"

"He's been working a lot," Rebel says. "Maybe I've over-scheduled him."

His boyfriend, Troy—and holy macaroni, those two make for a stunning combination—puts his arm around

Rebel's shoulder. "It's not your fault. He's a grown-ass man. If it was too much, he could've said something."

"Tank will take good care of him," Pixie says. "Did you see how sweet he was with him? Those two are so cute together."

My mouth pulls up in a smile at his infectious gushing, but Rebel's face doesn't quite show the same joy. He's worried, but there's something else. Something that looks a heck of a lot like guilt. I file that away as something I may need to ask Cameron about when it's just the two of us.

It takes us a bit longer to clear out Troy's apartment without Tank and Brewer, but we manage to get the job done. When everything has been carried into Rebel's place, I'm pretty sure we're all exhausted. I know I am, and I wipe my face off with a bandana.

I look sideways when I hear a snicker. "Is that a handkerchief?" Pixie asks.

"It's a bandana," I say as I tuck it back into my pocket.

"It's a Stars and Stripes handkerchief," Pixie insists, his eyes sparkling with mirth.

My face breaks open in a smile. "Oh, that's wrong on so many levels." I pull it back out and unfold it for him. "Honey, that's not the Stars and Stripes. That's the Texas Lone Star, I'll have you know. Big difference. Also, that's a bandana."

"I stand corrected on the Stars and Stripes, but that's a handkerchief if I've ever seen one. What's the difference between a handkerchief and a bandana anyway?"

"Bandanas are multi-purpose pieces of brightly colored cloth, perfect for tough cowboys like me. Handkerchiefs are for senior citizens. They're ironed, white or pastel cottons with hand-embroidered monograms in the corner, like my grandma used to make." I hold up my bandanna and flip it over. "See? No embroidery on this one. That makes it a bandana."

Pixie is laughing out loud now, holding his right side. "That's the funniest thing ever. I have to admit, it totally goes with the cowboy boots and the hats, though. Aren't you hot as hell?"

I shrug, then fold my bandana back up and stick it in my back pocket. "Of course I'm hot, but so are you and you're wearing shorts and..."

I cock my head to study Pixie's lithe body and the ridiculously tight jeans shorts he's wearing. I hear something that sounds a heck of a lot like a growl, and I find Bear looking at me, his eyes narrowing.

Isn't that interesting? There is definitely a possessiveness there that I spotted before as well. Duly noted, not that I have any interest in Pixie. I'll admit, watching that boy get ravished is sheer delight, but other than that, I have no interest in him at all. He's too young for me, too...needy. I don't know what it is he needs, but it's not me.

"You like my shorts?" Pixie asks, his tone flirting as he winks at me.

He has one hand on his hip, his butt sticking out like a magnet. And I do declare, that's one mighty fine behind that kid's got. He may not be my type, but I'm not dead, you know?

"Shorts? Is that what you're calling them? Why yes, I like them just fine. But the point I was trying to make is that you're just as hot in a shirt and shorts as I am in my jeans, boots, and cowboy hat."

There is a chorus of chuckles around me, and I realize the unintended double entendre of my words. Of course, Pixie jumps on it immediately. "I have to agree. You look definitely hot in that outfit, and the bandanna fits the whole cowboy-hotness you've got going there."

How can you not laugh at that blatant flirting? I don't know how he does it, but it's innocent and sexy at the same time. It's like you know he does it just for fun, not because he wants you to act on the signals he's sending out.

The quick look sideways he gives Bear confirms this for me. This kid knows what he wants, or I should say, *who* he wants. And I have to admit, even after having just met him, my money is on Pixie. I don't think he'll give up until he has tamed that bear.

Cameron has been watching this all with amusement. "You hitting on my roommate, Pixie?" he asks good-naturedly.

Pixie steps closer, then pets my biceps with one hand, batting his eyelashes at me. God, the kid is perfect. "Why, yes I am. You never told us he was this delicious. Maybe you wanted to keep him for yourself?"

I almost blurt out how ridiculous that suggestion is, but then I remember all these guys think Cameron is gay. It sobers me up quickly. Doesn't it bother him, to pretend and lie to these guys who are his friends? I'm not judging him, because I do understand he had little choice. And I can't help but admire the lengths he's willing to go to take care of his mom. But to live a constant lie, man, that would be so hard for me.

"Now that you've seen him, can you blame me?" Cameron asks, and I wonder if I'm the only one who notices that his flirty smile never reaches his eyes.

18

CAMPY

I'm not sure why I agreed to go out with Jackson again to be his wingman after last time was so weird. But when Jackson said one of his costars suggested a bar for him to check out tonight and asked me if I'd come with, I couldn't find it in me to tell him no. And I suppose I'd rather make sure if he goes home with someone they're not a creep. Even if the thought of him going home with someone makes that hot feeling rise in my stomach every time it occurs to me.

"About ready?" Jackson asks, tapping at my bedroom door.

"Almost," I call back, pulling my pants up and checking myself in the mirror. Once I'm satisfied that I'm not a complete mess, I yank my door open to find Jackson waiting for me in the hallway.

Jackson's eyes dart over me, and I swear I can almost feel them like a caress. "I'm hoping this bar is pretty casual like the other one we went to?" I ask, feeling momentarily self-conscious about my T-shirt and jeans.

"You look..." he starts, cutting himself off with a totally

fake cough as his cheeks pink. I'll certainly take *that* compliment.

"So do you," I smile, biting my lip and holding back the urge to reach out and smooth down the front of his shirt, not because it's wrinkled but because I want an excuse to put my hands on him for a few seconds. I can't even *begin* to unpack that insane hankering, so instead, I turn around to grab my phone off my dresser and then make a shooing motion to get Jackson moving. "Let's get going before all the good ass is taken."

He opens his mouth like he's going to say something, but snaps it closed again, leaving me wondering what it was going to be.

He opted for his favorite cowboy boots and I smile even wider at the sight of him. I hope like hell LA doesn't get to him and steal the country boy side of him from the world. I hope no matter how big of a star he becomes, he'll still wear cowboy boots to the bar.

This bar is a lot louder than Redd's was, but still not as bad as Bottoms Up. The first thing I notice when we walk in is the makeshift dance floor in the back corner where dozens of men are dancing to music playing from an old jukebox. There are certainly more guys here to choose from, and I can't decide if I'm happy about that for Jackson or not.

"What's the game plan? Should we get drinks and find somewhere to sit?" I ask, leaning close to Jackson so he can hear me over the noise and breathing deeply when the scent of his spicy body wash tickles my nose.

"Would you be opposed to dancin' for a few minutes?" he asks, his eyes fixed on the small sea of writhing, grinding bodies.

"You want to dance?" I repeat, a nervous flutter in the pit

of my stomach at the thought of pressing my body against his.

That shy look I've come to find adorable seeps into Jackson's eyes, and even in the dim light of the bar I can tell he's blushing a little again.

"It's just...I don't know how. I can line dance with the best of 'em, but that..." He tilts his head in the direction of the mating ritual we call dancing. "I don't know how to do that. I need to learn, right?"

"Yeah, you do," I agree. "But, to be honest, I've never danced like that with another man so I'm not sure how good of a teacher I'll be."

"Maybe we can figure it out together?" he presses. "I'd much rather look like a fool in front of you than some stranger." And then he busts out the crooked smile I can't say no to.

"Okay, yeah, let's do it." Grabbing his hand, I tug him toward the dance floor.

When we reach the group, a few men move aside a little to give us space along the edge to join in. Turning to Jackson with an unfamiliar feeling of uncertainty and shyness, I'm not exactly sure how to start. It's true I've never danced this way with a man, but I've never danced with a woman either. I danced with some girls at homecoming and prom, but nothing like this and not since I was eighteen. It's not like I've had a lot of time for clubbing. Sure, I go to Bottoms Up with the guys, but that's a work outing, not leisure.

The song on the jukebox changes to "Pour Some Sugar on Me" and Jackson's expression goes from nervous to eager as he grabs me and drags me to him, spinning me in the process so my back presses against his front.

"I love this song," he whispers near my ear, sending a shiver down my spine. His hips press to my ass and his arms wrap around my middle as he starts to move in time to the beat. Having nowhere else to put my hands, I reach them up and loop them around Jackson's neck, behind me. And, surprisingly, the position feels right. Sexual as hell, but right all the same. It's probably how comfortable I feel with him.

Jackson's hot breath cascades down the back of my neck as we both fall into a comfortable rhythm.

"I thought you hadn't danced like this before," I say accusingly, leaning further back into him.

"It feels more natural than I expected," he answers, his voice taking on a slightly gruff edge. "It feels kind of like... fucking," he admits, almost too quietly for me to hear over the music, and another shiver rocks me.

Have I ever heard Jackson say something so dirty before? Was that even all that dirty or did it just seem that way because I can feel his cock growing hard against the curve of my ass as we move? And why is it so hard to breathe all of a sudden?

"You must be good at fucking then," I blurt out and Jackson's laugh rumbles against my back, his arms tightening slightly around me.

"I'm not sure of that, but I'll certainly take the compliment."

"Hey, I would know," I point out and he laughs again.

The song ends too soon and when his arms loosen, we stumble apart awkwardly. *I* feel awkward, anyway. Jackson simply smiles at me with an air of casual confidence.

"You clearly don't need more practice than that. How about drinks?"

"Drinks, right, yeah." He makes an *after you* gesture.

My legs feel a little shaky as I walk away from the dance floor, and a coolness seems to surround me now that Jackson's large body isn't pressed up against me. Jesus, I need to get it together and stop acting so weird. I'm here to help him find a date, not muse about the way his muscled arms make me feel oddly safe when they're wrapped around me.

I order two beers while Jackson snags a table for us. But, by the time the bartender hands me our drinks, Jackson isn't alone at the table anymore. A couple of guys have taken it upon themselves to fill two of the chairs, leaving the fourth one free for me.

You're here to be Jackson's wingman. Now, stop being fucking weird and do what you promised. With a deep breath, I paste on a fake smile and saunter over to the table with our drinks in hand.

"Cameron, meet Mike and Baxter," Jackson gestures at the two men and I don't bother to try to figure out who's who.

"Hey guys, can I get you two something to drink?" I offer as soon as I reach them and set Jackson's beer down in front of him.

"Wow, what a gentleman," the blond man praises. He's cute in a pretty, femme kind of way. He sort of reminds me of Pixie and I immediately know he's not Jackson's type. Although, what did Jackson say last time? Something about *if you feel a spark, type doesn't matter so much.* I glance at the other guy and assess him as well. He's pretty average looking, but there's something sweet and alluring about his smile. It's a boy-next-door kind of smile.

"How about a round of lemon drops?" boy-next-door suggests and his friend nods eagerly in agreement.

"Coming right up," I agree, returning to the bar. While I wait for the round of drinks, I watch Jackson with Mike and Baxter and my stomach sours at the way he's laughing. Is he flirting? It doesn't look the same as the way he acted around whoever that old Texan dude was at the bar the other day, but it's hard to tell.

Returning to the table a second time with a round of shots, I have the urge to do something crazy like plant myself in Jackson's lap. Instead, I pass out the shots and make sure my fake smile stays in place.

Jackson

Dancing with Cameron was heaven and hell at the same time. I was hard as a rock, my cock pressed against him, and there's no way he didn't notice. You couldn't have put a sheet of paper between us, we were that pressed together, so yeah, he knows I had a raging hard-on. But he didn't protest. He didn't walk away. My plan clearly worked.

I might've lied to him just a little about me being uncomfortable with that type of dancing. Well, it wasn't so much a lie as more of an exaggeration, I guess you could say. It's true that I don't have a lot of experience with anything other than line dancing or the occasional school dance, but for some reason, I've always been comfortable on a dance floor.

Even as a teen, when my classmates were all gangly, awkward arms and legs, I was strangely elegant and coordinated. I get that from my dad, who could do a mean line dance as well as waltz my mom around the room. As conservative as they are, their strict rules never extended to the "no dancing" rules some of my Southern Baptist friends were suffering under. I guess they both loved music and dancing too much to give that up.

Of course, pretending I needed the practice was the perfect excuse to get Cameron on the dance floor as well.

I'm not above using all tactics at my disposal to get him to admit he's attracted to me. Because he is. He has to be. After my conversation with Ethan, I refuse to believe in a different truth than that one. He likes me, he's just scared to admit it to himself.

"You're a great dancer," Baxter says. He's cute as a button with his messy blond hair and a little makeup on. The lip gloss he's wearing makes you want to kiss it right off his full lips. "I just saw you two on the dance floor, and you were easily the best dancer out of everyone there."

The funny thing is that he's not even sounding overly flirty. He says it as if it's a fact, an observation. "Thank you," I say. "I love dancing."

"Well, if the mood strikes again, I'd love to dance with you," Baxter says, and this time, he does wink at me.

Clearly, I don't have a problem attracting men, I realize with a pleasant shock. Somehow, I had expected it to be harder.

"I'd love that," I say easily.

I debate winking back, then decide that's really not my style. At least, not with him, and not in front of Cameron. Baxter seems nice enough, but he's not my type. And I can't help but smile at the thought that I've come a long way since I actually am starting to realize that I do have a type. A very specific type. Type C, I think, and my smile widens.

Cameron shoots me a questioning look. "What's up?" he asks.

"Nothing. I just thought of something funny, but it's hard to explain."

"Okay," he says, smiling back at me. Then he adds, "You can tell me when we get home."

My eyes widen as it hits me. He's jealous. There's absolutely no other explanation for his behavior and this remark than him being jealous. I considered it when he and I went to the bar before, when we met Reed and Corey. Reed seemed so certain that Cameron was jealous, but I couldn't figure out why he would be.

This time, I can't reason away his behavior any other way. He's jealous. I can't figure out what's going through his head, but the conflicted emotions are clear as day. He really frigging likes me.

It may sound stupid, but as actors, we're trained in showing and recognizing subtle emotions. I'm not, like, Juilliard trained or something, but I have taken quite a few acting classes. Not as many as I would've liked, but then again, acting in my conservative college was focused mostly on putting on dramas aimed at sharing the gospel, so it wasn't like there was a lot of opportunity to go deep, you know?

But I happened to stumble across a local community theater in my college town that had a director who was formally trained as an actor. He worked on several movies and TV series until a horse-riding accident limited his mobility too much to work anymore. Man, I learned so much from him about facial expressions and body language. And everything I've learned is telling me that Cameron is jealous.

I can understand why he's conflicted about it. He's insisting he's not gay, or I should say, not attracted to men. From the moment I've found out, I've wondered how that's even possible, since he's clearly doing a good job working in gay porn. If he's really not attracted to men, he would have to be one heck of an actor to pull that off. There's a lot you can fake, but physical reactions are hard. But if he really likes me, and all evidence points there, then he must be so conflicted about it.

"You guys live together?" Baxter asks.

I wait for Cameron to answer. He's the one who brought this up, so now I'm curious to see how he'll talk himself out of it. He shoots me a look that's not exactly friendly.

"We're roommates," he says, and I'm weirdly disappointed he still qualifies us as that. Somehow, I had hoped he would continue his jealousy and suggest we were more than that, but that's ridiculous, of course. He's not there yet, not by a long shot.

"What do you guys do for a living?" Cameron then asks, and I have to give him props for trying to keep up the conversation.

It turns out Baxter is a paralegal, while Mike works at the county shelter. Cameron's eyes light up when he hears that, and seconds later, the two of them are involved in a deep conversation about puppy mills, rescue dogs, and the stupidity of people who would rather pay a couple of thousand dollars for a purebred dog than rescue a shelter dog.

I've seen it before, but it never fails to amaze me how Cameron changes when he talks about animals. It doesn't matter if it's giraffes, tigers, dogs, or even birds, when he talks about them, his whole face changes. It's not just that he smiles or talks more animatedly, it's that his whole body radiates energy and passion. It's a transformation, almost a metamorphosis, right before my very eyes.

It makes me realize all over again how unhappy he is doing porn, not just because he claims he's not gay, but because his heart isn't in it. He does it for the money, which is a valid reason, but I wish he could quit.

Maybe one day he can. A weird dream pops into my head, a vision of me and Cameron together, owning our own place. A quiet house, a ranch maybe, somewhere in the country. Me making enough money to support him going to school. It's so real, even as I'm sitting here in a noisy bar, that it takes my breath away.

And I realize with shocking clarity that my days of dating are over. I don't want anyone else. I want Cameron, and I'm willing to wait until he pulls his head out of his ass and sees how perfect we would be together. I'm his man. All he needs to do is open his eyes and see it. He likes me, that I'm sure of, and I think he does more than like me. He's just too confused or scared or something to admit it, but I have two advantages over him.

I have time and I have patience, and both will work in my favor.

19

JACKSON

It's two days before the pilot party, and Ethan's words haven't left my mind. I've been pondering them for days, until I realized he's right. I have two choices. Either I can forget about Cameron and try to move on, or I can go for it. The latter scares the living daylights out of me, because it's risky as all get out.

I'm almost one hundred percent sure he's attracted to me, but if it turns out I'm wrong or if he takes it the wrong way, I'm not only losing a friend, but most likely also a place to live. Still, I don't think I can live with any choice other than pursuing this. Just like I took a huge risk coming to LA and pursuing my dream to become an actor, this is something I have to do. My heart has made its choice. It wants Cameron, so now I need to figure out a way to make him realize he likes me.

So I've decided to be a little sneaky. Rather than declaring my intentions—holy cow, there's an old-fashioned expression I never thought I would hear myself use—I'm simply going to appeal to his friendship and his offer to help me.

I know he has a shoot today, which means he'll be tired when he gets home. He doesn't realize it, but on those days, I've been taking care of him a little more than usual. I don't mind cooking. It's a great way to relax after a long day of work. And since we started shooting early today, we're done by six, which means it's early enough for me to grab some ingredients and come home and cook.

I've discovered Cameron really loves Italian, so tonight I'm making lasagna. He already told me he wasn't expecting to be home before eight, but he still has to eat. When he walks in a little after eight, I already have the lasagna in the oven and I'm preparing a salad.

"That smells good," he comments as he walks into the kitchen, sniffing the air. Then as he peers into the oven, his face lights up. "You're making lasagna?"

"Yup, a triple portion so we have some leftovers for the rest of the week."

"If my lips weren't so sore from sucking dick half the day, I would kiss you."

If that's not the weirdest compliment I will ever receive, I don't know what could possibly top it. The strange thing is that it doesn't even bother me so much to think about him being with the guys he works with. It bothers me far more to think about him doing this only for the money, only because he has to. There is a level of sadness in that I find hard to swallow—unlike him, apparently, but I stop my thoughts before they focus too much on the word *swallow*.

He changes into something more comfortable, and by the time the lasagna is done, we're both lounging on the couch in sweatpants. Much to my surprise, he doesn't turn the TV on.

"How was work today?" he asks. "You had that fight scene with your uncle, right?"

I'm not able to keep the surprise off my face that he remembered. I had casually told him I wasn't looking forward to this scene because I like Ethan so much. It would be hard for me to fight with him on screen.

"It went really well. It took us a few tries, but man, he is so good. The way he looked at me, you would've put a million dollars on it that he hates my guts. That made it easy for me to look at him the same way. The director was elated with the results."

"Didn't you say he was happy in general with how things have been going so far?" Cameron asks with his mouth full.

"Yeah, he is, and so is the producer. They keep sayin' they got a good feeling about it, but I'm not sure if they're just being polite and this is something they're supposed to say, or if they really mean it."

"Two more days till the pilot airs, right? That means you guys should have some reviews the day after. Are you scared?"

"Yeah, I am. Not so much for the show, because I really do believe it's good, but I'm scared the reviews for my role or my acting specifically will be harsh. What if critics love the show but they hate me?"

Cameron nods. "I can understand why you would be scared of that. But I think if you had sucked that badly, your director would've said something, right? You said this guy, Patrick, had a lot of experience in this and won a bunch of awards. Surely he would've said something if your performance was so subpar."

See, this is something else I really appreciate about Cameron. He tells you like it is. He coulda told me that he knew I would do a good job, but he's not the type to lie to me. How could he know when he's never seen me act?

Instead, he chooses to focus on what he knows to be true, and he does have a point.

"Good point," I admit. "Either way, I think the whole cast will be happy when that first episode has aired and we've got some reviews."

"Do you want to watch it together?" Cameron offers.

He couldn't have given me a better opening if I had told him what I had planned. So I take a deep breath, fortify myself on the inside, and make him an offer he can't refuse.

"Speaking of that, the network is throwing a pilot party to celebrate the first episode being aired. Gonna watch it together and have some food and drinks. Do you want to come with me? It's kind of a cool thing, because you'll get to meet all the people you hear me blabber on about daily."

Cameron's hand stops halfway to his mouth, a bite of lasagna balancing precariously on his fork.

CAMPY

"Isn't that the kind of thing you might want to take a date to?" I ask, feeling like a complete ass when Jackson's face falls.

"I suppose it is," he agrees, setting his fork down and pushing his plate away. "I thought it would be fun to bring you, but I can—"

"I'll go." I cut him off before he can finish the sentence. "I want to go."

"You don't have to. I'm sure it's no different than parties thrown at the studio you work for."

"If everyone is fully clothed the entire time, then it won't be like the parties at Ballsy," I joke. "But if you want, I can return the favor and invite you to the next Ballsy Boys party.

You can see Brewer's dick in person if we get enough alcohol in him."

A blush spreads over Jackson's cheeks, and my stomach gives a little flutter at the pretty sight.

"So, you'll come to the pilot party?" he asks again, sidestepping the offer and the mention of Brewer's dick artfully.

"If you're sure you want me there, then I'd be honored to come. I'll just have to talk to Rebel and see if we can move the shoot that day up an hour or two so I can be sure I'm finished on time, no pun intended." Jackson snorts a laugh and blushes harder. "How fancy do I need to dress for this?"

"Nothin' too fancy, what you wore when we went to the bar is probably fine."

"Okay, thanks for the invite, I'm looking forward to it." I'm not sure why I do it, but I reach for his hand and put my hand on top of Jackson's. His eyes widen and so does his smile.

"Me too."

After dinner, I do the dishes, under protest from Jackson who tries to insist he can clean up, and then the two of us settle back on the couch. When he puts on one of the nature documentaries I like, I side-eye him curiously.

"Am I dying or something?"

"What?"

"Why are you being so nice to me?" I ask suspiciously. "Fuck, are you moving out and trying to find a nice way to tell me?"

"What? No." Jackson shakes his head rapidly. "I like cooking dinner and I know you had a long day, so I thought it would be nice to put on something you like to watch."

I narrow my eyes at him, my suspicion still simmering.

"You don't have to do nice things for me because you feel bad about my busy schedule and my sick mom."

"What are you talking about? I'm doing nice things because you're my roommate and my friend, and I like spending time with you, that's all."

"Oh." I blink in surprise at the sincerity dripping from his voice. "Sorry," I mumble.

Jackson just chuckles and shakes his head at me. "If you're done being paranoid, can we watch this show?"

"Yeah." I scoot a little closer to him without thinking about it. Jackson's nice to be close to, and nice to spend time with. "Thank you."

"No thanks required."

20

JACKSON

When our Uber stops in front of a huge mansion, protected by a heavy, black wrought iron gate, Cameron and I look at each other in surprise.

"Are you sure we're at the right address?" Cameron asks.

"I think so." I double-check the elegant invitation I received. Yessiree, we're exactly where we should be. "I think this may be the producer's house?"

Cameron grins. "Dude, we'll be hanging out with some high rollers tonight. You should've told me, I would've dressed a little fancier."

I think back to the moment he stepped into the living room in those tight-fitting jeans with that dark-blue, button-down shirt that clings to his body. If you ask me, he looks mighty fine. He couldn't have looked hotter in a tux.

"No worries," I say weakly. "You look perfect."

I wince inwardly at that last word. Am I giving away too much? I keep wondering whenever I blurt something like that out, but Cameron seems oblivious to my remarks. He's either seriously oblivious when it comes to flirting, or he is indeed as straight as they come. I'm still harboring a lotta hope for the first option.

We get out of the car, and just as our Uber drives off, another car pulls up. The chauffeur gets out, and seconds later he holds open the door for Ethan and his husband, Rick. Both are impeccably dressed in suits, and my stomach drops. Did I misread the dress code?

"Jackson," Ethan says with genuine warmth. "Let me introduce you to my husband."

Rick and I shake hands. "I've heard so much about you," Rick says. "It's a pleasure to meet you."

"Likewise. I've so enjoyed working with your husband, both professionally and personally. This is my friend Cameron, by the way. Cameron, this is my costar Ethan and his husband, Rick."

When Cameron and Rick are shaking hands, Ethan winks at me. I'm comforted by the idea that he knows what's going on. Maybe he can give me some impressions after he's observed us for a little bit. After all, a guy his age must have a well-developed gaydar, right?

"Did we underdress?" I ask him, which worries me more right now than anything else.

"You're fine. My man here likes me in a suit, what can I say?" Ethan says, sending a smile at Rick that makes my insides go weak. Gosh darn it, I want someone who'll look at me like that.

Before we can even ring the doorbell—or search for it, for that matter, because I have no idea where to even start—the gate slowly slides open.

"Prepare to be wowed," Rick says with a hint of humor in his voice. "I remember the first time Ethan took me to a party like this. My eyes about popped out of my head. Don't feel embarrassed if you get a little starstruck."

Campy 169

He says it as much to Cameron as to me, and I guess he has a point. Cameron may be completely new to this, but it's not like I've had a lot of experience. I think Ethan is the biggest star I've met so far.

The door is opened by what I assume is some kind of butler, and he ushers us in with practiced efficiency. "If you follow me, the guests are assembling in the theater."

Cameron and I share another look as we follow him. *Theater?* This house has a friggin' theater? The butler leads us through a long hallway, and I can't help but peek into the rooms we pass. There's a fitness room, what looks to be a library, an office, and a more casual family room, and that's just the ones we can see. This house is absolutely gigantic, and I can't even dare to guess how much it costs. Mind you, this is Beverly Hills. A shack costs a pretty fortune here.

The noise of people talking grows louder as we continue, and then the butler leads us into a foyer, I guess you could call it. And yes, I can now confirm the producer has a theater in his house. How's that for life goals?

"Jackson," Max, the producer, greets me. "I'm so pleased you could join us."

He shakes my hand, and I'm surprised he even remembers my name, having met me only once, but maybe someone made him a cheat sheet.

"And who is this?" he asks. "Your boyfriend?"

I'm amazed at the casualness of that question, and I once again realize how big the cultural difference between rural Texas and LA is. Being gay really isn't that big of a deal here. That being said, I don't want him to get the wrong impression.

"This is Cameron, my best friend and roommate."

Cameron's head jerks to the side at the mention of *best friend*, which I'll admit slipped out before I even realized how true it is. I've never had a friendship like this one, and it's not just because I have a crush on him. He doesn't judge, he doesn't criticize, he gives me the space to be myself and likes me just the way I am. He makes me feel at home, and I've never had that with anyone.

Patrick, the director, was right that everyone present here has brought a date. In that sense, I'm grateful I brought someone. It does raise eyebrows, however, the fact that I've brought not a date, but a friend. I spot some curious glances in our direction, but maybe I'm misinterpreting them and it's just because people are realizing I'm gay?

Rick and Cameron head off, bonding over a discovered shared love for animals. It turns out Rick is a vet. Which I guess I knew, but I somehow had forgotten, if that makes sense. Anyway, he and Cameron are chatting animatedly within minutes.

"Your previous statements that you were certain your roommate was gay make a whole lot more sense now," Ethan says softly.

I look at him quizzically. "What do you mean?"

He chuckles. "You didn't think I would recognize *Campy*? I may be old in your eyes, my young Padawan, but I still do enjoy good gay porn. And the Ballsy Boys deliver just that. Quality gay porn. Actually, Campy is one of my favorites. I don't know if you noticed, but he has a similar body type to Rick."

Ooookay then. We have now once again ventured into the weirdest conversation ever, one I never imagined I would have, especially at a Hollywood party. "Oh."

He lifts an eyebrow. "Jackson, you really didn't consider people might recognize him?"

I slowly shake my head. "No. I know that sounds naïve, but it never even occurred to me. Maybe it's because I've only watched one video of him, and that was when I discovered my roommate was a porn star. I mean, I know what he does, but to me he's just Cameron, you know?"

Ethan hesitates, then steps even closer to me. "Look, I'm not saying you should forget about him, but you need to keep in mind that Hollywood is, at its core, a very, very small town. Rumors spread quickly here, so if you don't want people to know you're close with a porn star, you may want to keep him away from parties like this."

It takes me a few seconds to recognize the nasty feeling in my stomach, because I haven't experienced it in a while. Still, I remember it all too well. It's what shame feels like. Shame for who you are, shame for the choices you're making, shame for the people you hang out with. It's the shame I felt for years before I found the courage to come out, and even after that, it took me a long time to let it go.

Ethan is suggesting I should be ashamed of being seen with Cameron because he's in porn. The hypocrisy of that in a town like LA, like Hollywood with all its crazy excesses and drugs and marital issues and the things people do to advance their career...I can't even describe it. And I've only seen slivers of this, know the rest only from the research I've done, the books I've read. No one in this town has any moral high ground to judge Cameron, and yet they will.

"I'm not ashamed of him." My voice is surprisingly steady, even if it's a little louder than it should've been.

Ethan sends me a terse smile. "I'm not saying you should be, kid. I'm telling you that people will make you *feel* like you should be. I just want you to be prepared for the backlash it could create if you go public with your relationship with him."

I shake my head. "There is no relationship. You heard me, we're just friends."

Ethan puts a strong hand on my shoulder, squeezing gently. "Then let me offer you some reassurance after the unpleasant news I just delivered. That boy is not straight. He may be confused, he may have not figured it out yet, but he likes you."

I can't conceal the joy that bubbles up inside me at those words. "How do you know?"

Ethan smiles, dropping his hand from my shoulder. "Because even when he's talking to Rick, his eyes constantly seek you out. Keep doing what you're doing, Jackson. It's working."

CAMPY

I SHOULD'VE KNOWN BETTER than to come to this party with Jackson. It didn't occur to me that people might recognize me. Sure, I get recognized at gay clubs, but I'm a *porn star*, why would people at an elite Hollywood party recognize me?

Maybe I'm being paranoid. Maybe all the looks and whispers are because I'm here with Jackson, not because they recognize me as Campy.

I glance over at Jackson and see him smiling brightly as he talks to his costar Ethan. His eyes dart to mine and our gazes linger on each other for a few seconds, sharing a smile that feels like it's just for the two of us, even though there are hundreds of people in the room.

"If you'll excuse me, I promised Jackson I'd get him a drink, I don't want him going thirsty," I say to the man who's been talking my ear off for the past few minutes. Ethan's husband Rick was nice to talk to, but this guy has been blabbering on and on. I figure the old excuse of getting someone a drink is bound to work, and it does.

"Of course, of course." He waves me off and I make my way to the small bar on the side of the room. There are servers making their way around with champagne as well, but I saw the way Jackson wrinkled his nose when he spotted them, which is why I figured I'd score us a couple of beers.

"Two beers, anything is fine," I tell the bartender when I reach him.

"Coming right up."

"Excuse me." A voice behind me has me turning my head. There's an attractive woman in a tight, red dress standing there, blushing and smiling at me. "Oh my god, it really is you. I thought my friends were messing with me."

I feel a frown forming on my face but force it into a phony smile.

"I'm sorry?" I decide to play dumb. There has to be a *tiny* chance she thinks I'm someone else, right?

"Campy, right?"

"Oh, um, yeah," I mumble, figuring there's no way she'll buy a lie.

"Did I see you walk in with someone? Is it your boyfriend? Is he on the show?" She asks the questions rapid-fire, leaving my head spinning.

"Here are your drinks," the bartender says, saving me from answering and making me want to kiss him for it.

"Thanks," I say to him, turning to grab the drinks and then giving the woman another quick smile. "It was nice to meet you, have a good evening."

Without waiting for a response from her, I start moving through the crowd, back in Jackson's direction, but I stop before I reach him.

If I go to him, she'll see and know who I'm here with. Not only that woman, but anyone else at the party who happens to recognize me. Jackson's trying to start his career as a serious actor, and being associated with me could ruin that before the second episode even has a chance to air.

I turn on my heel, nearly spilling the two beers on myself as I run into another guest directly behind me.

"Sorry," I mumble before sidestepping them and making a beeline for the nearest door.

My lungs feel tight and my heart is pounding too hard as I push through the doors to the back garden. To my relief, there isn't anyone else out here.

I set the drinks down on the garden wall and collapse on the wrought iron bench beside it. Leaning forward, I bury my face in my hands and try to breathe. I'm such an idiot, I should've realized the harm I could do to Jackson by being seen with him. Maybe no one noticed us arrive together. If I slip out now, I could save him from the association. I can send him a quick text and call a rideshare to get the hell out of here before I can do any damage.

I pull out my phone to send the text, but the door to the yard opens again before I can send it.

"I was wonderin' where you got to," Jackson says, stepping out into the garden.

"Hey, sorry, I needed some air. I was actually about to text you and tell you I was going to get out of here."

He frowns, coming to sit beside me on the bench, his concerned gaze roaming over me.

"Is something wrong? Are you not feeling well? Is your mom okay?"

For a second I consider lying and telling him I'm feeling sick. It's easier than the truth, but, looking into his trusting eyes, I can't bring myself to do it.

"I'm an idiot. I should've realized people here might recognize me. You can't be seen with me, it'll ruin you. If the wrong person saw us walking in together they might already be selling the story to every tabloid they can get ahold of."

His eyebrows furrow and his frown deepens.

"I don't care about that."

I scoff and shake my head. "You have to care about it, you're about to become a huge star. This is your dream, and I'm not about to be the one who wrecks it for you."

"So, what? You won't be seen with me in public anymore? We can't hang out? Are you going to make me move out?" he snaps, surprising me. I've never seen him so angry before. "I don't give a good goddamn what they might say about me for being seen with you. They think they know you just because they've seen you fuck? They don't know you, and they don't know me. You're a good person. You're strong and kind. I'd wager you're a hell of a lot better than half the people in that room who might judge you."

I blink in surprise at the curses falling from his lips, so passionate in his defense of me that he's not bothering with his usual politeness and niceties. His words shake something loose inside me and before I know what I'm doing, I'm leaning forward, intent on feeling his mouth against mine.

His warm breath fans over my lips as I get close, my heart beating an entirely different erratic rhythm now. His breathing is harsh from his rant, but it hitches when he realizes what I'm doing. There's no way I'm ready to admit it out loud, but right now I can admit to myself that I've been thinking about kissing Jackson for weeks. I don't know what it means, but it feels inevitable.

The lightest brush sends a spark through me. Our lips aren't even really touching, not yet, but I'm more than ready to rectify that. I lean even closer...

"Jackson, the show's about to sta— Oh, oops," Ethan's voice has us flying, the moment gone and disappointment settling over me. "Sorry, I didn't mean—"

"No, we're here to watch the pilot episode, we can't miss that," I say quickly, jumping up and darting my gaze around the garden, trying to look at anything but the two of them. "Come on, let's go inside."

"Right, the pilot," Jackson agrees, his voice huskier than usual as he stands as well.

We near the door and I reach out to grab Jackson's hand to stop him.

"Are you absolutely sure? I can still leave, let you enjoy your night without worrying what people might say about us."

His fingers tighten around mine and he gives my hand a tug.

"I want you here, anyone who says or writes anything negative can kick rocks. Come on."

I let him drag me inside and we claim spots beside each other in the theater where all the guests are gathered to watch the show. To my relief, everyone seems too focused on watching the show that's about to start to look at me anymore.

I notice Jackson doesn't drop my hand, and I don't say anything to draw his attention to it. Instead, I settle back in my seat and enjoy the rest of the evening.

21

CAMPY

Standing outside Brewer's apartment at the asscrack of dawn, with the rest of the guys half-asleep and grumpy just like I am, I have to wonder if we should start offering our services as movers, since apparently it's our new pastime.

Brewer sent out an SOS text telling us he was getting kicked out of his apartment and needed helping moving his stuff into Tank's place ASAP. I won't lie, I was surprised considering they *just* started dating and this seems ridiculously fast, but what do I know about relationships? Nothing, as evidenced by the whole thing with me and Jackson.

The near-kiss last night hung in the air between me and Jackson this morning, neither of us seeming to want to be the one to bring it up.

I tossed and turned all night, replaying our *almost kiss* over and over in my head, my feelings about it ranging from disappointment to relief depending on the time of reflection. Around four in the morning I settled on seeing it as a bullet dodged on Jackson's part. I'm a mess and he deserves so much better than me. All I do is lie to everyone around me. And *I'm not even gay*, I remind myself for the millionth time. Whatever last night was, it's a good thing Ethan interrupted us before we ruined our friendship.

If Jackson will let me get away with pretending it didn't happen, that's definitely the option I'm going to take for as long as possible.

The door opens and Brewer stands on the other side with a giant smile. Bear grunts something resembling a greeting and we all follow suit. Jackson has filming this morning, so he couldn't help this time, which means we have one less set of capable hands.

Tank is standing behind Brewer and when he turns around to whisper something to him and give him a gentle kiss, my stomach gives a weird dip. I never would've thought these two were capable of being so sweet to each other.

"You two are so sweet," Pixie sighs, echoing my thoughts.

"Thanks for coming, guys," Tank says.

"Who's in charge?" Bear asks. "Who's gonna tell us what to do?"

Brewer doesn't hesitate before answering. "Tank. He's got this all planned out."

Within minutes, Tank has divided tasks. Rebel and Troy are dismantling two of the bookcases in the living room, Brewer and I are packing the last stuff into boxes, Pixie is getting Brewer's stuff from the fridge, and Tank, Bear, and Heart have started bringing down the first big pieces.

"So, moving in, huh?" I say casually to Brewer as we work.

A guilty look crosses Brewers face before he nods. "Yeah. It's fast, but when I lost my room here it didn't make much sense to spend a lot of time and energy into finding a new place. We're moving my bed and stuff into Tank's guest room since that was empty anyway."

"That makes sense," I say. "Too bad it didn't happen a few months sooner though, I would have loved to have you as a roommate." But even as I say it, I know I wouldn't trade Jackson for Brewer if given the choice.

"Sure, but your new roomie is a pretty sweet deal, right?"

"What do you mean?" I feign ignorance, my jaw slightly clenched as we dance near dangerous territory with this line of conversation.

"Dude, the guy is hot as fuck with that whole cowboy thing he's rocking, including that Southern drawl. Don't tell me you didn't notice. His voice alone gave me a hard on."

Wanting to hide my reaction, I turn toward Brewer's closet and start gathering hangers. Obviously Jackson is hot, you'd have to be blind not to notice it. So why is it pissing me off so much to hear Brewer say it out loud?

"He's cool," I answer after a few tense seconds. "Jackson is hot, sure, but he's also super nice."

"No reason why he can't be both," Pixie pipes up, strolling in from the kitchen. "I wouldn't mind a roomie who looked like that."

"He's straight."

The lie falls off my tongue before I can think too much about it. I'm not sure if I'm saying it because I want them to leave it alone or to deflect from any future questions about why we aren't hooking up.

"That sucks," Pixie says, but then his eyes narrow. "I didn't get a straight vibe off him. He flirted with me."

"Everyone flirts with you, Pix," Rebel says. "That doesn't mean shit about being straight or gay."

"Huh. I never saw him flirt with you," Brewer says. "I thought he was straight as well."

I don't think I've ever been as grateful for someone's gaydar malfunctioning.

I shrug, doing my best to play it cool. "Either way, I'm not interested in him that way. You know I don't date." At least that part's true.

Pixie puts his hands on his hips. "And why *is* that? Why aren't you interested in finding a boyfriend?"

Another stiff shrug. "Who needs a boyfriend when you're a porn star and get to fuck the sexiest guys without any complications? Works for me."

"You know, I felt the same way," Brewer says.

I look up from the box I'm taping to study Brewer. "You're saying you feel different now?" Not that it matters. Our situations are *completely* different. But I'm still curious to know how he could've gone from total playboy to domesticated so quickly.

"Of course he does. He's with Tank now," Pixie says almost indignantly.

As on cue, Tank walks into the room, wiping his face with his shirt. "You guys about done in here? We've dragged the big stuff down, so we can fill it up with the boxes now."

"This is the last one." Brewer points to the box I'm finishing with.

"Good. We'll take a little break and then load up the boxes." Tank looks at Brewer for a few seconds, then walks into the kitchen and comes back with a bottled water and a banana. "Here. You need to eat something."

"I'm not—"

"I wasn't asking."

Brewer mutters something under his breath before uncapping the water bottle and drinking half of it before starting on the banana. "You happy now?"

Tank leans in and kisses him. "Get used to it."

I watch in stunned silence as Tank walks back out of the room, Brewer staring after him like a lovesick fool.

Pixie giggles. "And that's why Brewer now loves having a boyfriend."

I shake my head, not sure what to say. It *does* seem nice, what the two of them have. If only.

22

JACKSON

I'm not doing well this morning at the shoot. I'm fumbling my lines, missing cues, and creating a whole reel of bloopers and mistakes. Patrick, the director, is growing more and more frustrated.

"I'm not sure what crawled up your ass this morning, but you damn well better get your head screwed on right, Jackson," he snaps at me right before the lunch break.

"I'm sorry," I say, biting my tongue to hold back the *sir* he hates so much. "I'll do better."

He gives me a curt nod, then stalks off.

"Trouble in paradise?" Ethan asks as I take my usual spot across from him.

I chose a salad for lunch, but it's a sad affair, really, with browning lettuce drowned in too much dressing. "I don't rightly know," I say, feeling miserable.

"Correct me if I'm wrong, but I had the impression I was interrupting something last night."

"Can we not talk about this?" I try.

Ethan grins. "Oh my dear boy, that dog won't hunt, as

Rick would say. You can't clam up on me now. Come on, tell me what's wrong."

I let out another one of those deep sighs that seem to originate in my very soul. Man, I've got it bad. "Cameron may have been close to kissin' me," I admit.

Ethan raises an eyebrow. "And why would you feel mopey about that?"

I push back the salad. My stomach isn't interested in food right now. "Because he's makin' me so confused. He's not hot and cold, exactly, but he's giving off all these mixed signals, and I don't know what to believe anymore."

Ethan covers my hand with his in a sweet gesture. "Jackson, he's giving off mixed signals because he *is* confused. He has to be. If he's doing gay porn while thinking he's straight, that's gotta mess with his head. And then with you in the mix and the obvious attraction he feels for you, he's gotta be in knots inside."

There's nothing but warmth in his eyes, and it settles me. "You think he's attracted to me?"

Ethan removes his hand and sends me a big smile. "Kid, he couldn't take his eyes off you. He's smitten, he just doesn't know it yet."

The hope that I had before roars back up inside me. "So what do I do?"

"Wait. He's gotta be ready, so all you can do is wait, and be there for him when that lightbulb comes on."

Wait. I can do that, I think. Especially now that Ethan says he sees it too, the chemistry between us. I feel lighter now, my faith restored, and after lunch, I nail the most difficult scene of this episode in a single take.

When I come home, Cameron is spread out on the couch, looking ten kinds of exhausted. He helped Brewer move today, so we both didn't get much sleep.

"Hey," I say, a little cautious.

We managed to pretend the whole almost-kiss didn't happen this morning when we stumbled into the kitchen in search of coffee, both barely awake, but I'm not sure if that's how he wants to play it.

"How did shooting go today?" he asks. Okay then, pretending it is.

"Started off a little crappy but things improved after lunch."

"Oh, good. Sorry, I didn't go grocery shopping. I stopped by my mom's real quick and I was too tired after."

I shrug. "It's fine. We can grab something if you want? Or order in?"

"I'm in the mood for a burger," he says, and my mouth instantly waters.

I haven't had a burger in forever, too cautious with what I eat. But now that he mentions it, I'm craving one. "I'm in. What's a good place to get a burger here?"

He looks at me as if I'm mad. "In-N-Out, of course," he says.

"Okay, never been to one. And they have good burgers?" I double-check. Hey, I'm Texan. I take burgers seriously. Well, all meat, really.

"Dude, there's nothing like it."

After high praise like that, my expectations are high, so color me surprised when it's a regular chain-restaurant, not looking all that different from a McDonald's. Cameron's face is glowing though, so I keep my mouth shut as he orders something off the secret menu, as he calls it. I have no earthly idea why a restaurant would wanna keep a menu secret, but what do I know? It's California, people. And they say Texans are weird.

"What are we eating again?" I ask as I look at my food, a

thick burger with what looks like grilled onions on it, as well a massive load of cheese, and fries smothered in even more cheese and with a weird, pinkish sauce on top.

"Animal style burger and animal style fries with their secret sauce. There's about ten thousand calories in there, but I don't give a fuck. It's so good."

The look on Cameron's face as he bites into his burger is pure bliss, much like he looked in that video with Pixie, but nope, I'm not going there. Gotta keep my eyes on the ball.

I try a few fries, and I have to admit that sauce is amazing, though combined with the cheese it's a bit heavy.

"Oh my god, this is seriously the best burger ever," Cameron says with his mouth full, so I take a bite out of mine as well.

It's rich, the cheese, and I like the combination with the onions, but the burger itself is nothing more than okay. Honestly, I'll take a bacon-and-cheese Whataburger over this any day, but I'm smart enough not to spoil his fun.

He even ordered us a milkshake, and I gotta admit, that is fantastic. I'm gonna have to spend an extra half hour in the gym tomorrow to train this off, but it's worth it to see Cameron this happy.

He finishes off his food to the very last fry. "Man, is that amazing or what?"

I'm not big on lying, but I can't spoil this for him. "Best burger I've had in months," I say, which is technically true.

Just before we get into the car, he reaches for my hand. "Jackson, are we good?"

There's so much insecurity in his look that it hits me deep. Ethan was right. He is confused, and it's gotta be messing with his head. I can't push him and make it worse. And so I grab his hand and squeeze it.

"We're good, Cam. Better than ever. Let's go home."

23

CAMPY

"Hey, Campy, you want to go out and grab a drink?" Pixie asks as I'm pulling my pants on after a shoot with one of the not-so-regular guys, Otter.

"Oh, hey, I didn't even know you were around today," I say as I fasten the button on my jeans. "Are you scheduled to film this afternoon?"

"No, I had to swing by and talk to Bear. But he's in a meeting with some dude, who is hot as fuck by the way."

"Some dude?" I ask, cocking my head before pulling my shirt on. "A new hire, you think? I know Bear and Rebel have been interviewing."

"I don't think so. He's older and I overheard them talking business. It sounded like he might be starting his own studio or something? I don't know. All I know is he's a silver fox, and he apparently goes by the name Daddy, which *so* fits him." Pixie's eyes glaze over a little and I'd bet money he's enjoying a little fantasy about whoever this *Daddy* man is.

"Do you need a minute alone?" I tease, snapping him out of his thoughts.

"No," he replies, rolling his eyes at me. "So, drink?"

I bite my lip, trying to decide how to answer. It's rare for me to hang out one-on-one with any of the guys but any time I do, I seem to have trouble keeping myself from spilling my secrets. And lately I've been so desperate for someone to talk to, I'm not sure I can trust myself if Pixie were to push like Heart did a few weeks ago.

"Come on, I don't bite," he prompts.

"I had a sore nipple last week that said otherwise."

Pixie lets out an adorable little giggle that breaks down my defenses like no one else can ever seem to.

"All right, fine," I agree reluctantly.

"Want to go to Bottoms Up or somewhere more low-key?"

"Wherever." I shrug, not much caring either way. Pixie opts for chips and margaritas at a Mexican place down the street from Ballsy Boys studios.

"So, why the sudden desire to hang out with me?" I ask with forced lightness.

"Is it a crime to want to hang out with a coworker?" he counters.

"No, I'm just not used to being the one anyone asks to hang out with."

"Only because you give off a serious *back off* vibe. None of us are ever sure if you want us to leave you alone or what."

"Oh," I say, feeling like a bit of a dick for how I've kept everyone at arm's length.

"You've seemed kinda distracted lately, maybe a little down? We've all been worried about you," he confesses.

"Great." I groan in embarrassment. "You guys have been sitting around talking about what a wounded little bird I must be?"

"Not at all," he assures me. "I just thought maybe you'd like someone to talk to. But even if you don't, at least we can both get drunk on margaritas and eat a bunch of tacos."

I chuckle. "I like the way you think."

We reach the restaurant and I hold the door open for Pixie. When we get a table, we waste no time ordering drinks, along with chips and salsa.

"So, let's start with the good stuff," Pixie suggests once the server walks away. "You were totally lying about Jackson being straight, right? How's your cowboy in bed?"

I choke on a sip of water I just took and have to cough into a napkin to clear it from my lungs.

"Excuse me?"

"Oh please." Pixie rolls his eyes again. "You two were throwing serious vibes at each other. And we both know he damn well flirted with me, and that he's not straight. Are you really telling me you haven't fucked? Ooo, is this one of those really steamy slow-burn-type things?" he asks excitedly.

"My life is not a romance novel, Pix." I laugh and shake my head. "Jackson's a good guy, but I'm not—" I bite my tongue to cut myself off and Pixie eyes me curiously.

"You're not what? Not into him? Not looking for a boyfriend? Not sure he'd be okay dating someone in porn?" he lists off a number of possible concerns, and it would be easy to pick any one and let the conversation end with that. But for some reason, I really want to tell him the truth.

"I'm not gay," I blurt out.

It's clear by the way Pixie's eyes get huge and his mouth falls open that out of any possible excuse in the world, that was the last one he expected to hear. But after he recovers from his surprise, he starts to laugh. Not his normal little giggle, and not an awkward laugh one might expect when faced with such news. No, it's a full-on clutching-his-stomach, red-in-the-face, guffaw.

"Oh my god, that was too funny. You're not usually that funny," he says, wiping away tears and trying to catch his breath.

"I'm not joking, Pix."

"Okay, fine. So you're bi, how is that a reason not to date Jackson?"

"Listen to me. I. Don't. Like. Guys." I say each word slowly so he'll understand what I'm getting at.

"Um, yeah, you do," he responds confidently. "Sweetie, you're the best actor out of all of us, but no one is *that* good of an actor."

"The sex we have on set is a job, nothing more. I don't *feel* anything for any of you guys."

He shrugs, taking his drink when the server approaches and sets them down in front of us, not a moment too soon either. I'm going to need all the tequila this side of Mexico to get through this conversation.

"I don't feel anything for any of you guys either. But that sure as shit doesn't make me straight."

"I've never had feelings for a man though. Fine, I find some guys hot on occasion, but that's just because I'm secure enough in myself to appreciate how men look sometimes."

"That's all well and good, but you *do* have feelings for your roommate, and as far as I can tell, he's a man."

"He is," I agree. "And I like Jackson a lot. But, I'm not gay. I think if I was, I would've realized it before now. I like women."

Pixie rolls his eyes at me. "Bi erasure much?"

"What?" I scrunch my eyebrows together in confusion.

"There are options other than gay and straight," he says. "There's pansexual and bisexual too, not to mention a lot of other things that probably don't really apply here so I won't get into them."

It's my turn to roll my eyes. "I know there are pansexual and bisexual people."

"So then you know that liking women doesn't necessarily mean you're straight."

I roll the information over in my head for a few seconds. For all my condescension, it hadn't occurred to me before that maybe I'm not entirely straight, but that might not mean I'm *gay*. Sure, I've had a lot of sex with men, but that's all been professional. I don't *want* Tank, Brewer, Pixie, Rebel, or Heart. I don't mind fucking them or getting fucked by them, but at the end of the day, it's nothing more than a paycheck. Then Jackson came along and completely fucked up my head. Not that it's his fault, but damn is it inconvenient.

"I can see the wheels turning, so I'm going to leave you to sort that out," Pixie says with a cheeky smile. "If you have any questions or need someone to talk to after you think through everything, let me know."

"Thanks, Pix."

"Anytime," he assures me, giving me a kiss on the cheek before changing the subject to idle gossip and small talk.

Pixie's words sit heavy on my mind the rest of the night and follow me all the way home. *Bi erasure*. I'm not even sure I know what that is. For as much contact as I have with gay men day in and day out, I don't know much about a lot of the issues in the LGBT community.

Feeling annoyed by how much Pixie's simple sentence has fucked with my head, I grab my phone off my nightstand, rolling onto my back and holding it above my face, and type in *bi erasure*.

It turns out it's pretty much exactly what it sounds like,

the tendency in both the straight and gay communities to ignore the existence of bisexuality. I bristle at the implication. I know being bisexual is a thing. Okay, so maybe I've always sort of figured you're either *more* one way or the other, rather than being completely fifty-fifty with liking both, but that doesn't mean it isn't real.

An article titled "Myths About Bisexuality" catches my eye in the search results, so I click it.

MYTH 1: To be bisexual you must like both men and women EQUALLY

Reality: Even if you're only attracted to the same sex on occasion and otherwise see yourself as straight (or vice versa), that doesn't mean you aren't bisexual.

I GRUMBLE a little at how quickly that damn article undermined my entire view of bisexuality. I take a second to think about it. I like women, that has never been in dispute. But is it possible there's something to the fact that I was so willing to go into gay porn? How quickly I got comfortable having sex with men, and, if I'm being honest with myself, started to *enjoy* it? And then there's this whole thing with Jackson. It's obvious I have some kind of feelings for him, but does that mean I'm bi? Maybe I like Jackson as a good friend and my brain is confused because of all the men I have sex with?

I groan and toss my phone aside. I don't care if I am bi, but I hate feeling so confused. Confused about my feelings for Jackson, overwhelmed by my life, completely fucking drowning at this moment.

I sit up with a gasp, trying to catch my breath as my lungs seem to squeeze more tightly.

There's a rap at my door and I drag in a breath.

"Yeah?" I rasp. The door swings open and Jackson looks at me with concern before rushing over to kneel beside me.

"Hey, hey, are you okay?" he asks, his voice gentle. "Deep breaths, Cameron, come on now." His large hand rubs slow circles on my back and I manage to pull in a deep breath and hold it for a few seconds before slowly letting it out.

"Sorry," I mutter once I have my breathing under control.

"It's okay, I'm glad I came in here to check if you were hungry. What happened?"

"Panic attack, I think?"

"I figured that, I meant what caused it?"

I manage to lift my gaze, meeting his for the first time since he rushed to my rescue. His eyes are soft and full of concern, his normally crooked smile fixed into a frown instead. There's a worry line between his eyebrows that I reach out and smooth before I can think better of it.

"I don't think I'm straight," I confess, barely above a whisper, and just like that, the crooked grin is back.

"I kinda figured that too, Cam."

I'm not sure what possesses me to do it, but before I know it, I'm leaning forward and pressing our lips together. Jackson gasps against my mouth, tensing and then melting into the kiss, his lips molding to mine as his hand moves from my back to my neck, gently holding me in place. The stubble on his chin rubs my skin a little raw, and the spicy scent of his soap lingers on him, making my mouth water. Our lips move together, testing, exploring, answering questions I was too afraid to ask until now.

Unlike kissing Pixie, or any of the guys I work with, a fizzy, hot feeling bubbles in my stomach as Jackson's tongue sweeps over my bottom lip and I part them to let him in.

The hot, wet invasion into the depths of my mouth makes my cock hard faster than I've ever experienced in my life.

I twist my fingers around the front of Jackson's shirt, tugging him closer, needing to feel more of him. He takes the hint, getting off his knees without breaking the kiss, and pushing me backward on my bed so he can crawl on top of me. The feeling of his large, solid body covering mine sends more sparks crackling along my skin.

Our cocks line up, and even though we're fully clothed, there's something more erotic about the feeling of him hard against me than all the filthy sex I've had in my life, on set or off.

"Cameron," he gasps into my mouth.

"Is this okay?" I check, kissing down his chin and along his jaw, unable to keep my lips off of him now that I've started.

"You tell me," he chuckles, the sound making his throat vibrate against my mouth and his chest rumble against mine.

I roll my hips, pressing my erection against him.

"Feels pretty okay to me."

"You were pretty sure you were straight five minutes ago, are you sure you don't need a few minutes to think about this?"

I let my teeth graze against his pounding pulse point and he groans.

"I don't want to think about anything right now. You know very well I'm not a blushing virgin, and right now I just want to do the easy thing, instead of overthinking it to death." I reach for the button on Jackson's jeans and feel him tense, pushing away from me.

"Well, I need a minute to cool off and think anyway."

"Oh, right, of course." I sit up too, leaning forward to

hide the way my pants are tented and doing my best not to look down at his erection either.

"Is this just a hookup or is it more than that?" he asks after a few seconds.

"I...don't know." I put my hands over my face, dragging them up and through my hair before hanging my head.

Jackson deserves a better answer than that and there's part of me that wants to promise him things I've never promised anyone. But I'm not sure I can. It's not only that I'm not sure what it would be like to have a relationship with a man, or if it's even what I want. It's that I'm not sure a relationship with *anyone* would work given the way things are in my life right now. I have my mom to think about and two jobs, so I don't exactly have time to woo someone. And would he expect me to quit porn? Not that I want to do porn the rest of my life, but right now it's my only option to make the money I need for my mom.

"Let's do this."

24

JACKSON

It's crazy, of course. I'm crazy. I should say no for many reasons, but none come to mind right now. All I can think of is his mouth on mine, my body covering his, naked skin on naked skin. My blood hums with want, the force of it making it hard to breathe. Why did I put the brakes on again?

Right, I needed a minute to think. Well, I'm done thinking. I wanna go back to feeling, to kissing, to exploring. When I lean in for another one of those earth-shattering kisses, he gently places a hand against my chest.

"Jackson, wait. Tell me why. I thought you wanted more."

How do I tell him that he *is* more? That he's everything I want? When I look at him, I see it all. The ranch, the dog, the white picket fence, maybe even a couple of kids. But I know that if I tell him that, I'll lose him. He's barely ready to be with me, let alone hear what basically comes down to a proposal of marriage.

No, I need to move slow here, like you would with a skittish colt. Win his confidence. Get him to trust me. Then, put a saddle on him and ride him before he realizes he's been suckered. Well, in this case maybe the riding comes first, I think, and smile at him.

"I said I wanted more than a hookup, Cam. I was looking for a connection. Wouldn't you say we have one?"

He stares at me, his lips still slightly moist and swollen from our kissing, and his jaw red from my stubble. He's never looked more beautiful to me.

"I don't want to hurt you," he says, his voice barely above a whisper.

"I'm a big boy, Cam. You're under my skin...and I think I'm under yours, so let's see where this goes."

One, two seconds, and then he closes the distance between us and his mouth is on mine again. That fire from before that had simmered down flares up again. He willingly lies back on the bed again on his back, pulling me on top of him. His hands find my shirt and pull it out of my jeans, then dance over the skin on my back.

And his tongue, oh gosh, his tongue. Our mouths move in an intricate dance to music only we can hear, pushing and pulling, giving and taking, the speed building up until we're chasing each other.

I want to see him, touch him, feel him, and with regret, I let go of his mouth. I see my desire reflected in his eyes, almost black with want.

"We good?" he asks, his voice hoarse, and I realize he's asking for my consent to go further.

"We're very good," I assure him before I push myself up and whip my shirt over my head. "And now we're even better."

He grins at me, that blinding grin that does all kinds of funny things to my stomach. "I like that," he says. "I like that very much."

He reaches for his shirt and I have to move off him a bit,

then help him drag it over his head. "I can't get over how smooth you feel," I say, reveling in the sensation of his bare skin under my hand.

I run my palm over his chest, smiling when he arches his back to reach into my touch. "Needless to say, you're way ahead of me when it comes to sex, so tell me when I'm doing something wrong, okay?" I ask him.

Cam frowns. "You *have* had sex before, right?"

"Yes, Master Yoda, but your sexy ways teach me you must."

His grin is back after that or maybe it's because my hand hasn't stopped exploring his chest. His nipples are little pebbles now, and when I flick them, they get even harder. He watches me intently, a look on his face I've never seen before.

"I don't think I need to teach you a damn thing," he says. "Your instincts seem to be working fine."

I lower my mouth to his neck and lick a trail from his Adam's apple downward. Just above his collarbone, I find a spot that makes him squirm a little, so I suck it until there's distinct redness visible.

"I gave you a hickey," I say with a strange pride.

Cam laughs. "Marking your territory, are you?"

I touch the spot with my index finger, a rush thundering through me. "Just getting started."

His eyes darken even more. "You're so fucking sexy."

I'm a patient man by nature and I want to take my time with him, I really do, but there's a sense of urgency boiling inside me to hurry up. The need to be with him, to be one with him is stronger than anything I've ever felt before. And it's not just my dick talking though I can't deny it's ready and rarin' to go. No, it's something much deeper, something inside me that longs to connect with Cam on the most intimate level.

Leave it to me to make what's supposed to be simple sex into a romantic tale. I swear, there are days when I wear myself out with all the thinking I'm doing. Lucky for me, Cam doesn't share my patience, so when I'm stuck staring at him, trying to take it all in, he takes over.

With one gentle shove, he switches positions, and now it's me on my back with him leaning over me. "Your body," he says, licking his lips in a way that makes my heart swell, "it's so fucking perfect."

Then his mouth descends on mine again, and I can barely think as his tongue invades my mouth, claiming everything I can offer him and then some. His right hand deftly unbuckles my belt and his nimble fingers pop open the buttons on my jeans until he can reach inside. The moment his hand is on my cock, I let out an embarrassing moan. He smiles against my mouth, but never stops kissing me.

Cam's an expert at multitasking, I discover. His mouth is still kissing me in a way that makes my head swirl and his hand is firmly wrapped around my cock, not so much stroking as putting perfect pressure on it. He does this thing with his thumb on my slit, which is making me leak like crazy, and I can barely think with all the sensations assaulting my body.

With his lips against mine, he whispers, "Wanna take this further?"

I swallow. "How?"

"I want you inside me," he says, shocking me.

I'd expected him to want to top, what with him claiming he wasn't gay until, like, five minutes ago. And I woulda been fine with bottoming, I swear, but I'm not gonna turn down this sweet proposal.

"Yeah," I say, proving once again how eloquent I am when my brain is being fried by what he's doing to me.

He rolls off me and shows he's far more practiced at taking off his clothes in bed than I am, because he's naked within seconds, whereas I almost fall off the bed trying to take off my jeans. He shoots me an amused smile and pitches in, dragging them off and then my underwear as well.

And then he's on top of me again, but now we're both naked, and I can barely take it. He feels so good, and my hands have a will of their own as they find their way to his ass, caressing his soft skin there. He spreads his legs a little, and it brings our dicks together in a way that almost makes me swallow my tongue. Good thing he's got his wrapped around it, claiming my mouth all over again.

"If you don't stop rutting against me, this will be over in a most embarrassing way," I warn him.

"I haven't even tasted you," he teases.

"Cam, you can take your own sweet time next time, but please, if you so much as breathe on my dick now, I'll come."

My goodness, there's that smile again, the one that sends my heart all a-flutter. "We can't have that, now can we?"

He reaches over me into a drawer and pulls out a condom and lube. We're really doing this, and I'm so excited I can't hardly breathe. He rolls it on me with quick moves and slicks me up. I watch as he preps himself with fast strokes. "This one's on me," he says with a wink. "Next time, you get to do it."

He rolls on his back, pulls up his legs, and invites me by holding his arms wide. I feel clumsy when I climb on top of him, fumbling with where to position my knees and hands and how to get everything lined up. Then Cameron cups my cheeks and gives me a slow, soft kiss. "Relax," he says. "There's no rush."

The nerves flutter less now, and I manage to find a comfortable position—more or less. "Are you good?" I check with him and he nods, still with that adorable, encouraging smile.

I press against his hole and slide in with ease, nothing like the clumsy experiences with my ex—though I hate to even call him that, the two-timing, lying... Nope, not wasting any more time on him. I'd much rather think of Cameron, and how insanely good it feels to fill him.

I carefully push in deeper and he lets out a little sigh, his eyes drifting shut. "Mmm," he sighs.

He's so warm, so tight, but that's not what makes my spine tingle. It's knowing that it's him, my Cam, that I'm closer to than ever before. It's knowing that we get to share this intimate experience that will change me forever.

It's a strange realization, knowing that he's done this so many times, and yet I'm not threatened by that or jealous or insecure. Yeah, I'm a little concerned I won't be as smooth as I'd like to be, but that's got nothing to do with his job. That's because I wanna make this good for us.

I start thrusting carefully, repositioning myself until I've found the perfect angle that makes Cameron breathe out on little puffs and sighs, moans so soft I can barely hear them over the slick sounds our bodies make.

"Cam," I say, feeling my body lose the battle with my impending orgasm. I've become good at edging, I thought, but that was before I was inside the man I love. "I can't hold out much longer."

His eyes blink open and he smiles. "Feeling good?"

"Better than ever before. But I want you with me, Cam. Please."

He takes my right hand and wraps it around his cock, just the top. "Put your thumb on my slit," he tells me, and I follow his instructions. He's dripping with precum, which releases a flood of satisfaction inside me.

"Now squeeze, like you're massaging, while fucking me."

I'm not as good at multitasking as he is, and it takes me a few tries to get it right, which actually helps me stave off my orgasm. But when I do find a good rhythm, Cam starts thrusting into my hand, which is the hottest thing ever, also because every time he snaps his hips up, I can slam even deeper inside him. My balls make this little whack against him and the sound alone is enough to nearly send me over the edge.

I hang on with whatever willpower I have left, but then I lose the battle. My balls pull up tight, and I close my eyes as I jerk into him a few times, not even able to keep it coordinated. I let out a long moan as I unload, and seconds later, I feel Cam's dick tremble in my hands and he spills his cum all over my hand and his own chest.

I'm barely coherent enough to get rid of the condom and chuck it onto the floor with a reminder to myself to clean that up later, and then all I want to do is hold Cam and cuddle. The sex was everything I thought it would be, but the feelings? They're stronger and deeper than I had ever thought possible. Sweet mercy, I'm so in love with this man.

25

CAMPY

I wake up with Jackson's large body half on top of me, both of us a little sweaty under the blankets, his cock half-hard in his sleep as he snores near my ear. Well, at least I know last night wasn't a dream. Although, the ache in my ass may have been a clue too.

My ass isn't the only thing feeling it this morning either—my lips feel a little sore and swollen from our kisses, which lasted long after the sex was over, and I can feel everywhere Jackson's stubble rubbed my skin raw.

It's possible I should be freaking out right now, but when I close my eyes and try to find any sense of regret or fear, all I come across is a new lightness in my soul. How the hell it took me this long to figure this out, I'll never know. But maybe it's not so bad that I didn't figure it out until Jackson came along. I'm reluctant to slap a label on myself and I don't think it's necessary at this point. What matters is that we agreed to see where this might go.

My stomach churns a little at that in a way it didn't from the sex. I don't know what exactly that means, to *see where things go*. And I'm completely certain all my lies and bullshit are just *waiting* to bite me in the ass and send this whole house of cards tumbling before long. But that doesn't mean I can't enjoy it while it lasts, right?

"Ya freakin' out?" Jackson mumbles, his accent extra thick with sleep.

"Not like you think."

He yawns and stretches, then pulls me closer to him, running his nose along my throat. "Not regrettin' last night then?"

"Not at all," I assure him. "What time do you need to be on set?"

"Soon. What time is it?"

I sit up and lean over him to grab my phone off the nightstand. "Six-thirty."

"Shoot, yeah, I gotta get movin'." He throws the covers back and slips out of bed, gathering his clothes in his arms and then turning to give me a shy smile. "We're good?"

"We're good," I assure him, puckering my lips in invitation. Jackson leans down to give me a kiss that straddles the line between quick and lingering, clearly wanting to turn it into more if he had time.

"In that case, I'm takin' you on a date this weekend once we both have a day off work together."

My stomach flutters at the declaration and I nod happily.

"I'll be at the rehab center today, so I'll be home at my usual time."

After that, Jackson disappears into the shower while I make coffee and linger in the kitchen until he leaves.

I'm too restless to sit around the apartment all morning, so I decide to get dressed and go down to Ballsy to see if anyone is around.

When I get there, it sounds like Brewer and Tank are

filming a scene together, so I linger out of sight for a little while.

When the scene wraps, they walk off set with their arms around each other, bickering and teasing in a way that seems to have become pretty standard for them recently.

"Campy, hey," Brewer greets when he spots me. His gaze zeros in on my throat and he smirks. "Nice hickey."

"Shit," I mutter, putting my hand over the spot.

"I hope that's from your cowboy."

"Um...yeah," I admit. "We sort of hooked up last night."

"Sort of?" Tank asks, quirking an eyebrow at me.

"We fucked, okay?" I clarify with a hint of irritation.

"You're freaking out," Brewer observes. "Why are you freaking out?"

"I'm not," I argue. "It was great, he's great, everything is fine. Well, everything except for the fact that *I'm* a fucking mess and Jackson could do about a million times better than me."

"That's bullshit," Brewer says. "You're a catch, so don't ruin a good thing by letting self-doubt get in your way."

"Easier said than done," I mumble.

"Sure it is," he agrees. "But you have to make a conscious effort if you want it to work."

"Since when are you full of so much wisdom?" I joke.

"Must be from spending time with me," Tank teases.

"No, I spoke in full sentences without any grunting or growling, so that theory is out," Brewer deadpans.

"Well, thanks. I didn't mean to sidetrack you, I'm sure you want to get showered and everything. I appreciate the advice though."

"Anytime."

As I watch Brewer and Tank walk away, guilt churns in my stomach again. Sure, Pixie was cool when I told him about the whole *not gay* thing, but there's no guarantee the other guys would be. And what about Bear? How pissed will he be if he ever finds out I lied about doing straight porn before coming to work for Ballsy Boys? There's so much on the line and no matter how much I want to throw all the lies off and show them all the truth, I'm afraid of what will happen.

Jackson

FIGURING out what to do on my first official date with Cameron was easy. We were watching a documentary a few days ago, and they showed some park rangers on horseback. Cameron casually mentioned that he would love to learn how to ride. That, I can arrange, and even better, I can combine it with another invitation that was still outstanding.

"So where are we going today?" Cameron asks as we're in his old, beat-up car.

It's freaking miracle this thing still runs. I guess I could splurge some of my first paychecks on a car of my own, but so far, I've been doing just fine taking Ubers. It's not like driving is a lot of fun in this city. Cameron is following the instructions I give him, based on the navigation app on my phone. I don't want him to see our final destination just yet.

"You'll see when we get there," I tease him.

He shoots me a look sideways, then focuses back on the road. "Your outfit doesn't tell me anything either. You're dressed in the same jeans and boots you always wear. Hell, you even have your hat on."

"You have a problem with the way I dress?" I feign insult.

He grins. "Oh, I have no problem at all with the way those jeans hug your ass," he assures me. "I like those jeans just fine. And the boots kinda go with the whole cowboy thing you've got going."

"I've been debating whether I should stop wearing them," I say, sobering after chuckling over his remarks. "I got recognized a few times already, and it's making me stand out."

Cameron sighs. "I get it, but I would hate for you to have to change something that is such a part of who you are."

"Yeah. I guess dreams come true at a price, you know?"

We chat during the hour drive until my app tells me we've reached our destination, and I tell Cameron to take a right turn into the driveway.

"Where are we?" he asks, frowning.

There's a gated entrance, and Cameron stops the car. "There's a keypad," I tell him, repeating the instructions Ethan gave me. "The code is 65908."

With an adorable frown of concentration, Cameron punches in the numbers and the gate slides open. I've never been here before either, and I can't hold back a gasp as the driveway bends around the corner, opening up the view to a fantastic ranch. It sprawls amid a gentle rolling landscape, a pool and a tennis court already visible. I can see the horses Ethan gushed about as well, lazily grazing in a field surrounded by a white fence.

Ethan told me to park right next to the house, and by the time Cameron has switched off the engine, Ethan's already waiting for us, Rick by his side. Cameron spots them, then smiles at me.

"You could've just told me we're hanging out with some Hollywood superstar," he says, but I can tell he's excited. And he doesn't even know what else I have planned for him.

"We're so excited to have you guys over," Ethan says, and it hits me again how genuinely nice this man is. He's a star, but you would never guess from the way he treats us.

"Well, if I had known we were coming here, I could've maybe brought a present or something," Cameron says, and I realize he's a little nervous.

Rick elbows me. "He still has no idea?"

I shake my head, smiling.

"No idea about what?" Cameron asks.

I put my arm around his shoulder and pulled him close. "Rick is gonna throw us a Texan barbecue, which is the best thing you'll ever eat, but before we eat, you and I are going to do something else. Ethan and Rick have a number of horses, and they've given me permission to teach you how to ride on one of them."

His mouth drops open a little before he recovers himself. "Are you serious?" he asks, excitement bubbling over in his voice.

"Yes, sir," I say, and I've barely finished speaking when his arms wrap around me and he pulls me in a tight hug.

"Thank you," he whispers into my ear. "Best date ever and it hasn't even started yet."

My heart is singing with joy that I got this right, and with reluctance, I let go of him.

"One of their horses is a very meek one, perfect for beginners," I tell Cameron. "So all you have to do is decide whether you want to learn how to ride English or Western style."

He takes a look at me and does a slow perusal of my body, stopping at my boots. "Like you even have to ask."

Rick and Ethan take us to their barn, where they have stables for their five horses. Four are outside in the meadow, but one is inside, a gentle mare called Sunshine,

Rick explains. He thinks she would be a perfect fit for Cameron.

Cameron walks up to her without any hesitation, allowing her to sniff his hand, then nuzzle him. She lets out a little whinny, and it shouldn't surprise me how easily she accepts him. This man loves animals, so it makes sense that animals will love him as well.

Rick hands him some snacks he can feed her so they can get acquainted a little better, and then he leads her out of her stable by her halter. She's a beautiful, rich chestnut color, with gorgeous white markings on her nose.

I show Cameron how to put her bit in, and she takes it with ease, clearly used to this routine. Saddling her is a walk in the park as well. She doesn't even try to blow up her belly to avoid the saddle from getting too tight, like my horse Star would always do.

Together, we lead Sunshine outside where Rick and Ethan have a small paddock I can use with Cameron. Sunshine waits patiently as I show Cameron how to get on her back. It's takes him a few tries to get it right, but he's patient with himself as well, checking with me on what he does wrong.

And then he's on her, sitting high on her back with an intoxicating smile. "How do you feel?" I check in with him.

He beams at me, his whole face radiating joy. "This is so cool. I can't believe you arranged this."

I smile right back at him, my heart dancing with joy at his pleasure. "I'm glad you're enjoying it. Want me to show you how to use the reins?"

Sunshine really is perfect for him, as she shows no impatience while I teach Cameron the absolute basics of horseback riding. He's a fast learner, I have to give him that. After fifteen minutes or so, he's comfortable enough on

Sunshine's back for me to let him go, and the look on his face as he rides around the paddock by himself is priceless. He's gentle with Sunshine, not pulling the reins too hard, and she responds with eagerness.

"Want to try to go a little faster?" I ask him, and he nods. "Okay. Let go of the reins a little. I'll take them so you can focus on having a good posture. Try to sit as deep and low in the saddle as you can. The most important part is that you don't pull on the reins, because that will confuse Sunshine."

Two clicks of my tongue and Sunshine obediently speeds up into a little trot, and I run right alongside her. I keep a close eye on Cameron to see how he's faring. It takes him a little while to get the hang of what to do with his body, and the concentration on his face is super adorable. After a few minutes, I'm panting, because I have to keep up with Sunshine, and I let her slow down.

"That was awesome," Cameron says. Then he chuckles. "How much am I gonna feel this in my ass tomorrow?"

I laugh in between sucking in deep pulls of air. "Let's just say you won't be bottoming tomorrow. Or the day after."

He laughs. "Thank fuck you're vers, then."

After another fifteen minutes or so, I can tell Cameron is getting tired. No wonder, you use muscles with horseback riding that you don't use otherwise. With a little grunt, he climbs off Sunshine's back. "Holy fuck, I'm going to feel this tomorrow," he says, rubbing his ass. "But it was totally worth it."

"Yeah?" I ask as I affectionately rub Sunshine to thank her for being such a perfect learning partner for Cam.

"Totally." Then he cocks his head and looks at me. "Show me how you ride."

"This wasn't about me," I say, shaking my head.

He steps closer, then reaches up for a kiss, and of course

I oblige. "Indulge me," he says. "I want to see my cowboy ride an actual horse."

"You should ride Rocket," Rick says, who's been watching the whole time. "He's my horse, and if you're as good a rider as I think you are, the two of you will be amazing together."

With the two of them ganging up on me, there's no use in saying no, so fifteen minutes later, I find myself on horseback for the first time in months. It feels so familiar, as if I'd never been gone from home.

Rocket is perfect for me, indeed, the classic Texas quarter horse. He's well-trained, Rick assured me, but I guess I'll test that for myself soon enough. I take him out of the paddock and into an empty field where we have a little more space. All I do is click my tongue and off he goes, eager to please me by stretching his legs into a beautiful, steady gallop.

Within a minute, I've forgotten Rick and Cameron are even there. Rocket responds to my every signal. I don't even have to use the reins, a simple change in pressure from my calves makes him change the direction, just like that. He's fast, maneuvers like a quarter horse should, trained to herd cattle.

And as I ride him, lifting my face up to the sun, my hat tightened on my head so it doesn't get knocked off by the wind, I realize how much I've missed this. As much as I appreciate LA and the chances it's brought me, I'm not a city boy. I belong out here, in the fields, with the sun on my face. It feels like home.

26

CAMPY

The pure joy on Jackson's face as he rides makes my heart swell. It's been a week since the night of my panic attack and the sex that followed. Also known as *The Best Sex of My Life*. Intellectually, I've always known filming with the guys wasn't the same as *sex*, but to actually *feel* it was a world of difference. The way Jackson touched me with so much awe and passion set my skin on fire. And the way it felt to have him inside me was in a completely different category than what happens on set.

He may not have much experience, but he certainly doesn't lack skill. In the week since, we haven't had much time together between both our schedules, but every spare minute has found us with our hands and mouths all over each other.

Pixie had a field day when he saw the fading hickey on my neck yesterday and I'd been forced to admit that he was right. When he demanded details about Jackson in bed, I sidestepped the question, not wanting to make that night less special by turning it into tawdry gossip.

"You're crazy about him, aren't you?" Ethan says, startling me out of my thoughts.

"Probably too crazy about him, honestly," I admit.

"Is there such a thing?" he laughs.

"He can do better than me. I'm sure he'll figure that out all on his own, though." The words make me feel ill as soon as I say them. Jackson deserves better than a porn star living a double life who has to spend all his income taking care of his mother. And, there's still the issue of what associating with me could do to his career, which neither of us have brought up again since the pilot party. I know Jackson doesn't think it matters, but it does. He's a good man, if a little too starry-eyed about the world.

"He's a good man," Ethan says, echoing my thoughts. "Don't hurt him, okay?"

"I'll do my best."

Jackson trots the horse back toward us, skillfully dismounting with a huge smile on his face.

"I forgot how much I love this."

"Not going to leave us and head back to Texas, are you?" Ethan jokes.

"Not on your life. If the show renews, I may have to get me a nice little ranch like this, though, and a couple of horses of my own." Jackson casts a quick glance in my direction, as if he's checking my reaction to this idea. It sounds like heaven to me. Too bad I'll never be able to afford anything similar.

"You guys ready to eat?" Rick checks.

"I'm starving," I volunteer.

"Me too," Jackson agrees.

"Great, I'll fire up the grill."

Jackson leads Rocket back to the barn to take his tack off and I follow.

"This really was a great idea for a first date, thank you," I tell him as I help by removing the bit while he takes off the saddle.

"I thought you'd like it." He gives me that sweet, crooked smile I can't get enough of, and just because I can now, I grab the front of his shirt and pull him into a kiss.

Jackson sighs into my mouth, wrapping his arms around me and pulling me close as our lips move in tandem. The taste of sweat and dirt on his mouth makes me even hotter for him, imagining what it would be like to spend the day together sweating in the sun, taking care of a whole ranch full of animals, and then fucking in the barn. I know, I know, I'm sounding like I'm in a regency romance with fantasies of getting it on with the stable boy, but damn if it doesn't sound good.

Rocket paws at the ground and snorts impatiently, forcing us to part with a laugh.

"I think we'll have to hold that thought for later."

"Trust me, I won't forget," I promise with a wink.

Dinner with Rick and Ethan is wonderful and the food is even better than billed. Rick and I talk about animals while Ethan and Jackson talk about the show. It's comfortable and nice. I can almost imagine doing this for years to come, the two of us making time to spend with *couple* friends like Rick and Ethan. The two of us making a life together.

That thought makes my heart pound and my throat dry. Since my mom's diagnosis, I haven't dared to wish for something like that, but Jackson makes it all too easy. I meant what I said to Ethan though. Jackson can do so much better than me.

After dinner and another hour of conversation, we decide we'd better call it a night. But as soon as we get in my car, the last thing I want to do is head right back to the city.

"Mind if we take a detour?" I ask.

"Sure, where to?"

"Somewhere we can look at the stars?" I suggest, a wistful feeling in my chest.

Jackson types out something on his phone and then smiles at me. "We're not far from a state park. It's closed so we should be the only ones in the parking lot. We can sit and look at the stars as long as you want."

"Perfect, lead the way."

I start the car and let Jackson direct me until we reach our destination. We both climb out and get up on the hood of the car, scooting close and linking our hands together as we lean back to look up at the vast night sky.

"It takes your breath away, doesn't it?"

"Yeah," Jackson agrees. "It reminds me of home."

"Do you miss it?"

"Some things," he concedes, squeezing my hand and turning his head to look at me. Our eyes meet and my heart stutters. "I'm glad I came to LA though. I think I just need to find the right balance to keep my head on straight."

The thoughtful look on his face does something funny to my insides. Maybe that's what I like so much about Jackson: he's the opposite of me, he's what I *wish* I could be—honest and *real*.

I lean over and steal a kiss, only meaning for it to be a quick peck, but as soon as our lips touch it's like adding gasoline to a flame.

Jackson tangles his fingers in my hair, his tongue thrusting between my lips as he drags me onto his lap. I can feel him already getting hard, and I'm not far behind. It strikes me again just how different this is from filming. I don't have to *try* to get excited, I couldn't stop myself from getting hard right now if my life depended on it. Our hands wander and grope, tugging at each other's clothes and hair, sneaking over each other's skin as our tongues tease.

"Will you top me, Cameron?" Jackson pants into my mouth.

I pull back and look at him to gauge how serious he is. "Now? Out in the open?"

It's hard to tell if the blush on his cheeks is from embarrassment or arousal but either way he nods enthusiastically.

"We're all alone out here," he points out.

"Okay, but do you have condoms or lube?"

"Of course, I was a Boy Scout in my day," he smirks, shifting so he can reach into his back pocket to pull out a little lube packet and a condom to hand to me.

I slide off his lap and grab his hand to bring him with me.

"Drop your pants and lean over the hood."

Jackson unbuttons his pants slowly, holding my gaze with a little smirk, and then wiggles them down to his ankles, along with his boxers, and turns around to bend over the hood.

His gorgeous, round ass on display just for me makes my cock throb and my brain short-circuit.

"How do you feel about rimming?" I ask, stepping behind him and taking his ass cheeks in my hands, parting them so I can see his tight pucker. Sure, it's not all waxed and tidy like the guys on set, but somehow that makes it even hotter.

"No one has before."

"Can I?" I check, squeezing his globes in my hands, my mouth watering to taste him, to make him moan.

"Yeah," he agrees breathlessly.

Dropping to my knees behind him, I drag my tongue from his taint, all the way up his crack, over his entrance, eliciting a surprised gasp from him.

I do it again and he moans deep in his chest, pushing his ass back toward me. I flick my tongue over his hole, licking in long, slow strokes that have Jackson's legs quaking and his hips twitching as I work him over with my tongue until my spit is dripping down to his balls.

With my hands still on his ass cheeks, I brush my thumbs over his pucker, working them in tandem with my tongue and drawing more frantic moans from him. I slip one inside and feel the heat of his channel and the tight grip of his inner muscles wrap around it.

"Oh, Cameron, *fuck*," he gasps. I smile to myself. Apparently the key to unlocking Jackson's potty mouth is to get him so worked up he can barely think straight. "Please, ungh."

I work my second thumb inside, still licking around his rim and taint as I use my thumbs to stretch and relax his hole. When he softens again, I pull my thumbs apart and shove my tongue between them, licking inside him until he's all but riding my face, begging for more.

Jackson makes a strangled noise when I pull my thumbs out and reach for the condom and lube I set on the ground. It only takes me a second to get my pants open and ready to go before I get to my feet behind him.

"Ready, Cowboy?" I check as I notch the head of my cock against his hole.

"Yes," he groans, pushing back impatiently.

I thrust forward an inch, breaching his pucker and feeling it tighten around me as he adjusts to the feeling. I lean over him, resting my forehead against the middle of his back as I hold still and wait for Jackson to be ready for more.

My heart is beating hard, my pulse echoing in my ears in time with our ragged breaths. I feel him relax around me, so I give him another inch, testing his reaction. When he doesn't wince or tighten up again, I press forward until my hips are flush against his ass and my cock is buried deep inside him.

The tight heat of his channel surrounding me manages to feel different than I've ever felt before. Maybe it's the desperate little noises he's making, or the way he's trying to hold still beneath me and failing. No part of this is a performance for anyone else, not even me. This is Jackson, completely undone by my fingers and tongue, taken apart by my cock.

And as I pull out, thrusting back in with a snap of my hips that makes Jackson gasp, I feel the freedom of not having to perform either. This is nothing but raw, unadulterated lust. This is nothing but Jackson and me.

I fuck him slowly, deliberately, in no hurry for this to end. Now that I'm actually fucking him, Jackson settles, seeming content to go along at any pace I set as long as I don't stop fucking him.

I push his shirt up and trail kisses up and down his spine as I rock in and out of him, loving the way his ass squeezes around my cock. His skin is salty from sweat, his larger body feeling incredible under mine. I could get used to this, and that thought scares the hell out of me.

Eventually my slow pace isn't enough for either of us and I start to thrust faster, harder, and Jackson meets every one. The quiet night fills with sounds of slapping flesh and desperate grunts and moans. Reaching around him, I wrap my hand around his cock and milk the tip just like I showed him when our positions were reversed earlier in the week, feeling his pulse in the thick veins as he swells in my hand, the sticky stream of precum coating my fingers turning thicker until his inner muscles begin to flutter and then spasm around me, dragging my own orgasm from me.

I dig the fingers on my free hand into his hips and throw my head back, crying out to the blanket of stars overhead as I pump my release into the condom deep inside him, feeling it all the more intensely with his ass pulsing around me.

Aftershocks rock us both long after our orgasms fade and we stay bent over the hood of the car for a long time, until I have no choice but to pull out and get rid of the used condom.

Jackson pulls his pants up and I do the same, and then he pulls me into a tender kiss that settles in my chest.

"I suppose we should get home," I sigh.

"Do you want to stay out here a little longer?"

"Do you mind?" I check.

"Not at all." He climbs back onto the hood of the car and pats the spot beside him.

27

CAMPY

I'm in the middle of pouring a cup of coffee when a pair of large arms wrap around me from behind. I melt against Jackson's bigger frame as he presses his nose to the back of my neck, followed by his lips, before releasing me.

"Morning, darlin'."

"Morning," I reply. "What's your day look like?"

"I have to go on some talk show in a few hours to promote the show, and then I've got filmin' in the afternoon. What about you?" Jackson wrinkles his nose a little when he mentions the talk show. I know he's thrilled by the response viewers have had, the producers are even optimistic about getting renewed for a second season, but he's still adjusting to the limelight.

"Filming and then I was going to swing by my mom's tonight. Are you up for it or are you going to be on set late?"

"I think we're supposed to wrap around seven if you can wait that long?"

"I can," I agree. "I was thinking of telling my mom tonight actually."

"Tellin' her what? About doing porn?" his eyes go wide and I laugh.

"Oh my god, no," I laugh. "About me and you. If that's okay? Or is that too serious for what we're doing? Am I moving too fast?" I ramble, second guessing my decision until Jackson cuts me off with his lips on mine.

"You should know by now, I'm not afraid of serious. If you're ready to tell her, I'm happy to be there to support you," he assures me. "Do you think she'll be upset?"

"No. She might be surprised but she won't be an asshole about it. Strangely enough, when I was thirteen she sat me down and told me she would love me no matter my sexuality. Maybe she saw it even then. Everyone else seemed to realize it before I did, so it would make sense."

"It's possible," he agrees. "Either way, I'm more than happy to go with you. You know I love seein' your mama anyway."

"She likes you too. If anything, she might be upset that I got you before she could," I tease.

Jackson smiles and shakes his head at me before giving me one final kiss and releasing me.

"I should be home around seven-thirty and then we can go see your mama. Have a good day, darlin'."

"You too."

I practically float through my day with thoughts of Jackson on my mind. Being able to freely think about Jackson while I'm filming without guilt or confusion makes it a hell of a lot easier to keep an erection and show the necessary enthusiasm. And I'm not the only one who notices the difference.

"I take it whatever's been bothering you is resolved? My ass certainly felt the difference today," Heart jokes after we finish up.

"Yeah," I confirm, and then, just because I'm feeling bold and giddy, I tell him. "Jackson and I are seeing each other."

Heart chuckles at me, clapping me on the shoulder. "That's great, man."

I make my way to the showers with a pep in my step and a smile on my face. Telling Heart about Jackson felt *good*. It makes me want to tell everyone I see that Jackson and I are together.

While I wait for Jackson to get home, I do some cleaning around the apartment and then, on a whim, grab my laptop to log onto the UC-Davis website to look at the vet school information. I know it's a ways off, but I love looking at the class catalog and imagining what it would be like to register for classes, to excitedly page through text books in preparation. A longing ache starts in my chest and stays there while I look at all the pictures of the campus, and the clinic, and smiling students.

By the time Jackson gets home, my good mood from the day is waning thanks to my stupid idea to browse the vet school website, but as soon as I see his crooked smile, it perks me back up a little.

"What's wrong?" he asks as soon as he notices my face.

"Nothing, just bumming myself out," I wave him off. His gaze doesn't leave mine as he waits for further explanation. "I was looking at vet school stuff and just feeling pretty down that it's so far off."

Jackson's eyes soften with sympathy and he crosses the room to sit down beside me on the couch.

"I know it doesn't feel like it now, but you *will* get there. You have too much passion not to."

"I know," I agree, giving him a weak smile. "Thank you."

"Anytime. Now, let me get changed quick and we can go."

"Sounds good."

We spend the drive to my mom's singing along to the radio and talking about nothing. When Jackson is singing his heart out to *Bohemian Rhapsody*, terribly off-key I might add, I look over at him and my heart gives a violent flutter. Is this what falling in love feels like?

"What?" he asks, no doubt noticing the strange way I'm looking at him.

"Nothing, just don't audition for any musicals," I advise and he gives me the finger.

"Don't go flashing fingers around unless you plan on using them," I warn, my voice dripping with suggestion that makes Jackson blush like crazy. *God I like his easy blush.*

"Do you think of anything but sex?" he teases back.

"Hello, porn star," I point at myself and his smile falls a little. "Does it bother you?" I ask, my nerves ramping up as I wait for the answer. If he says *yes,* what would I do? I can't afford to quit. It's a can of worms I probably shouldn't have opened.

"Not the sex part, I get it's only a job and you don't make it sound particularly *sexy*. But it bothers me you aren't happy."

"Yeah," I sigh. "Me too."

Before we can dig into this discussion any further, we reach my mom's house. Pulling into the driveway, the anxiety that was absent this morning rears its head.

"Are you nervous?" Jackson asks.

"A little," I confess.

"It's going to be fine."

"It is," I agree. "Let's do this."

My mom is lying on the couch when we step inside, and she gives us a pained smile. I look around and I'm pleased to see the new health aide is keeping things clean.

"Hey, Mom, how are you doing?"

She grimaces, trying to sit up, and I rush over to help her.

"Fine. A little dizzy and weak today, but otherwise good."

"How's your new nurse working out?"

"She's helping a lot. I hate to admit it, but she's really making my life easier."

A knot of worry loosens in my chest. No matter what it's costing me, financially or otherwise, if it's making her life easier, it's worth it.

"Good, I'm glad to hear that."

"Jackson, I'm so glad you came," she says, noticing him and waving him over. "I've been watching your show. You are amazingly talented, and you look so handsome as a cowboy."

"Thank you, ma'am," Jackson says politely, bending down to give her a hug.

"I bet you have girls following you everywhere now, don't you?"

He laughs and glances over at me.

"I have an admirer or two," he admits. "But girls ain't exactly my type."

"Well, I'm sure you have plenty of men after you too."

He chuckles again but doesn't say anything. This is as good of an opening as I imagine I'll get, so I go for it.

"Mom, Jackson and I are dating."

She blinks in surprise for a few seconds before a bright smile spreads across her face.

"Oh, honey, that makes me so happy. I thought there might be something between you two, but I wasn't sure if you were still in denial."

"In denial?"

"Well, you've always been a little blind to the crushes you've had on other boys, I wasn't sure if you'd come to terms with that or not."

"What are you talking about? I'll admit, realizing I'm not exactly straight has been a newer revelation, but I haven't had feelings for any guys other than Jackson before."

"Sweetie, that isn't true at all. Your middle school best friend, Tucker? You used to absolutely moon over that boy. And the way you talked about that veterinarian at the wildlife rehab you volunteer at, I thought you two might've been dating and you were just afraid to tell me."

"Veterinarian?" Jackson asks, raising an eyebrow at me.

"I don't have a crush on him, he was just teaching me some cool things and he was interesting to work with."

"And handsome," she adds.

"What? You never even met him."

"I know, but you mentioned on more than one occasion that you thought he was handsome," she points out with a smirk.

"I did?"

"You did."

I look up at Jackson and find him watching me with lights dancing in his eyes. "I can't decide if I'm jealous or amused."

"There's nothing to be jealous of," I assure him, reaching for his hand. "Maybe I did have a crush on a couple of other guys without realizing it, but you're the only one I've liked enough to admit it to myself."

"That's so sweet," my mom coos.

With the confession out of the way, I head to the kitchen to get a late dinner together and the three of us spend a few hours playing cards and enjoying each other's company.

Maybe my mom was right, but I meant what I said to Jackson, he's the only one who's managed to get under my skin. I don't know what that means for us, but I do know he deserves dates and romance, and I'm going to make sure he gets it.

28

JACKSON

Ever since our phone call, Brax and I have resumed our usual texting, and I'm happy we've moved past it, especially since my folks are still chilly. We've spoken on the phone since, but they're struggling to understand why I would drop out of college six months before graduating. I get it, but they're not showing much understanding for my side of things.

Two weeks ago, Brax texted me he wanted to visit me during spring break. When I inquired whether he told our parents, he cheekily texted back that if I didn't need their permission to drop out of college, he sure as hell didn't need it to visit his own brother. That was followed by a snarky reminder that he was twenty, not twelve. Good point.

I said yes, of course, strangely excited to actually have a family member visiting me. Brax had planned to take the bus, poor college student that he is, but I surprised him with a plane ticket. That resulted in a few texts about me being rich, which I denied, but it was all in good humor, and he did accept my gift to him.

Since I still haven't bought a car, I asked Cameron if I

could borrow his. He was fine with it, as long as I dropped him off at the Ballsy Boys studio and promised to be there on time to pick him up again.

And that's where I find myself on a sunny afternoon, on my way to the airport to pick Brax up. Traffic to LAX is the usual nightmare, but that's all forgotten when I spot my brother on the curb, waiting for me.

His face lights up when he sees me exit the car, and people around us snicker as we hug each other. I guess it's easy to spot that we're brothers, seeing as how we're dressed almost identically, including our hats and boots.

"It's so good to see you," I say, hugging him tightly.

"Right back atcha, bro. That your car? I would've expected you to be able to afford a little more luxury."

Right, then. I had wanted to start with a little small talk before dropping this particular bomb on him, but I guess there was no time like the present. "It's my boyfriend's car."

His head whips around and he meets my eyes over the roof of the car. "Boyfriend?" he asks. "Last time we talked, you were still dating and playing the field. Any more surprises you didn't tell me about?"

I shrug. "A few, but we have a week to catch up."

"Tell me about your boyfriend," Brax says as soon as we drive off, and I'm beyond grateful he sounds genuinely interested.

"His name is Cameron, he's a few years older than me, and he wants to be a wildlife veterinarian."

"Cool. How did you guys meet?"

"He's my roommate, actually. Or I should say, I'm his roommate, since it's his apartment. We became friends, then more."

Brax makes an appreciative hum, not showing any sign of disapproval. "You're okay with all this?" I check.

"With you being gay? Hell yeah. I'm not Dad, Jax, you know that. I'm happy you're in a relationship. Is it serious?" Then he snickers. "Of course it serious. It's you, after all."

I shoot him a quick look sideways. "What's that supposed to mean?"

"No offense, but you're the most traditional guy I know when it comes to relationships, aside from the fact that you're gay. I'm pretty sure that if you'd been straight, you woulda been married already."

Isn't it funny, how Brax can see so easily what took me much longer to figure out? "As far as I'm concerned, it's serious, but I'd appreciate it if you kept that to yourself. Cameron needs a bit more time to get there."

"He's not in the closet, is he?"

It's an unexpected question from Brax, one that shows a heck of a lot more understanding for the issues gay men face than I would've expected from him. Has he read up on what it means to be gay?

"No, but he only recently came out," I say, then remember that as far as the public knows, Cameron has been gay all along.

I sigh inwardly with how complicated that makes things. It's not that I don't want Brax to know about Cameron's other job, but it's not something I want to lead with. I want to give him a chance to know Cameron first, before his opinion might be tainted by knowing he does porn. I know my brother is not the judgmental type, but it's a big step from our conservative background to being completely accepting and understanding, and I want to make sure he is before I risk telling him.

It's not because I care *that much* about what he thinks of Cameron, though I do care some because Brax's opinion matters to me, but mostly because I want to protect

Cameron. If my brother is gonna have an issue with Cam doing porn, then that's something I want to talk to Brax about first before Cam gets wind of it.

"Let's just say it's a bit messy, but he's a good guy, Brax. I promise you, you'll like him."

"Good," Brax says. "I can't wait. When am I gonna meet him?

That's when it sinks in, that I agreed to pick Cameron up from the Ballsy Boys studio... And I have Brax in my car. So much for keeping his other job a secret from him. I dictate a quick text to Cam, telling him we're on our way and that we should be there in about forty-five minutes. As I'm chatting with Brax and catching up on the local gossip in our little town, I try to find a solution for my problem in the back of my head. But I can't text while I'm driving, and I can't dictate anything either, because Brax will hear it. How can I let Cam know I want to pick him up elsewhere?

A few minutes later, a text comes in. Just to be safe, I don't let Siri read it out loud, but glance at it on the screen. Relief fills me as I read Cam's reply, telling me he'll meet me in a parking lot two blocks from the studio. It seems he was ahead of me already. Thank goodness for that.

By the time we're close to where we're picking up Cam, Brax and I have decided we're in the mood for pizza tonight. I rarely eat it anymore because of my strict diet, but I guess my brother being here is a good reason to splurge a little. Plus, Cam introduced me to this wonderful authentic Italian restaurant that makes the most amazing pizza with a super thin crust.

"There he is," I tell Brax and point at Cameron, who's standing in the parking lot of a convenience store where I can pick him up easily.

"He's cute," my brother says, and before the slight weirdness of that comment registers fully with me, he says something that makes my heart stop. "Holy crap, it's Campy."

Campy

I climb into the backseat of the car and it's immediately clear that I've missed something because Jackson is wearing a confused, stunned expression and his brother looks guilty as hell.

"Um...hey," I greet awkwardly, unsure if I should lean over the seat to give Jackson a quick kiss like I normally would or if that will freak out his brother. Maybe that's where the weirdness is coming from right now? Did his brother have a problem with meeting me?

"Hi," his brother finally breaks the silence, reaching back to offer me his hand, "I'm Brax, Jackson's brother."

"Cameron, nice to meet you."

Jackson clears his throat and forces a smile at me through the rearview mirror. "Are y'all hungry? I could eat a horse."

"Starved," I agree, settling for giving Jackson a quick peck on the cheek before sitting back in my seat. For his part, Brax doesn't look disgusted or freaked out by the mild PDA, so maybe the weirdness is related to something else entirely.

The brothers apparently already decided on a nearby Italian restaurant, and I direct Jackson on how to get there since he's still getting familiar with the city. When we get to the restaurant, Jackson opens my door for me and takes my hand when I get out of the car.

At the table, we make polite small talk about Brax's

schooling and Jackson's exciting new career, but the underlying thread of tension lingers under the surface while we wait for our pizza and sip beer.

When Brax gets up to use the bathroom, Jackson's shoulders sag and he turns to me with a somewhat panicked expression.

"What's going on? I clearly missed something."

"Don't freak out," Jackson says, a hit of pleading in his voice that makes my heart start beating harder immediately.

"Saying that has the opposite effect, just tell me what's wrong. Are your parents okay? Is your brother in trouble?"

"Nothin' like that," he assures me, reaching for my hand under the table. "Brax recognized you when he spotted you."

"He what?" I rasp, my gut twisting and my heart in my throat. "You didn't tell me he was gay."

"He's not, at least as far as I always knew."

"I can't believe this is happening." I yank my hand away from his and bring it to my face as a way to hide. "I did what I had to do because I knew I had to take care of my mom, but this is starting to feel like some sort of curse. Has every single person on the planet seen me fuck at this point? I didn't think this many people even watched porn, or at least they'd be polite enough not to talk about it in public."

I can feel a full-on panic attack coming on as it gets harder to drag in a breath.

"Cam, shh, it's okay," Jackson tries to reassure me, but I bat his hand away when he tries to touch me, making me feel like even more of an asshole than I already was.

"It's not okay. Even if I quit right now, the videos will be out there for the rest of my life. Every single person I meet on the street might have seen them. What if I can't get into vet school or can't get a job because of them? Have I completely ruined my life?"

"You need to take a deep breath, darlin'," Jackson instructs, pulling me into his arms despite my protest. "Your life isn't ruined."

"Is everything okay?" Brax asks, returning to the table looking startled.

"Fine," Jackson answers. I can't even bear to look at him. Here Jackson was so excited to introduce me to his brother, and now I'm sure I've embarrassed him. Who wants to tell their family they're dating a porn star?

"Is he having a panic attack? I have Xanax if it'll help," Brax offers.

I nod quickly, holding my hand out and swallowing the pills dry when they appear in my palm.

"Thank you," I mutter, still unable to meet his gaze.

"Is this because of me? Should I not have said anything?"

Rather than answering his question, Jackson suggests we get our pizza to go and Brax offers to track down our server and request as much.

It doesn't take long for the pills to make me feel calmer and a little sleepy. Once we have our pizza, we head back out to my car and Brax offers to drive so Jackson can sit with me in the backseat.

I close my eyes and rest my head against Jackson's shoulder during the drive, Jackson giving directions the whole way.

"I'm going to go lie down for a little while, you guys go ahead and eat," I say as soon as we're home. Jackson looks like he wants to fuss over me some more, but I wave him off and head to the bedroom.

I strip out of my jeans and crawl between the sheets of

the bed I've been sharing with Jackson for the past few weeks. The pillows and blankets all smell like him, so I burrow underneath them all, wanting to hide from the world for a little while. How will I ever be good enough for Jackson with this black mark on my life?

At some point I must've fallen asleep, because the next time I open my eyes it's dark outside and my stomach is growling. I push off the blankets and grab my pants to put them back on. Shuffling down the hallway toward the living room, I can hear Jackson and Brax's voices at a low rumble as they talk.

"I don't understand why you didn't tell me you're gay," Jackson says, making me stop in my tracks, not wanting to burst in on the conversation.

"I'm not gay, I'm bi."

"But you've only dated women, right?" Jackson clarifies.

"At this point, but that doesn't change the fact that I like both," Brax explains and a sense of kinship softens some of the embarrassment I'd been feeling. Not that I *love* the fact he's seen my videos.

"Right, of course," Jackson says. "But, why didn't you tell me?"

"I was going to. I recently came to terms with it myself. I was going to tell you during this visit anyway, but I'm sorry it came out in such an awkward way. If it helps, I was always more into Tank's videos than Campy's."

Jackson's laugh is a warm and comforting sound, which only makes my chest ache worse. I want so badly to be the kind of man who's right for him. But how can I with all this baggage? When my career could drag his through the mud?

Sensing the end of the conversation, I take the last step around the corner into the living room. Jackson gets up and closes the distance between us, pulling me into his arms and I melt into the hug.

"Sorry I caused you to freak out," Brax apologizes once Jackson releases me.

"It's not your fault," I assure him.

"For what it's worth, I don't think porn is anything to be ashamed about. It's a job," he says with a shrug.

"Yeah," I agree halfheartedly. That's just the thing though, I'm not ashamed about the porn per se, it's more what it could do to the people I care about.

29

JACKSON

The music swells as the camera flies higher and higher, showing the lush, green hills of Texas in the spring that are so familiar to me. Of course, by the time summer rolls around, that green turns to yellow, then brown, but it's gorgeous while it lasts.

"Damn, that show is good," Brax comments.

It's his last day here, and the fourth episode of *Hill Country* was on tonight, so we all huddled on the couch to watch it. I'm thankful the tension between Brax and Cam has dissipated, though it's still a tad weird that my brother has seen my boyfriend naked. Brax promised me he wouldn't watch his videos anymore, which I do appreciate.

"You killed it," Cameron says. "Man, that scene where you went to your father's grave, that was hitting me in the feels."

"How weird is it to see yourself?" Brax asks.

"Really freaking weird," I admit. "It feels like an out-of-body experience at times. Like I'm watching someone else playing me, you know?"

"I can't even imagine," Brax says. "Seeing yourself on TV,

that's so messed up in a way. But I gotta admit, the first episode, I had trouble not seeing you, you know? Like, feeling I was watching my brother. But after that, I really did feel like I was watching someone else. The show totally sucked me in."

"Same here," Cameron says.

I elbow-bump him companionably. "You got hooked because I'm shirtless half the time."

He sends me a blinding smile. "I'll admit that doesn't hurt. They did a nice job highlighting your...physique."

I snort. "Do you have any idea how weird that is? When complete strangers rub baby oil on you to make you look better? When they drag down your jeans an inch because they insist you need to show your V, whatever the heck that is? And yes, I was told to do a few push-ups right before those scenes because it made my muscles pop and gave me a fine layer of perspiration. As the director put it, which apparently is something sexy..."

Brax is dying with laughter now, but Cam just looks at me and shrugs. "Dude, I do porn. I am naked all. The. Fucking. Time. What you do is for fucking amateurs."

I stare at him for a second or two, my mouth dropping open at how casually he just owned that, and then I burst out laughing. He joins in seconds later, and we hang against each other, shaking with laughter.

"Very mature," Brax comments, wiping the tears from his eyes.

"You need to go, man," I tell him when we're done laughing, checking my watch.

He has a late flight out and because of that, I arranged an Uber for him rather than drive him to the airport myself, as I would get in too late. With an early shoot tomorrow to catch the morning light for an outside scene, I need my sleep.

"I know. I'm all packed," Brax says.

We walk him outside and wait till his Uber arrives, exactly on time, which in this city of a miracle in itself. With a last hug, Brax takes off.

"He's nice, your brother," Cameron says as we walk back up.

"He is," I confirm.

"I'm sorry that he saw my videos."

I close the door of the apartment behind us and turn toward Cameron, who's looking at me like a lost puppy. "It's okay."

He shakes his head. "It's really not, though, is it?"

I pull him close and wrap my arms around him. It always does something to me when he hides in my embrace, like he does now. It reminds me that I'm taller than him and while he's no twink, I'm also a bit more muscular. Call me old-fashioned, but I kinda dig that feeling of being his strong man, his protector.

"It's okay, darlin'," I say again. "I'll admit it's a bit awkward, but we'll get over it."

"What if your parents ever find out?" Cam asks, and an instant flash of shame fills me.

Oh dang, I hadn't even considered that. "Then we'll deal with that, too. I'm not ashamed of you, Cam."

He leans back to meet my eyes. "No?"

"Never."

He looks at me for a few seconds more, then rises up for a kiss. "You know what I really like about you?" he murmurs against my lips. "Your mouth. It's so damn kissable."

My lips curl up in a smile. "Wanna test that? Just to make sure?"

He presses his lips against mine, and the softest sigh escapes from my mouth. I lift him up and he wraps both his legs around me as I walk forward until he's up against the wall. His hands are wrapped around my neck, and that mouth of his, that devious, talented mouth, is kissing me for all he's worth.

"I know what we could do before bed," I say, my heart already racing.

I can't get enough of this man. He's under my skin, in my blood. He's a buzzing in my head, a warm feeling in my heart.

"Do you, now?" Cam teases, nibbling on my jawline. "And what would that be?"

I'm just about to answer him when my phone rings. We look at each other in surprise, and then I put him down to answer. It's Ethan, and worry fills my heart. Is something wrong with him?

"Hey," I answer.

"It's me, kid. Sorry for disturbing you," Ethan says.

"No problem. Are you okay?"

"Yeah, I'm calling with great news, actually. My agent just called me. She has an in with the network, and they gave her early access to today's ratings."

My heart skips a beat. "Oh?" I manage.

"We killed it, Jackson. *Hill Country* is the best viewed new show this week. Stellar ratings across the board on storyline, acting, everything."

My face breaks open in a smile so wide, my jaw hurts. "That's amazing! Oh my gosh, that's the best news ever."

I can hear Ethan laugh through the phone. "I figured you'd want to know. If this keeps up, they'll renew soon for a second season."

I hold on to Cameron, probably leaving some bruises

considering how tight my grip on his arm is. "I can't even..." I say, struggling to find words.

"I know. Also, my publicist arranged for an interview with the two of us in *People* magazine, a double feature. You up for that?"

Am I up for... I shake my head, overwhelmed by all the good news. "Ethan," I say. "Thank you. Thank you so much."

"You deserve it, kid. Now, go celebrate with your man."

As I hang up, I look at Cam, who's smiling at me broadly. I've never had celebratory sex, I think, and then I lift him up and carry him into the bedroom, eliciting a very unmanly squeal from him.

Campy

"I take it that was good news?" I ask as Jackson drags his tongue along my throat as he presses me up against the door of our bedroom.

"Great news," he confirms. "The show is killin' it. Ethan thinks we'll get renewed."

"In that case, we need to celebrate," I conclude, wiggling in his arms so he'll set me down.

"My thoughts exactly," Jackson agrees, putting me on my feet, but keeping me caged against the door. "Can I go down on you?"

One of the sweetest things about Jackson is even though we've been together a little while now and have covered all the bases numerous times, he still asks every time. Such a gentleman.

"Have you ever sixty-nined?" I smirk up at him.

"No, but I'm game."

We grope and kiss as we undress, taking twice as long to "help" each other get naked as it would've taken to do it ourselves, both of us getting sidetracked over and over finding interesting places to kiss and lick to draw the best sounds from each other.

Eventually we stumble over to the bed, falling onto it in a tangle of limbs, still unable to stop tasting all the skin we can reach.

Maneuvering Jackson onto his back, I climb on top of him and straddle him backwards, wrapping my hand around his thick shaft and stroking it. Licking my lips as precum oozes from the slit, I grind my erection against his chest.

Jackson runs his hands up the back of my thighs until they reach my ass, grasping my cheeks and kneading them.

"I didn't take into account our height difference. I don't think this is going to work so well."

"Well, I'm not gonna complain about the view." He slaps one of my ass cheeks lightly before returning to squeezing them in his hands.

"In that case, sit back and enjoy. And if your fingers happened to make their way into the action, I wouldn't protest," I tell him, looking over my shoulder and throwing in a wink for good measure.

As I take his cock into my mouth, my lips stretching wide around his impressive girth, I hear the rattle of the nightstand drawer opening, followed by the squelch of lube being squirted out.

The feeling of cold, wet lube being spread over my hole is so familiar I don't even flinch as I focus on running my tongue up and down his length, the head of his cock bumping against the back of my throat.

When the tip of his finger breaches my hole, I moan and

his cock slips deeper into my throat. I swallow and enjoy the groan of pleasure from Jackson as my throat briefly constricts around him. Bobbing my head, I reach between his legs to play with his balls, tugging gently at his sac and rolling them in my palm while I suck him.

Jackson works his finger deeper, adding a second before long and matching the pace of my sucking as he uses them to fuck me. I thrust back to meet his fingers, my erection dragging against his chest again with delicious friction. I suck and moan around his cock as I ride his fingers shamelessly and drink down the precum pouring from his slit.

He adds a third finger and my legs start to shake, the pit of my stomach tightening, along with my balls. His fingers crook down and if my mouth wasn't full of cock, I'd cry out from the electric pleasure of his fingers massaging my prostate.

"Cameron, I'm so close," he warns as I bury my nose against his balls and swallow again so he can feel the muscles of my throat squeezing him tight. I hum encouragingly, doubling my efforts while fucking myself on his fingers with abandon.

He's so deep in my throat I can't even taste his cum as his cock starts to pulse. I pull back so I can catch some on my tongue, the salty sweetness of it making my eyes roll back in my head. I suck him dry and then release him from my mouth with a pop.

Pushing myself up, I continue to ride his fingers, chasing my own release. Jackson reaches around and wraps his hand, rough from a lifetime of manual labor, around my cock and jerks me in time with the thrusts of his finger until I come undone, crying out and palming his chest with my release.

"Wow," Jackson breathes when I manage to get enough

feeling back in my legs to turn myself in the right direction and lie down beside him.

"You can say that again," I agree with a laugh, snuggling into his arms.

"Cam, I..." Jackson starts before cutting himself off and clearing his throat. "Sleep well." He buries his nose against the top of my head and tightens his arms around me. I almost want to push, but part of me is afraid of what he might've been about to say, so instead I kiss his shoulder and close my eyes.

"Night."

30

JACKSON

When I got the part in *Hill Country*, I not only signed with an agent, but I was assigned a publicist as well. Assigned being not entirely correct, since I'm paying her myself, but the network made it very clear I needed one.

So far, she's certainly had a positive effect on my career, I think. She's secured me some wonderful TV interviews, quite a few magazine interviews, a ton of online press, and even one commercial endorsement from the makers of the boots I wear every day. That was the easiest "Yes, please" ever for me.

We talk on the phone maybe once a week or so, with the strict instruction I should immediately call her if anything is wrong. I never quite understood what would constitute *wrong*, but I guess if I ever got involved in any type of scandal, my first call should be to her.

She's nice enough, Katie, even if she's super businesslike and very goal-oriented. That's not a bad quality in her line of work, but she's not one to chitchat or waste time with small talk.

That's why I'm a little surprised when she calls me out of the blue, because we spoke two days before. "Hey Katie, what's up?" I ask when I answer the phone.

"I heard some interesting news about you and wanted to verify."

As I said, she rarely wastes time on small talk. "Sure. What did you hear?"

"Look, there's no subtle way to ask this, so I'm gonna come straight out, okay? Are you gay?"

It's not so much the question that takes me back, as the timing. Why has this come up now? An uneasy feeling settles in my stomach. Still, my answer is swift and definitive. "I am." I wait a few beats, then when she stays quiet, I add, "Is that a problem?"

Her sigh is audible on the line. "No, but I wish you would've told me."

"Why is it even important? I thought being gay wasn't that big of a deal here in Hollywood?" I ask, frowning.

"It's not a problem at all, but if you had told me, we could've capitalized on it. Maybe we still can, if we act fast. Are you publicly out? Does your family know?"

"Whoa, backup. What do you mean by capitalizing on it?"

"Jackson, when timed right, coming out as gay can gain you a lot of sympathy with fans. Younger viewers adore you, especially women, and they're the ones with the highest tolerance for LGBT issues. Not just tolerance, but affection, even. If we can utilize your coming out, we could get you some new fans."

I'm still not quite sure what she means, but maybe I'd better answer her question first. "I am publicly out. There is no one important who doesn't know I'm gay, including my family."

"And are you dating anyone right now?"

My thoughts immediately go to Cameron. I have no idea what we are. Boyfriends? He's introduced me to his mom and he's met Brax, so I guess we are, but I'm not sure if he's comfortable yet with the whole world knowing. Plus, *boyfriends* seems too simple for what we are, too cliché a term to capture how I feel about him.

"Let's just say there is someone important in my life, but leave it at that. "

She hesitates for a bit before she answers. "Look, Jackson, I'm gonna be honest with you here, okay? I heard a rumor that you might be dating a gay porn star, is there any truth to that?"

My heart skips a few beats. How the hell does she know this? The answer comes quickly. The pilot party. Enough people recognized Cameron as Campy. If only one of them said something to a tabloid, that would've done the job. Plus, we've hung out in public enough, like in the gay bars we went to. If people recognized either of us...

"Does your source have a name?" I ask, wanting to know how much info they have.

"Not yet, or they're not telling me. But if they start digging, that won't take long. I take it it's true then?"

How can I confirm this without talking to Cameron first? I can't decide for him if he's okay with this, though I have a sneaking suspicion he won't be on account of the panic attack he had when Brax recognized him. He's not gonna want to come out and publicly date me. That would mean giving up his private life even more. Any chance he has of staying under the radar for his porn work will be gone then. What an unholy mess this is.

"Can you give me a few hours so I can talk to him? I don't want to say anything without his permission."

"Yes, but call me before the end of the day. If this breaks, it could hurt you. Viewers may not have an issue with you being gay, but porn stars are still not seen as a respectable partner."

"Katie, no matter what he says, I'm not gonna stop seeing him." That much I can tell her. "So honestly, I don't care what viewers think."

Her tone is surprisingly warm when she answers. "I understand that, so all I'm saying is that I need as much time and information as you can give me so I can spin this. Anything is salvageable, but we have to break the news ourselves."

I guess that's good news in some way, but I'm still feeling heavy-hearted as I hang up. What a nightmare. How naïve of me to never even consider the ramifications of dating a porn star. That's because that's not how I see him. At all.

To me, he's Cam. Sweet, sexy, kind Cam. The man who can look at me with eyes that betray much more than he's ever put into words. The man who can make my body feel things I've never felt before. The man who does everything for his mama. The man who I'm in love with and who I want to grow old with.

What I said to Katie is true. I don't care what it will cost me in terms of negative press. I'm not giving him up. If the choice comes down to him or my career, it's him. It will always be him. I know he's not there yet, but I have faith he will be. All he needs is time, but after Katie's call just now, we may not have that time.

Dear God in Heaven, I hope this won't make him run.

CAMPY

. . .

I'M sore and tired when I step into the apartment but sporting a smile a mile wide because today wasn't a Ballsy day, it was a wildlife center day. I may smell like the wrong side of a donkey, but I got to hand-feed a bald eagle and that was absolutely the coolest thing I can imagine.

Jackson is sitting on the couch and as soon as I see him, the joy inside me boils over and I fling myself onto his lap. He laughs as he catches me, his large hands grasping my waist and his lips soft and warm under mine. He must not have shaved today because the slight stubble on his cheeks rubs against my chin, sure to leave me red and raw if we kiss too long. But I don't care. Right now all I want is to get lost in Jackson for a few hours.

I flick my tongue along the seam of his lips and he opens for me, granting me access to lick into his mouth and suck his tongue—the latter being a little trick I learned from Heart. He's not usually the best kisser during scenes, but every once in a while, it feels like he drops the act for a few seconds and I get a more real version of him. That's when his kissing is *much* better. It's also when I start to wonder who he must be thinking about and if he's seeing anyone. He's almost as cryptic as I am about his personal life, but I like thinking there's someone at home taking care of him the way Jackson takes care of me.

"Mmm, I love kissing you," Jackson mutters against my mouth.

"You're not so bad yourself, Cowboy."

His hardening cock presses against my thigh, tempting me to grind against him and then swallow the moans he gives me. When his hands tighten and he pulls back from the kiss, I frown.

"We need to talk," he says and my heart plummets rapidly.

I may not be a relationship expert or anything, but I've seen enough TV to know nothing good comes from the phrase *we need to talk*.

Climbing off his lap, I settle on the couch beside him with a lump in my throat and a hard knot in my stomach.

"Okay, well, if you're dumping me, can we make this quick? I'd rather we just rip the band-aid off."

"What?" Jackson's eyes go wide and he reaches for my hand. "Why would I break up with you?"

"I don't know. If that's not what this is, then what do we need to talk about?"

His smile tightens as he twines our fingers together, his gaze dropping to our hands and staying there as he seems to search for the words. It feels like an eternity of waiting, counting my own heart beats simply to have something to do other than speculate about what he wants to tell me.

"I talked to my publicist today," he starts, and it does nothing to ease my fear. "There are rumors going around about the two of us being together. I'm guessing someone spotted us dancing or something and sold the story to the tabloids," he gives me an apologetic smile as he explains.

"I fucking knew this was going to happen."

I shake my head and try to tug my hand out of his, waiting for the metaphorical axe to fall. He *is* dumping me, or at least his publicist told him he has to. Maybe he's hoping I'll do it for him so he won't have to.

"It's not that bad," he assures me. "She told me it was salvageable as long as we—"

"Break up?" I guess.

"Cameron, would you stop yammerin' and listen to me?" Jackson snaps and for some reason, his irritation is cute as hell. He's always so patient and sweet, it's kind of nice to see a different side of him for a few seconds.

"Sorry." I mime zipping my lips so he'll continue.

"As I was *sayin'*, she says it's totally salvageable, but we need to come out as a couple. She said if we get out in front of it with a public statement, it'll be for the best. She didn't say for certain, but I get the feelin' if we make it the kind of gooey, sweet love story the public loves then no one will care about your job."

"So, if we want to stay together we have to tell the world we're madly in love?" I repeat, feeling a little sick.

I've spent the past year living a lie, and now I need to pile on more? Not that I don't love Jackson. How could I not? He's good to my mom, he's cute and sweet. He's the kind of genuine person I didn't think existed in real life. He's amazing, of course I love him. But how could he feel that same way about me? I'm just a porn star with dreams I'll never be able to reach. And the thought of Jackson telling the whole world he's in love with me just to save his career honestly makes me want to vomit.

"I know it's a lot to consider..."

"It's more than a lot," I counter, as the weight of it all really sets in.

If we go public with our relationship, it means I'll be going public about doing porn too. There will be pictures of Jackson and I together in every magazine in the world with the headline *Television Star Dates Gay Porn Star*. Julie and everyone at the wildlife rehab will know. Oh god...my mom will know.

My throat feels too tight and every breath is a struggle as I lean forward and put my head between my knees in an attempt to calm myself down. My life will be ruined, Jackson will become a laughing stock for dating someone like me, and everything will fall apart.

"Deep breaths for me, Cam," Jackson instructs in that

magically calming voice he somehow manages every time I need it. His hand lays on my back, warm and soothing as I struggle to draw slower, deeper breaths.

He doesn't seem to get impatient as he coaches me through breathing for what has to be at least ten minutes, and I add that to the list of reasons I'm head over heels for him. And that's really the crux of it, isn't it? My choices are to tell the world I'm a porn star or lose Jackson.

I sit back and turn my head to look at Jackson. He reaches over and wipes his thumb across my cheek, brushing away tears I didn't realize were there.

"We don't have to do this," he assures me. "I'll tell Katie we need to keep it quiet, and if it means I end up having to leave the show, or whatever other consequences there are, I'll deal with those."

"No." I grab his hand and kiss his rough, calloused palm. "I'll do it. Do you think we have a couple days so I'll have a chance to warn my mom ahead of time though? I don't want her to find out reading *US Weekly*."

"Are you sure? I'm serious, Cam, we don't have to do anything you aren't comfortable with."

"I'm not really comfortable," I admit. "I don't care about telling the world I'm...bi, or whatever. But telling the world I take it up the ass for money? Yeah, that's a bit embarrassing."

"I didn't even think about it that way," Jackson confesses. "I forget about these two separate lives you have."

"I know, it's okay," I assure him. "It'll be fine. I should probably warn Bear too," I muse. "Oh man, I bet Rebel's going to have a joygasm when I tell him. If this isn't good publicity for Ballsy, I don't know what is. People will be buying subscriptions by the thousands to watch your boyfriend suck dick."

Jackson frowns before pulling me closer and pressing a kiss to the top of my head.

"I'm going to make sure Katie spins this in a positive light. No one is going to write a single negative word about you."

I chuckle against his shoulder. "Pretty sure you don't have a say in that, but thank you." I turn my head and kiss his cheek. "Do we really have to lie about our feelings though? All the love stuff I mean…"

My heart hurts all over again at the idea of having the world think Jackson is in love with me when he's not.

He tenses and stills and then clears his throat. "Right… I'll…uh, talk to Katie about that part."

"Thank you." I sigh, settling closer to him and letting the rhythmic feeling of his breathing soothe me, until I start to realize just how bad I smell. "My god, how are you holding me right now when I reek of animals?"

Jackson laughs, tightening his grip.

"It's kinda nostalgic, I like it," he teases, pressing his nose against my neck, followed by his lips.

"That's just nasty," I complain, pushing him away playfully. "I'm going to go shower, and then I'm going to think about how to tell my mom I'm in porn."

"I'll come with you to your ma's," he offers.

"Of course you will, I'll need you to talk her off the ledge after my confession."

I'm only half-joking on that one. The thought of telling my mom the truth and shattering her image of me sits like a stone in the pit of my stomach all through my shower and for the rest of the night.

31

JACKSON

I'm worried about him. He called his mom, and the nurse picked up to say she was having a bad day and was asleep. He said he'd stop by tomorrow.

I can tell how torn up he is about it, how scared of her reaction. And not just hers, but everyone's. In a way, it's like coming out, I guess. He has to tell everyone he's doing porn and then possibly face their scorn and rejection. And as much as I would like to tell him it'll be okay, I can't.

His mom will love him no matter what, of that I'm certain. She's too loving and accepting to react any other way, though it may shock her to hear what he's been doing to pay the bills. If I have her pegged correctly, she'll be more guilty than angry. It's quite something to hear your son has been doing porn just to make sure you're taken care of.

But his coworkers, I don't have a clue how they'll react. He makes them sound nice and friendly, but that may change when his secret is out. Gosh, I wish I could protect him from this...but I can't.

He's barely said a word to me since he showered and went to bed early. When I peek around the corner, I see he's still awake, lying on his back and staring at the ceiling. I could ask if he's okay, but that would be useless, since he's clearly not. Instead, I undress and slide under the sheets next to him.

When I reach for him, he allows himself to be pulled close, and he nestles his head on my shoulder. A rush of emotion courses through me. I love him so much, and it breaks my heart to see him in pain. But is he ready yet to hear that big word for me? Will it help him now?

Honestly, I don't think it will. It'll only make him feel more guilty for possibly ruining things between us, for making things harder for my career. He said it himself, he doesn't want us to pretend about the love stuff, as he called it. He has no idea of the depth of my feelings, that much is clear.

So no, I can't tell him just yet…but maybe I can show him? I turn on my side, bringing our faces an inch apart. He looks so forlorn, and I raise my hand to brush through his messy hair, then cup his jaw and gently kiss him. It's like I gave water to a dying plant, and he opens up for me, leaning into my touch, my kiss. He needs me, and the thrill of that makes me shiver.

"Cam," I whisper. "You're so beautiful."

He smiles a little.

"I mean it, darlin'. You take my breath away."

He lets his forehead rest against mine for a few seconds and then kisses me with a need bordering on desperation. "Jackson…"

"I know, darlin'," I say. "I've got you."

We kiss until our bodies are on fire, but it's a slow burn tonight, a kindling that grows stronger and stronger until it burns brightly. I pour out all my love for him in my hands, my mouth, as I explore every inch of his body.

His ears, which I love to suck on for some weird reason. His lobes are sensitive, but it drives him really crazy when I nibble on his ear shell. He shivers under my touch, clinging to me as if drowning.

His nipples, which are so wonderfully sensitive to my mouth. They become little pebbles when I suck on them, and the noises he makes are so gorgeous. I'm becoming quite the expert at multitasking, sucking one while teasing the other with my fingers, and then switching until he's moaning.

His bellybutton, which I discovered is an erogenous zone for him. I tongue it for a little bit until he's writhing beneath me. My hands are under him now, grabbing his ass and kneading those firm globes gently. I love how soft his skin is there, but I love even more how he spreads his legs for me, so eager for more.

His faint happy trail, which I follow with my fingers, then my mouth, making him squirm. I roll his balls in my hands as I lick the precum off his cock, and he bucks up from the bed.

"Jackson," he says again, and his voice breaks.

"You want more, darlin'?"

"I need you. Fuck, I need you so much."

My fingers loosen him, slick with lube, and he opens up for me so easily, so greedily. We don't speak another word as I carefully slide inside him, my breath catching in my lungs. Will this ever not feel like a miracle, like a gift I get to treasure?

He sucks me in, pulling his legs up and folding them around me, holding on to me with both hands. *I love you.* The words are on the tip of my tongue and I force them back, choosing instead to kiss him. I slide in and out of him as our tongues dance, but then that gets too slow for me.

Cam works his hips upward to meet my thrusts, an indication he wants me to speed up as well. And so I increase my rhythm, filling him with deep, steady strokes. My right hand wraps around his cock, just the way he likes it, and keeps the same pace.

"Jackson..."

My name sounds like a sob now.

"Let go, I'll catch you. I'll always catch you."

He cries out, then releases all over my hand. He's still shaking, his eyes closed, when I feel my own orgasm barrel through me. I grunt as I fill up the condom, my hips moving in a rhythm that's completely instinctual. I hold him for a long time, the condom quickly thrown away, until he stops clinging to me.

He's already half-asleep when I wash his cum off myself and him and clean him up. When I slip back under the sheets with him, his deep breathing indicates he's asleep. I pull him close and finally release the words I've held back the entire time.

"I love you, Cam."

32

CAMPY

It's a familiar moment, sitting in my car in my mom's driveway with Jackson holding my hand, telling me it'll be okay. Unsurprisingly, this coming out is much more stressful than the last. I knew she wouldn't care about me not being straight, and I knew she already liked Jackson so there wasn't much risk. But, telling her I've been doing porn to pay for her medical bills? Yeah, this is scary as fuck.

"It's not going to change how much she loves you," Jackson says, giving my hand a reassuring squeeze.

"I know. But what if she doesn't respect me anymore? What if she's not proud of me anymore?"

"Darlin', look at me," he says, cupping my chin and turning my head away from the house and toward him. "The fact that you've done what you had to do to take care of your mama is admirable as hell. No one could possibly look down on that. And, I know I don't know her as well as you do, but she doesn't exactly strike me as the prude type. Even if you were doing porn simply because you enjoyed it, I don't think she'd look down on you for that either."

I take a deep breath and reach for the door handle to get

out of the car, reluctantly letting go of Jackson's hand so he can do the same.

When we enter her house, her caretaker is still there finishing up for the day, and we spend a few minutes chatting and getting updates from her before she leaves and I go in search of my mom.

I'm not surprised she's in her bedroom, but I'm happy to see she has a finished tray of food on the nightstand and looks much better cared for than she was before I hired her nurse. Jackson is right about one thing, there's no way I can feel ashamed of my job when it's given me the ability to take care of her like this.

"Hey, Mom," I greet her, bending over the bed to give her a hug and then letting Jackson do the same.

"Hi, how are my boys doing today?"

"Good," I assure her.

"Then what's with the frown?"

"No frown." I paste on my best fake smile.

"Please, you don't think I know my son's fake smile when I see it?"

"Okay, fine. There's just something I need to tell you about," I confess, settling at the foot of her bed while Jackson grabs the chair from the corner of the room and pulls it closer.

"That doesn't sound good."

"It's not so bad," I lie. "Here's the thing..." I reach for Jackson's hand, needing to feel his steady presence while I say this out loud for the first time. "You know how I told you I work as a vet tech while I'm saving up to go back to school?"

"Yes."

"Well, the truth is, I could never make enough to support you and pay my own bills working as a vet tech. I tried at first, but I was hardly scraping by and I wasn't able to pay for all your different meds and everything."

She struggles to sit up, a look of concern on her face. Jackson jolts forward, dropping my hand to help her get into a sitting position.

"If you tell me you've been doing something illegal to get the money, I'm going to kick your ass six ways to Sunday."

"It's not illegal, Mom," I assure her. "It's just...um...god this is embarrassing..." I put my face in my hands, unable to look at her when I say this. "I'm in porn."

"Porn?" she repeats.

"Yes," I confirm. "For a while now, I've been working at a gay porn studio. It pays well and the owner of the studio is really nice, so we're all treated well there. It's obviously not my dream job or anything, but it's really not so bad. The other guys I work with have become good friends and it's given me the ability to pay for everything you need and still keep up with my own living expenses."

My mom sniffles and I lower my hands from my face to check on her. There are tears streaming down her cheeks that Jackson wipes away just as gently as he always wipes mine away. He reaches for a tissue from the nightstand and hands it to her.

"I'm sorry, I didn't mean to disappoint you."

"Oh, baby," she reaches for me with a shaky, weak arm. "I'm not disappointed in you. I'm hating myself right now for this stupid disease that's stolen my independence and taken your dreams with it."

"It's not your fault. We're both just trying to get through this," I assure her. "I've never blamed you."

"I want to see you achieve your dreams. I don't want you to spend your life doing something just to pay my bills. You should stop worrying about me and go back to school."

"Mom," I reach for her hand. "I'm never going to stop worrying about you. I *am* going to go to school and become a veterinarian, but right now, you're my top priority. Eventually everything else will fall into place. I really believe that."

"I'm going to do everything I can to make his dreams come true," Jackson vows, handing her another tissue.

"I'm glad he has you," she says, giving Jackson one of those sweet, moony looks.

"Me too," I agree, smirking at Jackson and loving the blush forming on his cheeks.

~

Two days later, the headline seems to be on every magazine and gossip website: *Hill Country Star Shacking Up with Popular Gay Porn Star!*

By the way, don't even get me started on there being an exclamation point in an article title. Of course, the wording varies in some of them, but the message always comes across loud and clear—handsome, up-and-comer star slumming it with a Ballsy Boy.

As predicted, Rebel was completely thrilled with the development since our subscribers have increased by fifteen percent, and views on my videos have doubled in some cases. Comments like "I wonder if Jackson will ever guest star in a video with Campy" make me cringe every time I catch sight of them on a video. That would be a *hell no*. But, Rebel told me I can't say that when someone tweets it at me. My approved response is "You never know ;)". The winky face makes me feel extra gross about the whole thing.

I'm glad I told my mom ahead of time, but I wish I'd found a way to tell Julie and everyone else at the wildlife center too so they wouldn't have to find out this way. I can only imagine what they're all thinking about me now. I wonder what Dr. Marx and his boyfriend think. Are they disgusted? Amused? Have they watched my videos together?

Bile rises in my throat and I toss my phone aside, promising myself for the countless time that I'm going to stop looking at the articles and comments.

I flop sideways on the couch, committing fully to feeling pathetic about my life, when my phone rings. When I see my mom's name on the caller ID, my heart leaps into my throat and I hurry to answer it.

"Mom, are you okay?"

"I'm fine, honey. I was just calling to check on *you*. My nurse, Tiffany has been reading me these articles about you and I was worried about how you might be feeling."

I let out a long breath. "They're not saying anything *bad* about me at least."

"Of course they're not. What bad could they possibly say? You're an honest, hardworking young man."

"Yeah," I mumble, unconvinced.

"Cameron Michael Wallace, you listen to me right now," she says sternly, the use of my full name making me sit up and pay attention. "I am proud of you."

My breath catches as her words sink in and, to my embarrassment, tears prickle at my eyes. "You don't have to say that just to make me feel better."

"Have I ever been the kind of mother who bullshits you?"

"No," I admit with a watery laugh.

"You are an amazing young man, and I couldn't be more proud to call you my son."

I mean to laugh again, but it comes out as a sob this time, fat tears forming at the corners of my eyes and rolling down my cheeks as my response completely gets away from me. On the other end of the phone, my mom makes soothing noises while I cry out all the fear and shame that have grown so vast inside me they were becoming suffocating. Each tear feels like a baptism or maybe more of a bleeding of all the darkness to make room for the light.

I'm still crying when Jackson steps through the door, his expression going from neutral to panicked in an instant.

"Mom, Jackson's home."

"Okay, make sure he hugs you for me. I love you."

"Love you too, Mom."

I hang up and drop my phone on the cushion beside me before launching myself into Jackson's arms.

"Is everything okay?"

I nod with my face pressed into his chest. "My mom said she's proud of me," I explain through sniffles.

"Of course she's proud of you," Jackson says as if that was a foregone conclusion. "I'm proud of you too. You're an incredible person. I—"

He cuts off whatever he was about to say, instead tightening his grip around me and holding me closer.

"Enough of this emotional bullshit, I think." I laugh at myself, using the back of my hands to wipe my cheeks dry. "Why don't we make dinner together and you can tell me about your day?"

Jackson

CAMERON FELL ASLEEP EARLY when we were watching a movie together and I carried him into the bedroom, where he's now softly snoring in my arms. It's a soothing sound, and he's even more adorable and cute when he's asleep, but I can't sleep.

It's been such a rollercoaster, these last few days, what with all the news about his porn career breaking. I hate that he was forced to go public with it, and at the same time I'm grateful that it's now out in the open. Secrets grow nasty, bitter roots deep inside you since they fester in the dark, and I hope that now that it's out, he can let go of his self-doubt and shame about it. The crying he did tonight felt cleansing to me, and I can only hope he won't come to regret it.

It's not been how I pictured a relationship would be like, but then again I've been known to be a tad over-romantic. Heck, I was ready to ride off into the sunset with Cam the day after meeting him, so my expectations *may* have been too high. But heck, I do hope this is it when it comes to storms and setbacks. I want some time to just be happy together, is that too much to ask?

Maybe it is, I ponder. After all, this is what happens when you become famous...and I'm just getting started. I'm getting recognized more and more in public, which is flattering and super awkward at the same time. And Ethan said that'll only get worse. Or better, depending on how you look at it.

When I signed with her, Katie made me practice a signature, which made me snicker back then, but now I'm grateful. She told me to make it short, because I'd have to sign it many, many times, and boy, am I happy I listened to her. I'll be signing stuff for a long time, I hope.

Then it hits me. This news about me and Cam, this will reach Texas as well. Darn, my parents will find out about me having a boyfriend from the tabloids, if I'm not careful. And that he works in porn. No, they shouldn't find out like that. I made that mistake last time, when I didn't tell them about dropping out of college, and my father is still barely speaking to me.

No, they need to hear this from me. My stomach already turns upside down at even the thought. I have no choice. Cameron is not a fling. I'm dead serious about him, about us, and that means telling my parents, and the sooner the better.

I carefully turn Cameron on his side and sneak out of bed. There are a million things I can think of that I would rather do than this, but I don't allow myself to think about them. It's not even ten, so still early enough to call.

My mom picks up on the third ring, "Hi, Jackson," she says, careful warmth in her voice.

"Hey Mama, how you been?"

After she has filled me in on the latest gossip about the neighbors, she asks, "Were you just calling to catch up or was there something you wanted to tell me?"

I take a deep breath, then blurt it out. "I have a boyfriend."

It's deadly silent for a few seconds, and then she lets out a soft gasp. "Oh Jackson."

"I love him, Mama," I say, putting it all on the line. "He's not a phase, not something I will get over or outgrow. I love him, and I want to spend the rest of my life with him."

A wave of nausea barrels through me as I wait for my mama to respond.

"I don't know what your dad will say," she finally says. "This will come as a shock to him."

There's something in her voice I've never heard before, something awfully close to insubordination. "What about you, Mama?" I ask softly. "How do *you* feel about it?"

It takes a long time for her to respond, but I wait patiently, knowing I can't rush her on this.

"All I want for you is to be happy," she says finally. "I'll admit, Jackson, I don't understand. I reckon none of us do if we're not wired the same way. But I love you, and I want you to be happy. But your dad…"

"I know, Mama. This will be hard for him."

"Is he nice, your man?" my mom asks, and with that question alone she shows me how far she's come.

"He's wonderful. He's kind and smart, and he has a great sense of humor. His mama is quite sick, and he works very hard to take care of her. He's a good man, the best. I love him so much."

"It's wonderful to hear you gush about him," my mom says, affection clear in her voice.

And Heaven help me, I'm about to make things even worse. "Mama, he's working hard to make sure his mom has the best medical care, but that doesn't come cheap. Their insurance doesn't even cover half of it. He's had to take on a job to pay the bills, and it's not a respectable job, as Dad would put it. Do you understand what I'm saying?"

I want to give her the opportunity to wrap her mind around it by using code words, rather than coming right out and confronting her with the word *porn*.

"Oh Jackson," she says again. "I assume you mean he's somehow working in the…adult entertainment industry?"

A rush of love and pride for her fills me. That must've taken a lot for her to even say that out loud, and I'm a little surprised she even knows what it's called.

"Yes, Mama. The *gay* adult industry."

"Is this something we can keep hidden from your father?" That one question speaks volumes about how far she's willing to go to protect me, because she has never kept much from my dad, as far as I know.

"I'm afraid not. I'm becoming quite well-known, and

some people have found out about our relationship, and it's already in tabloids everywhere. I didn't want you to read about it in the news or hear it from neighbors."

"Your dad is going to be so upset," she says. "Oh my gosh, I don't know how I'm gonna tell him."

I fight back tears that burn in my eyes, the bitter result of knowing I've disappointed my parents. "I'm sorry, Mama. I love him."

"You don't have a problem with him doing...that?"

"He's not doing it because he loves it. He's doing it because he has no choice. He needs to take care of his mama, and this was the only thing he could think of that would make him enough money. I can't help but think there's some redemption in that, don't you think?"

"I suppose you're right," she says, her voice soft. "But your dad isn't going to see it the same way."

"Will you tell him?" I ask.

It's weak of me, maybe. Cowardly. But I can't do it. I can't face the rejection and disappointment, not after last time.

"I reckon I have little choice. He ain't gonna be happy, and it might be a while before things get back to normal. Just know that I love you, and don't forget to reach out to your brothers. I'm worried about Brax, Jackson. There's something troubling him, and he ain't talking to me. Just make sure he's okay, will you?"

That I can promise her with all my heart. "I've got him, Mama. He's okay, don't you worry."

She lets out a little laugh, but it doesn't sound happy. "That's my job as mama, my sweet boy. I worry about all of you."

I wipe away a tear at her term of endearment. "I never meant to hurt or disappoint you."

"Hush now. I love you, Jackson Bedford Criswell. You're

my oldest, my sweet boy. You've got a heart bigger than Texas, and don't you forget it. We'll survive this storm, so don't you fret now."

Despite my sadness over how my dad will respond, my heart lightens a little. "I love you too, Mama."

33

CAMPY

It feels strange walking into Bottoms Up with Jackson's hand in mine, but also pretty awesome if I'm being honest.

I'm still bracing for what it will be like to walk into the wildlife center next time with everyone now knowing I do porn, but after my talk with my mom, I already feel more prepared to face whatever judgement I may get. I've done what I've had to do and there's nothing shameful about that. But all of that's a problem for later. Tonight is about the two of us going out together to celebrate our relationship being out in the open.

"Want a drink?" I ask, having to get up on my tiptoes to talk into his ear so he can hear me over the pounding bass.

"Sure."

His hand on my lower back as we weave through the crowd feels as hot as a branding iron and I find myself hoping everyone notices, sees that he's mine. God, this is a crazy feeling, and I absolutely love it.

Ryan, the bartender, smiles as we approach, his eyes

darting between Jackson and me, and then dropping to Jackson's hand on my back.

"I see you two finally worked things out."

"Huh?" Jackson cocks his head and then looks at me to explain.

"Two beers please," I order, attempting to end this awkward line of conversation.

"What did he mean?" Jackson asks as soon as Ryan turns away to get our drinks.

"He's a bartender, he sees hundreds of people every night. He probably has us confused with other people," I attempt to explain, but the arch of his eyebrow tells me he's not buying it. "Okay, fine..." I sigh. "Remember when you met that date here?"

"I remember."

"I may have, kind of, followed you to make sure the guy was on the up and up."

"You followed me?" he repeats, his eyebrows going even higher and a smile spreading across his lips. "Were you jealous, darlin'?"

"Maybe," I mutter.

"You were," he teases, putting his arms around me and pulling me closer. "I knew it. You had a *crush* on me."

I roll my eyes and give his shoulder a playful shove. "You had a crush on me too, Cowboy."

"I know, it was because you were so sweet and irresistibly cute."

"Well, my crush was because you had an ass that wouldn't quit," I joke and he bends down to kiss me, slow and sweet in spite of the heat building between us with every sweep of his tongue against mine.

"Here are your drinks, guys. And the club has a strict policy about public sex, you're going to have to take that somewhere more private," Ryan says, giving us a wink when we pull apart.

"Oh please, it's not like everyone in this club hasn't seen me at it before."

"Well, I'm not about to give the tabloids anything else to salivate over so soon," Jackson laughs and I reluctantly wiggle out of his grasp to take our drinks, inclined to agree that fucking in public wouldn't be so good for his brand-new public image.

"Fine, how about if we drink and dance instead?" I suggest.

"I like that plan."

We find a place to sit and drink our beer, leaning close together to talk and flirt while we people watch. When our drinks are finished, Jackson stands up and offers me his hand.

"Let's dance."

It's not so different than the first time we danced together, except this time I'm not lying to either of us about how the feeling of Jackson's body moving against mine makes me feel. I'm not afraid to press my ass more firmly against the bulge he's grinding against me, or to turn my head and kiss him as our bodies rock in time to the music. Jackson wasn't wrong before, dancing really is like fucking, and I'm painfully hard in no time.

When his hands slip under my shirt, hot and rough against my skin, I'm not sure how much longer I can keep from jumping him.

"Is a blowjob in the bathroom considered public sex?" I ask.

"You're so bad, Cam," he accuses against my ear.

"That doesn't sound like you're telling me *no*," I point out and his laughter rumbles against my back.

"What if we get caught?"

"We'll be quick," I promise. "I want to suck you so badly, please don't make me wait until we get home."

Jackson groans, pressing the length of his erection against the curve of my ass again.

"You're such a bad influence," he grumbles, grabbing my hand and dragging me through the crowd toward the bathrooms at the back of the club.

Luck must be on our side because the bathroom is empty when we get there. I turn the lock and then shove Jackson against the nearest wall before dropping to my knees.

Jackson's head falls back against the wall as I undo his pants and pull his cock out.

"You know, this is my first club hookup," I muse, stroking his cock, milking his precum until a large drop is gathered on his slit.

"Mine too, obviously."

I dart my tongue out to lap at the head of his cock before the precum can drip. Jackson moans, his fingers tunneling through my hair. I relax my head and let him tug me closer, his cock sliding easily down my practiced throat. It's different than when I'm on camera though— hotter, more exciting, and definitely more fun. There's something about knowing that every gasp and moan is real and only for me that drives me wild.

I grab Jackson's well-sculpted ass, digging my fingers into it and encouraging him to thrust, to fuck my mouth however he wants. He does exactly that, burying himself deep before drawing back until the head of his cock rests against my tongue, and then doing it all over again. I drag in a breath through my nose every time he pulls out and look up at him with heated eyes so he can see just how much I love having my face fucked by him.

"So good, Cam," he grunts, pushing in deep so my nose is pressed into the tuft of hair at the base of his cock. My eyes water a little but if I had my way, I'd fucking live in this position with Jackson.

I press my tongue against the throbbing underside of his cock and swallow so he can feel my throat constricting around him. I'm rewarded with another gravelly moan.

This time, when he draws back, he slams back in harder, his pace quickening and his cock thickening between my lips. Drool drips down my chin and tears leak freely from my eyes now as he lets loose, chasing his orgasm as it nears.

"I'm close," he warns through gritted teeth, loosening his hold on my hair so I can pull away if I want to. Like hell would I waste his cum by letting it spurt onto the bathroom floor rather than down my throat.

I hum and grasp the globes of his ass harder.

"Oh...Oh...Cam...oh, *fuck*," he groans, his muscles tightening and his cock pulsing hard against my tongue, emptying himself into my mouth as I greedily suck every last drop from him.

Jackson

I HAVE to hold onto Cam with both hands, my legs feeling like cooked spaghetti. The only thing that's keeping me from sagging onto the floor is that we're in a public bathroom and that would be just ew. Cam licks his lips, smacking them in a way that tells me he enjoyed it, then proceeds to clean the last remnants off my cock.

His brown eyes are still dark with lust as he looks up. "You like?"

"Fuck, yes. That was…orgasmic."

He chuckles as he tucks me back in. "You know what makes me laugh?"

I can't imagine him laughing over anything after he's just made me come like that, but what do I know? "No?"

"You curse when you're having sex." He rises to his feet and smiles at me, his eyes twinkling.

"I don't curse," I say almost automatically.

"You rarely curse," he corrects me. "And while I find your *gosh darn it* and *oh my goodness* adorable as fuck, there's something deeply satisfying about making you swear when you're all hot and bothered."

I try to think back on what I said while he was sucking me off, but I have to admit my brain wasn't rightly working. "What did I say?" I ask weakly.

"You said my name, and then *fuck*."

"You say that all the time," I point out.

His grin broadens. "I do, but it never sounds as sexy and dirty as when you say it. It's as if your lips feel guilty for even uttering it, and they push it out as if to get rid of it quickly, making it sound filthy."

I can't help but smile at that. "You put a lot of thought into me saying a simple word."

"Say it for me," Cam says.

"Say what?"

"Say *fuck* for me. Come on, let me hear it one more time."

I shake my head. "I'm not saying it just so you can laugh at me some more."

Cam bats his eyelashes at me. "Pretty please?"

"You're gonna have to find your entertainment elsewhere, darlin'," I say.

His eyes narrow, and I see something bubble in there that I don't quite trust. "I see how it is. I'm gonna have to force it out of you, am I?"

"Force it?"

"Yes. By making you so *hot and bothered* again that you can't help but swear."

"Not gonna happen," I declare, crossing my arms. "I may have slipped up once or twice, but it won't happen again, especially now that I know that's your intention."

Cameron takes a step closer to me, our bodies only inches apart. "Is that a challenge?"

"You made me come only minutes ago. I'm confident I can endure whatever you bring." How difficult can it be to resist cursing? I mean, granted, when he kisses me it's hard to think, but not that hard. Pun intended.

Cameron winks at me, before he pulls my head down and kisses me. Oh my, I can still taste traces of myself on his lips, in his mouth, on his tongue. It's filthy and perfect, and I kiss him back with all I've got. I love the way he fits against my body, all lean muscles and strength.

I close my eyes, sinking into the kiss that leaves my head spinning. The world around us fades away, and all I can hear is my own heartbeat racing, thundering through my veins. He sucks on my tongue, then uses his teeth to nibble on my bottom lip.

"Fuck, your mouth is so damn perfect," he says with a growl, accentuating it with a little nip. "I'd love to see those full lips of yours wrapped around my dick, but some other time."

"Some other time," I agree, focusing hard in order to form words.

"You've got me so hard," he groans, putting my hand on his dick.

Even through his jeans, I have no trouble feeling how aroused he is. It's pulsing against my hand, his cock, and for a second, regret floods me. How I wish we were at home, so he could fu—. I catch myself just in time. Fill me. That's a better word. No swearing necessary.

I put a little pressure on my hand and he rubs against it, seeking friction. "Mmm, that feels so good," he says, his voice low.

I increase the pressure, cupping my hand slightly so I can squeeze him through his jeans. My reward is a low moan, so I do it again.

"Jackson..." Cam sighs. "Fuck, I wish we were home so I could fuck you into the mattress. Would you like that, baby? For me to fill you up again with my perfect cock and make you lose your mind with how good it feels?"

I swear I can feel my hole flutter at the thought, and my cheeks heat up. He makes it sound so dirty, so provocative. My dick is well on its way to being fully erect again, apparently not caring I just came.

"I would really like that," I admit, my voice hoarse.

Cam is now rutting against me without shame, his cock so hard it feels like iron against my hand.

"You're gonna make me cream my pants, that's how sexy you are," Cam says in that gravelly voice that shoots straight to my balls. "Is that what you want? For me to shoot my load in my pants?"

"My hand," I manage. "I want to feel you."

Cam unzips his jeans, then pushes my hand in. "Oh fuck, Jackson, please."

I don't think I've ever heard him beg like that and it feels so needy, so big. My hand wraps around the velvety soft skin, my thumb finding his wet slit like he taught me. He's working his dick into my hand, faster and faster, and I increase the pressure, creating a tight fist.

"Oh fuck, oh fuck," he chants. "So fucking close…"

I can't stop watching him as he throws his head back, abandoning himself fully to the pleasure of my hand. He's so hot right now, so beautiful, it's intoxicating. I slam him with his back against the wall as I take his mouth, needing to capture every little sigh of him as he comes. My hand's pressure is unrelenting now, and his body shakes against mine. I swallow his low moan.

"Jackson!" he grunts into my mouth and then he comes, shooting hot ropes of cum into my hand. His body shakes and shivers and he collapses against me with a last deep sigh.

"Fuck, that was so hot," I say.

Dammit.

34

CAMPY

I'm shaking all over as I get out of my car at the wildlife center. *Whatever they think about me being in porn, I can handle it*, I tell myself over and over as I double-check that I have my work gloves and everything else I need with me before accepting that I can't stall any longer and head inside.

Everything feels normal when I enter the main barn—Julie is in the kitchen area preparing some meals, Gerber the Goose tries to peck at my knees as I walk past, the donkey's bray loud enough to be heard from the arena. It's almost unsettlingly normal.

Julie glances up from the counting little fish into a bowl and smiles at me. "We're fighting," she informs me cheerfully.

"We are?"

"Yeah. I can't *believe* you're dating the hottie from *Hill Country* and you didn't tell me."

I cross my arms and arch an eyebrow at her. "Really? *That's* what you want to talk about after you've obviously read the articles about me this week?"

"What do you mean? Oh, the porn thing?"

"Yes, the *porn thing*."

"Cameron, sweetie, that's like the worst-kept secret of the century."

My mouth falls open and my arms drop to my sides as my mind reels. "You *knew*? Wait, are you saying *everyone* knew?"

"I don't know if *everyone* knew, but a lot of people did."

"But...how?" I think back, trying to come up with some way I might've given myself away.

"Facebook suggested Campy as a friend. At first I thought someone stole a picture of you to use as their profile image, but when I tried to look it up to find out what Ballsy Boys was, well...it was pretty obvious what was going on."

"Ugh, fucking Facebook," I groan.

"If it makes you feel better, I didn't watch any of your videos."

"Mildly," I confirm. "Who else knows?"

"A few people," she shrugs. "I think people mostly found you on their own. It sounds like Ballsy Boys has been advertising hard over the past few months, showing up in ads on Twitter and stuff."

"Fucking Rebel," I mutter. "Does...um...what about Dr. Marx?"

"Oh yeah, he knows."

My stomach drops.

"He knew before I did. I have a feeling he was a subscriber before you even joined."

"That figures."

I run my hands over my face, taking a deep breath. All things considered, this is better news than I'd dared to hope for. Most everyone knew long before this week and no one seems to be judging me or freaking out about it.

"Anyway, Tootsie the owl has an eye infection and needs ointment applied but she hates me. Do you mind doing that?"

The knot in my chest eases as we get back on familiar ground and I smile. I'm still the same Cameron to Julie as I've always been. And why shouldn't I be? Nothing about me has changed.

"I'm on it," I assure her, heading for the med room to find the ointment with Tootsie's name on the tube and the instructions.

I spend the next five hours getting lost in my work, as I always do—mucking out stalls, preparing meals, giving meds. One of the newer volunteers asks me to teach her how to prepare a follow-up fecal sample for the racoons to tell if they still have roundworms or not. Everything feels completely right and all my worries about my life being upended fade into the background.

By the time I'm driving home, I can hardly remember what I'd been worried about to begin with, all my focus on getting home to see Jackson. He's waiting with dinner when I walk through the door and the words *I love you* nearly tumble out of my mouth before I can stop them.

"How was your day?" he asks.

"It was great. Let me go shower quick and then I'll tell you all about it."

"Need a hand?" he offers with a smirk.

"Absolutely."

∼

Campy

EVERYTHING WAS PERFECT, and then a few days later, it all went to hell.

This can't be happening. This is one of those horrible dreams that *feel* real, but then you wake up and everything is exactly as it should be. I pinch myself and wince. *Fuck*.

The comments on the video just keep ticking up, more and more by the second. *Rex Groves?? I thought he went by Campy. And since when is he straight??? I wonder if Jackson knows his boyfriend isn't even gay? Maybe he's pretending to be gay to get to Jackson's money!* That last one garnered a lot of likes and comments in agreement.

I scroll back up and the stupid video is still playing, the views increasing by the second. I have no doubt King is behind this. He had to have been the "source close to Cameron" who told the tabloids about my brief stint doing hetero porn under the name Rex Groves.

Now this damn video is popping up everywhere and getting so many views it's slowing down X-tube.

"Fuck my life," I mutter. I should've known telling the world about us would lead to this little tidbit getting out.

"So, uh, straight porn, huh?" Jackson says, startling me into nearly dropping my phone.

The expression on Jackson's face doesn't give anything away and my heart starts to pound. He wouldn't dump me over this, would he?

"Yeah, before I got the job at Ballsy. I only filmed a couple of videos and I was underwhelmed with the payout, to say the least. I heard whispers that gay porn paid a hell of a lot better, especially if you're willing to bottom. So, I started looking into the studios in town. Ballsy had by far the best reputation, so I applied," I explain. "I probably should've told Bear about doing straight porn, but I was afraid he wouldn't hire me if he knew I wasn't gay. It's not like I was some sort of *star* in straight porn, I was nobody. I figured no one who mattered would ever see these videos."

"That makes sense," he says, face still carefully blank.

"Are you mad?"

Jackson hangs his head and shakes it a little.

"Honestly? I feel pretty blindsided. I don't understand why you didn't tell me about this."

"I should have," I agree. "I'm sorry." Standing up, I step into his arms and press my face into his firm chest. His body is stiff, which is the only sign he's giving that he's not thrilled with me right now. "When I got hired at Ballsy, I lied to Bear about it. He asked if I had any experience in porn and I told him no. Now, every time I think about it I feel sick to my stomach, worrying that Bear will find out and fire me. So, I try not to think about it."

"You already know I don't care about how you make money. I understand you do what you have to do. But I don't want to be lied to or kept in the dark. I may not be a relationship expert, but I know that's not how they work."

"I know," I assure him. "I promise, there aren't any other secrets."

The tension in his body eases and he finally hugs me properly, brushing his lips against the top of my head.

"No more secrets."

I nod against his chest in agreement. "Is Katie pissed?"

"A little, but she says it's fixable," Jackson assures me. "She says you may have to do a magazine interview to explain things."

"Whatever you need me to do," I assure him. "But first, I have to head down to Ballsy and explain things to Bear. If he fires me, I have no clue what I'm going to do."

"It'll be fine." He kisses the top of my head and squeezes

me tight in his arms. "No matter what happens, it'll all be fine."

The words *I love you* are on the tip of my tongue again, but I bite them back just in time. This isn't the time for that, not when my porn career has once again put his acting career in jeopardy for the second time in two weeks.

"I'll be back in a few hours. You can tell Katie I'll do whatever she thinks is best to minimize the backlash on you."

After a slow lingering kiss, I leave Jackson and go to face Bear.

"Come in," Bear calls when I tap at his office door. "I thought I might be seeing you today," he says when I open the door.

"Yeah, well..." I give him a wry smile, closing the door behind me as I step inside and take a seat. "I take it you've seen the video?"

"I have," he confirms. I can't tell from his tone how he feels about the whole situation, and he doesn't give me any more to work with, simply waiting for me to say what I came here to say.

"I should've been upfront with you about doing straight porn before you hired me," I say and then launch into the explanation of how I came to do porn in the first place and what lead me to Ballsy Boys. When I'm finished, it feels like there's a huge weight off. All that's left is for the axe to fall.

"I understand," he responds when I stop talking. "And you can go ahead and breathe because I'm not firing you."

"Oh, thank fuck," I let out a relieved breath along with a laugh.

"I don't give a good goddamn if you're gay, straight, bi, or whatever else. You do your job and you get along with everyone here, that's what matters," he assures me. "However, Rebel *is* concerned that some of our viewers may want an explanation, so he had the idea of filming a round-table-type video where you sit down with the rest of the guys and explain the situation to them, then he'll post that for our subscribers."

"Okay, I can do that," I agree. "When?"

"I should be able to get everyone in here tomorrow, if that works for you?"

"Sure, might as well get it over with."

I leave Ballsy studios feeling a hell of a lot better than I've felt in ages. Every single one of my secrets is finally out in the open. Now it's only a matter of absorbing whatever reactions everyone has now that my last card is on the table.

∼

I'M ABOUT DONE with nervously awaiting reactions from people. I'm glad my final secret is out in the open and this will be the last time I have to deal with it. Obviously, the rest of the guys don't have the power to fire me like Bear did, but in some ways their reactions feel more important. We're supposed to be friends and I can only imagine how betrayed they felt finding out I was keeping this from them.

With a deep breath, I push through the door and step into the studio. The main set looks like a living room today and for a second I enjoy the comforting feeling of my body assuming we're going to film a scene with group sex on the couch, rather than sitting in a circle and sharing our feelings.

All the guys are there, chatting and smiling while they wait for me. As soon as they realize I've arrived, conversation grinds to a halt and all eyes are on me.

"Hey guys," I say awkwardly.

"Hey, come sit down." Pixie pats the open spot on the couch while Rebel jumps up to mess with the camera pointed at the set.

"Nothing to stress about, this is just a chance to clear the air and answer questions our subscribers may be having," Rebel assures me. "We can keep this casual and light, and if we need to cut at any point, let me know."

He presses some buttons and then returns to his own seat.

"I want to start by apologizing. I felt horrible keeping this secret from you, but after I lied to Bear in the interview, I was afraid if I admitted the truth I would lose my job. I thought if he knew I wasn't gay, he wouldn't want me working here," I explain.

"You thought he'd fire you for being bi?" Brewer asks.

"Actually, at the time I thought I was straight," I confess.

The guys share skeptical looks with each other. "But you are bi?" Heart checks.

"Yeah. I've only recently figured that out."

"Because you fell in love with Jackson?" Pixie supplies, even though he already knows more about this than the rest of the guys.

"Yeah, and a really smart guy yelled at me about bi erasure," I joke, shooting him a wink. "I think I didn't fully understand what it meant to be bisexual, which was why I didn't realize that I was until Jackson came along and kind of messed up my world."

"In a good way, right?" Heart checks.

"In the best way."

"But, I don't understand, if you thought you were straight, why do gay porn?" Tank asks.

"It pays more. Women can make good money in hetero porn, but men don't make much at all, unless they're big stars," I answer with a shrug. "My mom is sick and I needed all the money I could get, and Ballsy Boys is the best paying studio in the city, gay or straight."

A murmur of understanding goes through the group.

"Is your mom going to be okay?" Pixie asks.

"She's...well, she's better than she would be if I was making minimum wage."

Pixie wraps his arms around me and squeezes tight and it's not long before the rest of the guys join in, all surrounding me in a giant group hug.

"Thanks for understanding, guys. I'm so sorry I lied for so long. I didn't know what to do and I was carrying so much guilt over it. I thought the lies made it easier to keep Campy separate from my real life, but I think it was really just tearing me apart."

"No more lies," Pixie concludes.

"Oh yeah? So what's going on with you and Bear?" Heart asks with a cheeky grin in Pixie's direction.

"I meant no more secrets from Campy," Pixie answers, sticking his tongue out at Heart. "And I have no idea what you're referring to."

"Riiiight."

A laugh goes through the group and any lingering tension seems to fade. After Brewer and Tank's recent confessions about their relationship and going to school, and now with my own shit out in the open, it feels like we're all closer than ever.

"You know what would be fun?" I say, looking at Rebel. "We should film a giant orgy. You could even come out of retirement for just one day for it."

As the idea sinks in, everyone starts to talk animatedly about the possible positions and combinations of it and Rebel suggests into the camera that viewers should weigh in on what they think of this idea, adding a wink before getting up to shut off the camera.

"Thanks again for understanding, guys."

"You're not the only one who has struggled with reconciling these two parts of your life. We're all good. And if there's anything we can do to help with your mom, let us know," Rebel says.

"You don't have to do anything," I wave the suggestion off.

"You know, Bear's always looking for charities for Ballsy Boys to donate to. Remember, we went to the breast cancer one in honor of my mom?"

"Yeah? You think he'd donate to MS too?"

"I'm sure he would. Pick out a foundation you want to donate to and I'll get the whole thing set up. We can do an event or just donate, every little bit helps."

"Thanks, Reb, it means a lot."

"Anytime."

After filming the sit-down with the guys and having it posted all over our social media, Katie had it edited so the part about the orgy was cut out and sent that to all the mainstream media outlets as well as attaching a "statement" from me about the whole thing, which seems to be smoothing everything over.

With all of my secrets finally out in the open, it feels like the wall between Cameron and Campy is crumbling. And, to my surprise, it feels a lot better than I expected it to. Maybe because it was never two separate people, it was me tearing myself in two to keep everyone I cared about in the dark. I'm whole again and it feels fantastic.

35

JACKSON

When my agent calls me and says we need to talk, my first thought is that I'm about to get fired from the show. Color me stupid, but I can't think of any other reason why she would call me in for a meeting. And not just any meeting, but a meeting that has to be scheduled with some urgency.

Please, no more surprises, is all I can think. Cameron and I finally have that whole horror of his porn career and that video leaking behind us. We're in a good place, and I want to keep it that way. How many more bad news days can there be?

Well, my parents still aren't talking to me. My mom does text me every day, God bless her. I'm sure my dad doesn't know. She's just telling me to be patient, that it's gonna take time. I know that, and I haven't lost hope, but it still hurts. Luckily, Brax is on me like white on rice, texting me every day and keeping my spirits high that everything will be all right. All I can do is hope that whatever news my agent has, it's not gonna make things worse.

When I show up at her office, I'm more than a little

nervous. In hindsight, I should've asked her what the meeting was about, but I didn't. I'm not sure if it was because at the time she called I was too scared or what, but I never even thought to ask. I just assumed it was bad news. Turns out, I'm wrong.

"So, Jackson," Marsha says, leaning forward in her chair. "I've heard some really interesting rumors."

My stomach drops. *Rumors.* That can't be good news, can it? What has she heard about me?

"No need to look so worried," she says, sending me an assuring smile. "It was a good rumor. A very, very good rumor."

I can't prevent a sigh of relief escaping, but then the meaning of her words registers. What could she have possibly heard that is that good? Luckily, she doesn't make me wait long.

"I heard from a reputable source that the network has agreed to a second season of the show," Marsha says, her face beaming.

It takes a few seconds before it sinks in, but then I let out a loud whoop of joy. "You're kidding me!"

Her face mirrors the joy that has to be visible on mine. "I assure you, I'd never be so cruel as to joke about something this important. The network was overjoyed with the ratings for the first season so far, and to keep the fans engaged, they've decided to renew for another season and announce this as soon as possible. And they want you on the show for the second season."

Oh. My. Goodness. My head dazzles with the implications. "What does this mean for me? Will it be the same contract?"

Marsha shakes her head. "Don't you remember when we discussed your contract that we put in a clause that if there was a second season, you will get a substantial raise? This is why we did that. Now, it's not official yet, and we'll have to wait until the network formally contacts you, but when they do, we can negotiate a rewarding contract for you based on the provisions in the existing one. You're a viewer favorite, Jackson, and we'll capitalize on that."

My mouth is suddenly very dry, and I have to swallow before I can speak. "I am?"

"Didn't you see the breakdown of the ratings I sent you?"

To be fair, I did look at her email, but all I saw was that I was doing well with viewers, particularly with women. I never bothered to look at the numbers of the others on the show, figuring I only needed to focus on my own performance.

"You're the highest-rating star on the show, especially in the core demographic, which is women between twenty-five and fifty. They used terms like hot, sexy, and attractive to describe you, and nearly ninety-five percent said you were a major reason for them to watch the show."

My mouth drops open a little. "Really?"

Marsha chuckles. "Kid, there were many demands for more sex scenes for you. My guess is you'll be spending a ton of time without your shirt on next season."

I consider if I should feel even slightly offended at that, then decide I don't care. "Thank you. That's amazing news."

Marsha nods. "It is, and the fact that you're so popular is why you'll be able to basically set your own terms for your contract renewal. I'm not saying you should buy a mansion in Beverly Hills just yet or go shopping on Rodeo Drive, but you won't have to worry about your credit card bills anytime soon."

I close my eyes, the feeling so overwhelming that it's hard to even breathe. This is everything I have ever dreamed of, and it's right here, right now. I can't believe my luck. I can't wait to tell Cameron about this. He'll be so happy for me.

And then it hits me.

"Marsha, not to sound too greedy, but can you give me a ballpark of what I can expect in terms of a salary increase?"

She nods briskly. "Sure. I've already made some calculations based on various scenarios. It all depends on whether you prefer to lock yourself in for multiple seasons or not. Usually, when you are willing to negotiate on a season by-season basis, you're able to get a better deal. The higher payment offsets the lack of job stability, obviously. Here," she says, pushing a sheet of paper toward me.

"Here are three likely scenarios for what you can expect, based on a season-by-season negotiation, a contract for two seasons, and a contract for three."

I have to take a deep breath before I dare to look, but when I do, the numbers in front of me are so staggering, I'm short of breath anyway. It's overwhelming and impossible and inconceivable that they would pay me this much money to do something I love so much.

I've done it. I've followed my dream and made it come true. This money is the proof that I did it, that my gamble paid off.

But more than anything, this money represents my future with Cameron. With what I will make, it will be enough for him to stop working for Ballsy Boys and go to veterinary school. Call me sappy, but that means more to me than any Porsche or house I could buy. I don't need a mansion or expensive clothes. All I need is for him to be happy, for us to be together.

I can't wait to go home and tell him.

. . .

Campy

Jackson bursts through the door like a kid at Christmas, practically glowing as he crosses the living room in two strides and lifts me off the couch, surprising a decidedly unmanly squeak from me. Clutching at his broad shoulders to keep from falling, I laugh as he spins me around until I'm dizzy.

"Oh my god, I'm going to puke if you keep this up," I warn, and he stumbles to a stop, dropping me onto the couch and then leaning down for a kiss just as enthusiastic as his entrance. "Someone's in a good mood today," I say once the kiss ends.

"I got some incredible news," he explains.

"Oh yeah? Tell me." I scoot over a few inches and pat the cushion beside me. Collapsing onto the couch, he tugs me onto his lap, still smiling like a maniac. "Come on, the suspense is killing me."

"The show's gettin' renewed," he finally reveals.

"That's great. I knew it would, I'm so proud of you."

"That's not even the best part."

"It's not?"

"Well, it is, but there's more than that," he says. "Apparently I'm a fan favorite and my agent thinks we can ask for more money. A *lot* more money."

"Holy shit, seriously?" His excitement is infectious. "How much?"

"More than enough," Jackson huffs out a laugh. "Plenty to buy a ranch like you wanted, and move your mom out there with us, and pay for round the clock caretakers for her, and pretty much anything else she could possibly want or need. Enough to send you back to school and let you quit doin' porn."

My smile slips as he lists off all the things he wants to do with his newfound wealth, my stomach twisting and my heart thundering.

"What are you talking about?" I slide off his lap back onto the couch.

"I'm talking about bein' able to take care of you and your mama."

"Who asked you to do that?" I snap, finding myself getting to my feet, unable to sit there calmly while he goes on about rescuing me or some shit. "I've been taking care of the two of us just fine. I didn't ask you to swoop in and *Pretty Woman* my ass."

"Cam," he reaches for me, my mood finally seeming to break through his jubilance.

"No." I jerk back so he can't touch me. "Do you even know what you're talking about? You think you want to throw all your money at us like we're some kind of charity case, but what about when the novelty of the whole thing wears off? What happens if I quit my job and lay all my responsibilities on your shoulders and then you realize you can do better than a desperate porn star and his sick mother?"

"That's not—"

"You don't know that." I cut him off before he can try to make a promise he might not be able to keep. "You can't see the future and you have no idea what's going to happen in a year, two years. Hell, I have eight years of school before I'd have my DVM, you think you want to support me for *eight* years when we've known each other less than a year?"

I'm shaking from head to toe, and in all honesty I feel like a bit of a dick as Jackson sits there, completely stunned. But the utter fear gripping me keeps me from apologizing. I'm sure he thinks he means everything he's promising, Jackson's far too good of a person to make false promises on purpose. But there's no way it could all be true. Life doesn't work that way, with some handsome, perfect man coming along to sweep you off your feet and make everything perfect.

"Cameron," he tries again, and I shake my head, holding up my hand to stop him.

"I shouldn't have yelled, but I'm serious about this. I'm not going to take charity from you. I'm really happy for you about your show getting renewed, but I need a little space right now. I think I'm going to go stay with my mom for the night."

Jackson doesn't try to say anything else as I head to my bedroom and throw a few things into my duffel bag and then head out the door.

My heart aches as I get into my car. The urge to go back inside and throw myself at his feet, beg him to forgive me and forget everything I said. God, I want it all to be true—a nice little ranch outside the city, caretakers for my mom, going back to school, and best of all, Jackson by my side for the long haul. I can see it so clearly and I fucking *want* it. But goddamn am I scared that it's too good to be true. Sure, Jackson thinks I'm shiny and fun now, but soon enough he'll realize just how famous he's becoming and he'll find some glamorous, rich boyfriend. I'll only hold him back if I take what he's offering.

By the time I get to my mom's I'm not shaking anymore, but I'm far from calm, and I'm feeling like more of an asshole than ever. Jackson was so happy and I went ahead and shit all over it.

"Did I know you were coming by?" my mom asks in lieu of a greeting.

"No," I sigh, flopping down on the couch beside her, suddenly feeling all of five years old because the urge to cry and say *I needed my mommy* is way too strong.

"Uh-oh, is something wrong?" she guesses and all I can manage is to nod my head, tears burning behind my eyes and a lump in my throat. "Do you want to talk about it?" I shrug.

Rather than pushing, she unpauses the show she was watching before I barged in, and we sit in silence for a while, watching fictional characters deal with their own problems.

"He's getting a huge raise with his contract renewal and he thinks he can just throw all kinds of money at us, like we're a charity case or something," I blurt out without warning.

She pauses the show again and turns to look at me.

"I assume we're talking about Jackson?"

"Of course. He came home talking about buying me my dream house and paying for everything you need like he's some sort of genie granting wishes," I grumble.

"I'm not sure I see what's so wrong with all that."

"I don't need someone else taking care of me, that's what. I've been taking care of the two of us just fine. It makes me feel like he thinks I'm helpless."

"And how do you think I felt when I had to start letting my son give up on all of his dreams to take care of me?" she counters and I wince.

"That's different," I argue.

"I'm not so sure it is. Family takes care of each other. He does this for you now, and there may well be a time when Jackson needs you to take care of him one day, and you'll be there for him too. It's what you do when you love someone."

I swallow around the thickness in my throat.

"You think Jackson loves me?"

My mom scoffs. "I have eyes, silly boy. Haven't you noticed the way he looks at you? That poor man has been in love with you since the first time he came over here to cook for me."

"We weren't even together then," I argue.

"Trust your mother on this one."

"But what if I let him do these things for me and then he changes his mind about us?" I ask in a small voice.

"Like you said, we're getting by just fine now. We can figure it out again if need be. But love is about trust, it's about taking that leap and having faith the other person will be there to catch you."

"I was an asshole to him today," I admit.

"That's part of love too. I'm sure he'll forgive you. Why don't you give it the night and in the morning you can go grovel?"

"In the morning he has a TV interview."

"How fun, we can watch it together, *then* you can go home and grovel."

"Sounds like a plan. Thanks, Mom."

"Anytime."

36

JACKSON

The makeup artist, a pint-sized woman who's an absolute master with concealer, meets my eyes in the mirror, sending me a friendly smile. "What do you think, honey?"

I turn my head to both sides to check my appearance in the mirror. It's amazing what a little makeup and some strategically placed concealer can do. If you saw me now, you'd have no idea I barely slept a wink last night. How could I, after the way Cameron left?

The makeup artist is still waiting for my answer, so I smile back at her. "That's looking mighty fine, thank you."

She nods with satisfaction, then packs up her supplies and gestures me to a waiting area where a director-style chair has my name on it.

It broke my heart, what Cameron said. Not because I think we're over. Of course we're not. I refuse to let that wonderful, sweet man walk out on me that easily. No, my heart broke because underneath it all, he's so darn insecure, so convinced I could do better. And I get where he's coming from, but that's not how this works. That's not how *love* works.

Back in high school, we learned about Greek mythology. There was this myth that explained how humans had gotten so arrogant, became so full of hubris that Zeus decided to cut them in half to teach them a lesson. After that, humans spent their whole lives trying to find their other half—literally.

And that's what Cameron is to me, my other half. I can't explain how I know, but I do. In hindsight, I think I knew from the moment I met him. My heart recognized him as my other half in some way.

So what happened yesterday is nothing but a setback. I won't deny it hurt me, seeing him be so defeatist about our relationship, about our future together. But I've said it before and I will say it again. I have time and I have patience, and both will work in my favor.

But right now, I have to focus on this show. All around me, there's busyness. Multiple people are hurrying back and forth, talking quietly into headsets, carrying coffee or furiously typing into phones. And I'm sitting here, on a chair that has my name on it, looking all spiffy and ready to perform.

I wonder if I will ever get used to this. There's something so surreal about getting this much attention when I still feel like a nobody inside. But I guess that being on the biggest morning show in America means I am really past being a nobody, even if my brain and feelings haven't quite caught up with that.

"You're on in five minutes," a production assistant tells me, and I nod.

It's a great opportunity the network arranged for me here. They've procured three consecutive segments on the show, starting with me. Tomorrow, Ethan will star, and the day after will be Brenda, who plays my mom. But I guess my agent was right that I've become the biggest name on the show, which in itself is mind-boggling.

Katie is now sending me a daily digest, as she calls it, of media clippings. She neatly arranges them in files labeled positive, critical, and tabloid. The latter category, she warned me about. She compiles them, but it's up to me whether or not I want to read them, she explained. She would keep an eye on things and promised to make me aware of anything she felt I needed to know. But she assured me it was my prerogative to ignore that category specifically.

The first few days she sent me these clippings, I read them. And good heavens, there is some unbelievable nonsense out there. And I'm not even talking about anything to do with alien babies, though I admit that made me chuckle, at least. No, it's the stories that have no factual basis whatsoever that leave me baffled. The ones where they use grainy pictures of me in a most unflattering form, taken with a zoom lens from heaven knows how far away. The whole thing is as unattractive as it can be, which perfectly matches the tone of the articles.

Three days of those, and I decided to let Katie handle that file. The positive ones are pretty sweet to read, though, if still highly surreal. Me in *People* magazine, come on, how insane is that? There was even a suggestion I'm a contender for "Sexiest Man Alive," and if that's not the biggest joke ever, I dunno what is.

The production assistant gestures at me it's showtime, and I follow her to the edge of the set. The show's anchors are joking around with each other, laughing and at least pretending to have a good time. Then Jenni, one of the anchors, turns toward a camera and does my intro.

"*Hill Country* has been the breakout hit this season. If you haven't watched this engrossing drama show about a family in Texas dealing with the loss of their husband and father, start watching now. Eight episodes in, we can't stop obsessing about it. We have questions, lots of them, and let's see if the show's new superstar can help us find some answers. We're happy and excited to welcome Jackson Criswell to the show!"

With a steadying breath, I walk onto the set, exactly as instructed. I kiss the show's two female anchors, Jenni and Shonna, and shake hands with the male one, Brian, then lower my frame on the high chairs they use. I've watched the show enough times to know that shorter guests have issues looking elegant on these chairs, but with my long legs, that's a problem I don't have.

"Jackson, thank you so much for being here," Jenni says.

"It's my pleasure, ma'am."

She lets out a giggle, then gently elbow-bumps Shonna. "He called me *ma'am*," she stage-whispers.

Shonna laughs, then turns to me. "We have to ask, your accent, is it real or did you learn it for the show?"

Katie made me practice for questions like this, which at the time I thought was ridiculous. But now I'm grateful, because I can dial up the charm just as she advised me. "Why, yes, ma'am, that's all me. I grew up in a small Texas town, so the show's setting is like home to me."

They lob softball questions at me for a few minutes, and by the time the first commercial break arrives, I'm feeling good. But after the break, Brian turns toward me. He's known for more critical questions, especially considering this is a morning show focused more on entertainment than hard news.

"Now Jackson, it's no secret that you're gay."

Since that's not really a question, I merely nod, but on the inside, I tense up. Where is this going? This wasn't in the prep questions Katie sent me.

"And you're in a committed relationship, am I right?"

That is a question, so I have to answer. "Yes, sir."

He chuckles at me. "You know you can call me Brian, right?"

I swear I'm not doing it on purpose, being this polite. It's so ingrained that I would have to work hard not to do it. Katie says it's part of my charm and that I should stop worrying about it. That's good, because right now, I am far more worried about where Brian is going with these questions than I am about how I address him.

"My mama raised me to be polite, sir," I say, shrugging.

"Nothing wrong with good manners," Shonna says, coming to my aid.

"Earlier this month, a video was released that caused a bit of uproar for your boyfriend and his chosen *career*. Now, this is a morning show, so we won't get into specifics, but how do you feel about this?"

Oh, he's sneaky, that one. He knows there's a heck of a lot I can't say, what with this being broadcasted during daytime. It's gonna be mighty tricky to deflect without getting into trouble.

"You know, Brian, I'm always a little confused about people's reactions to his *career*, as you refer to it. It has such a stigma, and people are so quick to condemn it or belittle it, and I don't understand that. He works hard, he's good at what he does, it's a legal job that pays the bills, and I think we can all agree it fulfills a need. If people didn't want to watch the kind of videos he makes, he wouldn't have a job, now would he? We all know just how popular his videos are, so why yes, I do have an issue with people judging him for that. Why would you look down on people who provide something others need or want?"

Brian blinks, a subtle twitch near his eye signaling he wasn't expecting that response. I've managed to subtly criticize people for attacking porn without saying porn. And without really getting into the whole debate about that video.

"So you're saying you have no problem with his profession?"

Of course I do, but not for the reasons he thinks, but that's not something I can explain on national television. "I would never judge someone for working hard in any kind of legal job to pay their bills," I deftly evade the question again.

He knows it too, and so do Shonna and Jenni, who share a meaningful look. My guess is they didn't know Brian was gonna ask a question like this.

"The pictures that were posted of the two of you certainly made you look like you're in love," Jenni says, confirming that she's eager to change the topic to something more friendly.

The screens behind me show a picture the paparazzi took of us last week, with me and Cam walking to the farmers market, our arms around each other. We look like we're lost in our own world, our little bubble of happiness, and I guess we were. How can I not be happy when I'm with Cam?

"That's a great photo," I admit, and I feel my mouth curl up in a goofy smile.

I don't know why, but I think of a selfie we took right after we came back from that farmers market. We'd cooked together, or rather, I had cooked for Cam with him distracting me in the kitchen. We ended up eating on the couch together, with him seated between my legs, because for some reason, we just couldn't let go of each other, and we were goofing around and kissing and being silly. I took this selfie of us, this snapshot of pure joy.

I don't even think about it, but I whip out my phone and say, "You should see the picture we took the other night."

And then I pull it up and show it to her. She takes my phone and holds it sideways, so Shonna can see it as well.

"Aw," they both say in a perfectly timed chorus. "What an incredibly sweet picture," Jenni continues, then angles my phone so a camera can capture it.

"So are you in love?" Shonna asks.

I say what's in my heart, not caring how many millions of people are watching. "He's the love of my life, the man I want to grow old with. I'm an old-fashioned guy, and I have no interest in playin' the field, or whatever you want to call it. He's it for me, and all I want to do is marry him, buy us a home with a white picket fence, and spend the rest of our lives together."

37

CAMPY

My heart skids to a halt as I hear the words come out of Jackson's mouth.

"He's the love of my life, the man I want to grow old with. I'm an old-fashioned guy, and I have no interest in playin' the field, or whatever you want to call it. He's it for me, and all I want to do is marry him, buy us a home with a white picket fence, and spend the rest of our lives together."

"What...um...*what* did he just say?" I ask my mom, my mouth dry as I continue to stare dumbly at the brightly lit morning show and its hosts with their toothy grins.

"He said he's in love with you, sweetie," my mom answers and I shake my head, still unable to believe it.

"That's...that can't be what he meant."

"And why not? I told you last night, it's obvious he's been in love with you for months."

My heart races with longing. I want it to be true so badly, but I'm not sure I can believe it until I hear it from Jackson himself...in a situation that can't be construed as a publicity stunt.

"I have to go." I jump up and look around wildly for my

shoes. "Wait, are you okay? Can I go?" I say, realizing I can't just leave my mom.

She rolls her eyes and me and makes a weak shooing motion. "My nurse will be here in half an hour, go."

"Okay, I love you, Mom."

I give her a quick kiss on the cheek, finally spotting my shoes across the room and darting for them, not even bothering to put them on, simply picking them up and jogging out the door to my car.

The drive home is excruciatingly long. As Murphy's Law would have it, I get caught up in traffic from two different fender benders, and hit every light on the way. I realize as I sprint up the steps to our apartment that Jackson may not even be home. I don't know if he was supposed to have filming after the interview or not.

I stop outside the door, taking a second to catch my breath before putting my key in the lock and opening it.

When I see Jackson sitting on the couch, staring at his phone with indecision on his face, I stop dead in my tracks just to stare at him for a few seconds. He looks up at the sound and meets my eyes, his uncertainty morphing into a shy, hopeful smile.

"Cam." Somehow, he makes my name sound like a prayer as I cross the apartment in three quick steps and scramble into his lap, kissing him soundly.

"Please tell me you meant it, that it wasn't just something Katie told you to say." My heart beats faster even considering the idea isn't true. I *want* it to be true, more than anything.

"I meant it," he vows, his arms tightening around my waist. "I love you so much, Cameron. Maybe I went about sayin' it wrong yesterday, but I wasn't trying to give you any of that stuff out of pity or charity, it's because you're my heart and my future. As far as I'm concerned, everything I have is yours too, because that's what you do when you love someone."

Hearing those words makes me feel even worse about how I reacted yesterday. I fiddle with his shirt, having a hard time meeting his eyes. "I'm sorry I was such a dick. I got scared and that's no excuse, but it's the truth."

"What were you scared of?"

"That I wasn't good enough for you and that you'd give me everything and then realize how much better you could do, and then what would I do?" I confess.

"You are so wrong about that, darlin'. You're incredible and worthy."

I finally meet his eyes again, and I see nothing but truth. And love. I don't even think twice as the words spill out of my mouth.

"I love you, Jackson."

With his hand on the back of my head, Jackson pulls me into a kiss that starts out slow and sweet but quickly boils over as tongues slide against each other, hot and wet as we fuck each other's mouths, our hands tugging blindly at clothes without making any progress, both our own and each other's, and our cocks growing hard, pressed together through our jeans.

Jackson drags his lips away from mine, kissing along my jaw and down my neck.

"Let's take this to the bedroom," I suggest.

He wraps his arms tighter around me and stands with me wrapped around him. His muscles flex under my hands and a shiver of want runs through me. No, not want...*need*. I need Jackson like I need air, and as much as that scares the shit out of me, I have no doubt I can trust him because he needs me in the same way.

He drops me on the bed and we both struggle out of our clothes, only breaking our kisses when absolutely necessary, drinking each other in like water in the desert. When his bare skin slides against mine, goosebumps erupt all over my skin and I moan into his mouth. Our hard, leaking cocks line up and we thrust against each other in a lazy way, completely at odds with our frantic kissing, both craving the contact but unwilling to end things too soon by getting off.

I run my hands over the broad expanse of Jackson's chest, his hair coarse under my palms and his muscles hard as I dig my fingers into them. I wrap my legs around his waist and give in to the feeling of his cock, hard and heavy, fucking against mine.

Jackson nibbles at my ear, my jaw, my throat, moaning my name over and over, intermixed with declarations of love that I return every time. Sweat and precum slick our cocks as we writhe against each other, sucking bruises onto each other's skin.

Eventually, our unhurried rutting gives way to faster thrusts, my hand slipping between our bodies to wrap around our erections for added friction. I arch into every thrust, the pressure of my grip and Jackson's cock trapped against mine pushing me closer and closer to the edge. My balls tighten and I dig my fingers into Jackson's thick bicep, his moans vibrating against my flesh and his legs quaking with each thrust.

"Cam...Cam...Cameron," he groans out, biting down on my collar bone as his hot, sticky release coats my hand and my own cock still pumping against his, every pulse of his orgasm beating against me until I let go as well. Our cum mixes and manages to cover both of us as we continue to grind against each other through the aftershocks.

It's not long before Jackson's arm tires of holding him up

and he collapses on top of me, burying his face against my throat and wrapping his arms around me, not seeming to care about all the sweat and cum smearing between us.

"When we get that ranch you talked about, we'll have to make sure it's big enough that my mom's bedroom is far, far away from ours."

Jackson laughs against the crook of my neck. "Deal."

Jackson

ONCE AGAIN, we're driving to Cameron's mom, but this time, we have good news.

"I can't wait to see her face," Cameron says with a smile.

"Same here."

He reaches for my hand. "That was a lucky day, that day you decided to respond to my ad for a roommate."

He's radiant, as if a weight has fallen off his shoulders. I guess it has, now that his secret life is over. Everything is out in the open, no more surprises. Only happiness, our happily ever after.

"Best decision of my life, darlin'."

We've spent the entire morning looking at houses, which is crazy and exhilarating. Even outside the city, they're expensive, especially if you want a bit of land like we do. But we saw some options that would work for us, and I've made a quick list of things we need to research.

"I love you," Cameron says for maybe the twentieth time this morning.

It's as if he's held it in for so long, it needs to come out now. I'm not complaining, mind you. There's no way I'll ever grow tired of hearing those words.

"You're my heart, Cam," I say, lifting his hand up and pressing a soft kiss on the back of it. "I'll love you forever."

He sighs with contentment and we ride in silence for a while.

"You do realize I made you curse again yesterday, right?" he then says, and I groan.

"Shut up," I say with a grunt.

He laughs at me. "I love making you curse."

I shoot him a side-eye, then surrender to the truth. "I love it when you make me curse."

His mom is, as always, happy to see us. She's looking a sight better, has gained a little weight, I think.

"We have some great news, Mom," Cameron says.

He's helped his mom onto the couch, where's she's comfortably settled under a thin blanket.

"I was hoping that would be the case, seeing as how you hightailed it out of here after this one," she waves at me, "made such a romantic declaration of love."

I've never seen Cameron blush, but he does now, both his cheeks growing red. "Aw, darlin', don't be embarrassed," I say, reaching for him.

He grumbles a little but allows me to pull him on my lap, his mom beaming with that show of love.

"I love your son very much," I tell her, and that makes her smile even bigger. "And seeing as how I want nothin' more than for him to be happy, we're gonna find ourselves a home outside the city. Something a little more country and quiet, where Cam can have his animals and where I can ride."

"I'm gonna quit porn, Mom," Cam says, and I watch as her eyes fill up. "And Jackson is gonna pay for my degree."

"Oh Cameron, that is wonderful news. I'm so happy and proud that you'll be realizing your dream," she says. "I'll never stop being grateful for what you did for us, but it's time to put that behind you and look to the future."

He nods. "I have every intention of being happy. Annoyingly happy," he says with a laugh.

"And we'd be honored if you'd move in with us, as soon as we find something suitable," I say. "We want to have you close so we can be there if you need us."

She's crying now, big, happy tears that speak volumes. Her hand shakes as she stretches it out to me, and I take it with care.

"You chose well," she says, and at first, I think she's talking to Cameron. But then she looks at me with such motherly pride, that it makes my heart hurt, and I feel myself tear up as well. "You picked a wonderful man, Jackson, and I'm glad to see you taking such good care of him."

"He deserves it, ma'am," I say, and I mean every word.

"Call me Ma," she says, and then I lose the battle with my tears.

She looks at me a bit worried, but Cam wraps his arms around me and hugs me tight. I miss my mama something awful right now, and all I wish is that I could share this moment with her. I say as much to Cameron in between some deep breaths that are close to sobs.

"Maybe someday you can," he says quietly. "But for now, maybe text Brax so he can celebrate with us?"

And that's just what I do. We huddle on the couch, the three of us, and take a selfie. I send it to Brax, with the news that we're moving in together. When he texts back with the cheeky question which of the two will share my bed, I know that all will be right in the world.

EPILOGUE (CAMERON)

Sweat trickles down my back as the early morning sun beats down the back of my neck. I carefully place the eggs our hens have laid into the basket and check their feeders and water trough to make sure they have everything they need. The chickens were a recent addition and I have to say, it's awesome to have fresh eggs every day.

Passing the field on my way back up to the house, Jackson's horse, Walker, whinnies at me.

"I don't have any apples with me, I'll bring one back for you before I leave for school," I promise her, receiving an unimpressed snort in response.

I take a deep breath of the fresh air and smile as a familiar peace settles over me. I spot Jackson standing on the front porch with a steaming mug in his hand and a smile on his lips that mirrors mine.

"I thought you had to be on set this morning," I say as I jog up the steps, stopping to give him a kiss.

"Nah, in the afternoon. They're filmin' some scenes I'm not in this mornin'."

"Well, if I'd known that, I would've stayed in bed a little longer," I tease, sneaking my hand under his shirt.

"Then who would've fed all your pets this morning?" he jokes back, smirking against my lips.

"They're not pets, they're livestock."

"Darlin', I know farm animals and I assure you, these are pets. If you give them names and regularly kiss them, they ain't livestock."

"Are you complaining?"

"Never," he assures me with another kiss.

When I remove my hand from his stomach, Jackson takes it with his free hand, running his thumb over the ring on my left ring finger. He surprised me with the proposal on my birthday last month, although the only surprise was that he managed to wait a whole year before insisting on putting a ring on it. At least, that's what Brax said when we called to tell him.

"After class, I'm meeting with the guys for an early dinner, do you want me to bring something home for you?"

"Nah, maybe I'll rope Ethan into grabbin' a bite with me."

The guys were understandably disappointed when I left Ballsy, but we still get together often to hang out. There was nothing funnier than the look of panic on Bear's face when they all came out to the ranch and Pixie asked to ride one of our horses. And, I often see Brewer and Tank on campus now that I'm taking classes full time to work toward getting into vet school. And, of course, I still work at the rehab center, but only part time still, thanks to school.

"You know what I was thinking?"

"What's that?" Jackson asks.

"We should have the wedding here. All those venues we

looked at last week were fancy and all, but they really weren't us."

"I like that idea. We could set up a tent in the back for it."

"That sounds perfect."

"It really does," Jackson agrees, giving me one more kiss. "Absolutely perfect."

KEEP AN EYE OUT FOR MORE BALLSY BOYS!

Will Pixie find a daddy? And will Bear finally pull his head out of his ass or risk losing the best thing to ever happen to him? Find out in the next book in the series, **Pixie**.

Check out **Ballsy**, FREE Ballsy Boys prequel on Prolific Works (Instafreebie)

How did Rebel manage to catch commitment-phone Troy? Find out in **Rebel**.

Don't miss Tank and Brewer's sizzling enemies to lovers story in **Tank**.

Find out how cool-as-ice Heart lost his heart to not one, but two men in **Heart**.

MORE ABOUT K.M. NEUHOLD

Author K.M.Neuhold is a complete romance junkie, a total sap in every way. She started her journey as an author in new adult, MF romance, but after a chance reading of an MM book she was completely hooked on everything about lovely- and sometimes damaged- men finding their Happily Ever After together.

She has a strong passion for writing characters with a lot of heart and soul, and a bit of humor as well. And she fully admits that her OCD tendencies of making sure every side character has a full backstory will likely always lead to every book having a spin-off or series.

When she's not writing she's a lion tamer, an astronaut, and a superhero...just kidding, she's likely watching Netflix and snuggling with her husky while her amazing husband brings her coffee.

Stalk Me
Website: www.authorkmneuhold.com
Email: kmneuhold@gmail.com
Instagram: @KMNeuhold

Twitter: @KMNeuhold

Bookbub: https://goo.gl/MV6UXp

Join my mailing list for special bonus scenes and teasers: https://landing.mailerlite.com/webforms/landing/m4p6v2

Facebook Reader Group Neuhold's Nerds: You want to be here, we have crazy amounts of fun: http://facebook.com/groups/kmneuhold

MORE ABOUT NORA PHOENIX

Would you like the long or the short version of my bio? The short? You got it.

I write steamy gay romance books and I love it. I also love reading books. Books are everything.

How was that? A little more detail? Gotcha.

I started writing my first stories when I was a teen...on a freaking typewriter. I still have these, and they're adorably romantic. And bad, haha. Fear of failing kept me from following my dream to become a romance author, so you can imagine how proud and ecstatic I am that I finally overcame my fears and self doubt and did it. I adore my genre because I love writing and reading about flawed, strong men who are just a tad broken..but find their happy ever after anyway.

My favorite books to read are pretty much all MM/gay romances as long as it has a happy end. Kink is a plus... Aside from that, I also read a lot of nonfiction and not just books on writing. Popular psychology is a favorite topic of mine and so are self help and sociology.

Hobbies? Ain't nobody got time for that. Just kidding. I

love traveling, spending time near the ocean, and hiking. But I love books more.

Come hang out with me in my Facebook Group Nora's Nook where I share previews, sneak peeks, freebies, fun stuff, and much more:
https://www.facebook.com/groups/norasnook/

Wanna get first dibs on freebies, updates, sales, and more? Sign up for my newsletter (no spamming your inbox full… promise!) here:
http://www.noraphoenix.com/newsletter/

You can also stalk me on Twitter:
https://twitter.com/NoraFromBHR
On Instagram:
https://www.instagram.com/nora.phoenix/
On Bookbub:
https://www.bookbub.com/profile/nora-phoenix

BOOKS BY K.M. NEUHOLD

Stand Alones
   Change of Heart

Heathens Ink
   Rescue Me
   Going Commando
   From Ashes
   Shattered Pieces
   Inked in Vegas
   Flash Me

Inked (AKA Heathens Ink Spin-off stories)
   Unraveled
   Uncomplicated

Replay
   Face the Music
   Play it by Ear
   Beat of Their Own Drum
   Strike a Chord

Ballsy Boys
- Rebel
- Tank
- Heart
- Campy
- Pixie
- ***Don't Miss The Kinky Boys Coming Soon***

Working Out The Kinks
- Stay
- Heel

Short Stand Alones
- That One Summer (YA)
- Always You
- Kiss and Run (Valentine's Inc Book 4)

BOOKS BY NORA PHOENIX

Perfect Hands Series

Raw, emotional, both sweet and sexy, with a solid dash of kink, that's the Perfect Hands series. All books can be read as standalones.

- **Firm Hand** (daddy care with a younger daddy and an older boy)
- **Gentle Hand** (sweet daddy care with age play)

No Shame Series

If you love steamy MM romance with a little twist, you'll love the No Shame series. Sexy, emotional, with a bit of suspense and all the feels. Make sure to read in order, as this is a series with a continuing storyline.

- **No Filter**
- **No Limits**
- **No Fear**
- **No Shame**

- **No Angel**

And for all the fun, grab the **No Shame box set** which includes all five books plus exclusive bonus chapters and deleted scenes.

Irresistible Omegas Series

An mpreg series with all the heat, epic world building, poly romances (the first two books are MMMM and the rest of the series is MMM), a bit of suspense, and characters that will stay with you for a long time. This is a continuing series, so read in order.

- **Alpha's Sacrifice**
- **Alpha's Submission**
- **Beta's Surrender**
- **Alpha's Pride**
- **Beta's Strength**
- **Omega's Protector**

Ballsy Boys Series

Sexy porn stars looking for real love! Expect plenty of steam, but all the feels as well. They can be read as standalones, but are more fun when read in order.

- **Ballsy** (free prequel available through my website)
- **Rebel**
- **Tank**
- **Heart**
- **Campy**

- Pixie

Ignite Series

An epic dystopian sci-fi trilogy (one book out, two more to follow) where three men have to not only escape a government that wants to jail them for being gay but aliens as well. Slow burn MMM romance.

- Ignite

Stand Alones

I also have a few stand alone, so check these out!

- **Kissing the Teacher** (sexy daddy kink)
- **The Time of My Life** (two men meet at a TV singing contest)
- **Shipping the Captain** (falling for the boss on a cruise ship)